A Moment in Time

Annette Mori

ALSO BY ANNETTE MORI

Single Books

The Invisible Woman: A Lesbian Superhero Tale
The Kitten Trap
The Love Demand
Compound Interest
Georgetown Glen
Artist Free Zone
Disconnected
The Others
Sculpting Her Heart
One Shot at Love
The Panty Thief
Pleasure Workers TWC2
A Window to Love
The Book Witch
The Book Addict
The Dream Catcher
Unconventional Lovers
Captivated
The Termination
The Review
The Thanksgiving Baby Caper
The Ultimate Betrayal
Locked Inside
Out of This World
Asset Management
The Incredibly True Adventure of Two Elves in Love
(Affinity 2014 Christmas Collection)

Love Forever, Live Forever
The True Story of Valentine's Day
Vampire Pussy...Cat
Nicky's Christmas Miracle X3
(It's in Her Kiss, Affinity's Charity Anthology)
Donner Junior Saves the Day

Series

San Diego Series
Undercover Love
Politics of Love
Love Bonds

The Next Generation Series

The Next Generation Book 1
Love Hacks Book 2
Love Sins Book 3

Co-authored

The Organization with Erin O'Reilly

Co-authored with Ali Spooner

Humbug
Heart Strings Attached- TWC3
Free to Love
Trouble in Paradise -TWC4

A MOMENT IN TIME

ANNETTE MORI

Affinity
Rainbow Publications

2026

A Moment in Time

Affinity E-Book Press NZ LTD
Canterbury, New Zealand

1st Edition

ISBN: 978-1-991357-36-6 (paperback)

Editor: A Koenig
Proof Editor: S Lee
Cover Design: Lisa M
Production Design: Affinity Publication Services

ACKNOWLEDGMENTS

A huge thank you to Ali Spooner, who was the only beta reader. I would also like to express my gratitude to the Affinity Rainbow Publications team, who provide assistance and support in so many ways. I am eternally grateful for the opportunities they give me to let my stories see the light of day. Thanks to Angie for her magic as the final editor to further tighten the story. She is a delight to work with. Inevitably, those pesky errors slip through, and I am thankful that the final proof editor, Sue Lee, caught those before the book went to print. A huge thanks to all the other readers and fellow writers who have sent personal emails, written reviews, and posted nice things on Facebook (you know who you are). The Affinity authors are an incredibly supportive group and often share posts or send words of encouragement. Finally, my wife, Jody, continues her support even when it interferes with our time.

Dedication

To my fellow science fiction nerds who appreciate a good time-travel romance novel.

TABLE OF CONTENTS

Prologue

Saron Bahl relaxed on her utilitarian bed and absently twirled the ring with her thumb and forefinger. It had become a habit soon after she'd purchased the symbol of her love. She was utterly oblivious to the fact that everything in her life was about to change.

Jasmine was off on her first mission, which Saron had also volunteered for, but the Ministry strictly forbade fusion partners from going on rare team missions. Sergeant Grimes had diplomatically reminded them of the rule—behind closed doors, of course. That hadn't sat well with Saron because she knew this mission was critical and subsequently more dangerous than most routine assignments.

She and Jasmine had graduated from the academy in the same year, both jockeying for the top spot. Jasmine had inched her way ahead of Saron by one measly point, which had earned her the distinction of top of her class. Since it was the largest class in history, that was quite an honor.

Jasmine had wondered how they would juggle their new responsibilities as rookie Time Enforcers. Not that either was prone to break the rules, but they'd kept their love a secret, hoping to go on missions together. Unfortunately, Sergeant Grimes was a particularly observant leader and had made it clear that, while they could continue to keep their relationship secret, joint missions were never an option. That had thrown cold water on Saron's plans.

She'd never met anyone more beautiful than Jasmine. It was love at first sight for Saron, and she'd bought the ring after only three vibradates. Of course, she kept that fact to herself, knowing Jasmine would deem her impulsive and completely ridiculous. But after four years, she was ready to make her argument for them to become legally bound fusion partners. They could do this. She was sure of it. So what if they went on separate missions. Love always prevailed. Didn't it?

The buzzer to their assigned pod interrupted her train of thought. She quickly returned the ring to the titanium box and pushed the button for the hidden drawer. Glancing at the Dynamic Surface Display, she frowned when she saw Sergeant Grimes in her dress blues at the door.

"Come," she announced before hopping from the bed to greet the imposing woman.

One look at her face and Saron knew.

Sergeant Grimes removed her hat and solemnly began, "Saron, I'm sorry. Jasmine…"

CHAPTER ONE

Ten years later…

"The entire Sapphite culture is at risk unless we prevent impending changes to the timeline," Captain Grimes announced. "The time blip turned bright red on our time map, and intelligence has confirmed that a group of rebels obtained access to time-travel technology. Mid-21st century. I know that isn't anyone's favorite time to travel back to because of the upheaval during that period with the resistance to the Age of Enlightenment, but I need someone to take this mission. The Sapphites are too important to our future civilization for us to ignore. Millions of humans will suffer if we don't correct this at the point of origin. Unfortunately, we're a bit short-staffed and cannot afford to send a team even though this type of assignment normally calls for one."

"I thought our Time Enforcers captured the mercenaries many years ago. How the frak did that fringe group of Traditionalists get ahold of time-travel technology? I assume they're behind the impending breach," Officer Hernandez grumbled.

"Don't you worry about that. It isn't our concern. The Ministry of Time Politics is looking into it."

"I'll do it," Officer Saron Bahl announced in her usual quiet confidence.

As one of the more seasoned Time Enforcers, the Ministry could always count on Saron to handle with maximum efficiency whatever mission they assigned her to or for which she volunteered. The fact that her direct familial ancestor was one of the founding members of the Sapphites made it even more fitting that she would be the one to volunteer for what was guaranteed to be a delicate mission. The mid-21st century was not a timeframe that any Time Enforcer eagerly agreed to visit.

Saron had a commanding presence on her worst day, but today, she appeared ready to take on the entire galaxy if needed. Many fellow Time Enforcers hoped to catch her eye, only for her to gently rebuff them. She was never cruel in her refusal to engage in divine connection with prospective bond initiators. Still, many felt the deep disappointment that their overtures had not been the key to unlocking the mystery behind her simmering sensuality, which all had recognized, yet none had managed to unleash. It was as if she were savoring her power, only to release it once she'd discovered "the one."

None of them knew she'd found and lost "the one" ten years ago. Captain Grimes had honored her one request and allowed her the space to heal without sharing the reason.

Grimes had granted the leave, and they'd never spoken of it again. When Saron returned to duty, all of her focus shifted to her various assignments, earning her a reputation for brutal efficiency.

"I had hoped you would be the one to volunteer for this critical assignment, Saron." Captain Grimes offered a warm smile. "Of course, you are shrewd enough to recognize that your entire existence depends on this mission's success."

Saron nodded once. "That is accurate, but not the reason I believe I am the person for this job." No additional explanation was forthcoming, but Captain Grimes understood all too well why Saron was volunteering for the mission. She only hoped this assignment would not result in her greatest fear. Losing Saron would be an incredible cost to the elite Time Travel Enforcement Unit. The mid-21st century was a dangerous time for women.

Captain Grimes watched with interest as Saron, appearing to sense someone focusing on her, turned her gaze onto Officer Graves. She narrowed her eyes at Officer Graves. He was a relatively new transfer into the elite Time Travel Enforcement Unit, and Captain Grimes didn't have a good handle on his skills.

One thing she knew about Saron was that she didn't appreciate anyone scrutinizing her. Unwelcome interest from women was one thing, but Saron had considerably less tolerance when the interest came from a man. She'd made it abundantly clear that even if she were in the market for a fusion partner, it would never be with a man.

†

Before Saron created a scene, Captain Grimes hurried to close the meeting and distract Saron from any confrontation. She needed to brief Saron further on the mission, anyway.

"With that settled. Dismissed." Captain Grimes rushed over to Saron. "Officer Bahl, a moment, please."

Saron shifted her focus from Officer Graves. "Captain, what can I do for you?"

"I'd like to provide additional information about the mission that we've deemed highly classified." From the corner of her eye, she noted that Officer Graves seemed to perk up and lean closer in an attempt to listen to their conversation. "This way to the Collaboration Nexus. I set the room up for a private conversation."

"Of course." With one last glare at Officer Graves, Saron followed Captain Grimes as they exited the Enforcement Strategy Nexus. The captain noted with interest the sudden appearance of Jude, the assistant to Minister Gabrielle Barnes, a high-ranking minister.

Jude approached, appearing overly deferential. "Beg your pardon, Captain. Minister Barnes suggested you might need administrative support in your infosync with Officer Bahl."

Captain Grimes narrowed her eyes and took a moment to respond patiently, attempting to hide her annoyance. She made a mental note to follow up with Minister Barnes to ensure she had sent her assistant. It seemed unlikely she had, knowing the highly confidential nature of certain aspects of the mission.

"That won't be necessary. I'll be able to capture the data required to supply the Ministry with a knowledge synthesis report and will personally deliver it to her."

Jude bowed his head. "As you wish, Captain."

†

Saron knew the rules. No advanced technology, lest it fall into the wrong hands. The only exception was the tiny devices for quick transport back to her time—one for herself and enough for ten Traditionalists. She assumed ten would be a sufficient number to complete her mission. The Ministry also allowed the standard-issue Universal Temporal Watch with numerous tools to make the mission easier.

She'd have to make do with the crude weaponry from the 21st century. Securing more of those primitive weapons would be the first task upon her arrival in that time frame. A small footprint was preferable, but if she had to take out an aggressor to preserve her primary target, she only hoped it would not drastically alter the timeline.

The Traditionalists were a pain in the ass, and they were smart. Whoever they sent to 2045 might whip up the far right to do their dirty work. "Your body, my choice" was a phrase that had endured. If they informed the early Traditionalists about the scientific breakthroughs on the horizon, where men were no longer needed for reproduction, unfettered violence against women would undoubtedly follow.

Perhaps the suspected cloak agent had already attempted to send the founding Traditionalists to the location of those early scientists, and that was the reason for the blip on the time map. In that case, Saron might have more assholes to deal with besides whichever future Heritage Warrior had been sent.

Thankfully, those pioneering Traditionalists were woefully inadequate. Unfortunately, neither the Heritage Warriors nor the original Traditionalists were known for their finesse. They'd take out more than the one she was sent to safeguard. She couldn't worry about protecting all of them. Her focus had to be on Avery Simpson.

Saron shook her head as she geared up with the crude vest and antique sidearms. One in her boot and another strapped to her side. Grabbing a knife, she tucked it in her other boot.

She was only authorized to neutralize her opponents, but experience had taught her that sometimes that lofty notion wasn't possible. Slipping the ModuPak over her shoulders, she was ready.

Gazing at the picture of the beautiful woman on the cellphone popular in that era, Saron wondered what she'd be like in person. The physical resemblance was uncanny, even in the grainy picture the Ministry had provided. Saron hadn't really needed it; she saw that same face in her dreams nearly every night. Avery had a larger-than-life reputation for grit and determination. That was good. She would need it. It was time.

She stuffed the phone in one of her pockets and turned the dial on her Universal Temporal Watch. The Ministry of Time Politics had a version for every era. Hers resembled the old-style smartwatches. *Not the worst design*, she thought.

†

Pushing the button, she prepared herself for her preferred setting of a five-second delay. This was the part she hated most but would never admit to. Traveling back in time created the worst motion sickness a person might ever experience. Even the veterans did not escape the effects on their bodies. The feeling was nearly instantaneous. The contents of Saron's stomach promptly landed on the bed of pine needles in the forest where she'd appeared. She'd eaten before the journey because a dry heave was worse than simply giving in to the need to purge.

Looking up, Saron saw a flash of light. *Shit.* The intel had been off. Their Heritage Warrior was already here. At least she hoped it was a Heritage Warrior and not their more impulsive and brutal elite counterparts. The Heritage Warriors were savage enough to have to deal with.

The sun hadn't even risen yet. Saron thought she had more time to track down Avery and get her to safety. It was time to improvise.

Another flash of light let Saron know she was in deep trouble. They had sent more than one Heritage Warrior. She'd have to get creative or regroup.

Taking off in a dead run, she headed to the first flash of light. There was no time to recover from the journey. Perhaps that would give her an edge. She might catch him before he had a chance to adjust to the new time.

†

The burly man had his head between his knees, groaning. A fresh pile of vomit, still steaming, lay in front of him. He wobbled as his head popped up, and bleary red eyes found Saron's steely gaze. Before he could say a word, Saron kicked with all her might. His head snapped back, and he toppled over, continuing to groan. Thank goodness for steel-toed boots, still used by construction workers in the 21st century.

"Hey, asshole. How many?" Saron asked.

The man spat out blood and a few teeth. "Frak you," he growled.

"No thanks, you're not my type." With the knife in her hand, she pressed the tip against his groin. "Even without your penis, I wouldn't be interested. Which, I might add, you're about to lose unless I get an answer to my question. I'm not authorized to use enhanced interrogation, but I have a mission and will use whatever force is necessary to accomplish my goals. Besides, when dealing with the Traditionalists, I tend to make exceptions to the rule. Don't think for one minute I won't do it." Saron was bluffing, but this man didn't know that.

The man had the gall to reach for the phaser, a nasty invention that literally vaporized a person with one shot. The Traditionalists had no compunction against using modern weapons. It put the Time Enforcers at a disadvantage, but Time Enforcers were much better trained. While still keeping the knife pressed against his penis, Saron stomped on his hand.

Hearing the satisfying crunch, she shook her head and calmly uttered, "Unh uh. I wouldn't do that if I were you." Grabbing the phaser, she tossed it out of reach. "I'm losing my patience. I can send you back to our time with your junk intact, or…" She let the words dangle in the air.

The man spat at her, and a glob of blood and phlegm landed on her jacket. "Go to hell, dyke."

A promise is a promise. The Ministry of Time Politics didn't always like her tactics, but they occasionally looked the other way. They had a strict "no enhanced interrogation" rule, and some might consider what she was about to do a clear violation of that rule.

Time travel always made her a little grumpy for the first few minutes, so she reconsidered her bluff. Besides, he'd pissed her off by soiling her jacket with his disgusting spit.

She hoped they would understand in this particular instance. She shrugged. Even if they didn't, the worst that might happen would be another demotion. Oh well, she didn't want to climb the ranks, anyway. Being a bureaucrat was not her idea of a good time.

In a lightning-quick move, Saron cleanly sliced through his pants, divesting him of his manhood, then slapped on a transport device that would send him to the main building in the Ministry of Time Politics. He'd be puking again and would be minus one essential body part, but he'd live. Let the Information Retrieval Agents in the Neuro Analysis Unit deal with him.

†

Two more flashes of light caught her attention. Yup, she was in trouble. She needed to find the fledgling compound for the Sapphites before the Traditionalists found Avery.

Fortunately, Saron knew the compound's coordinates. She prayed they did not. Hopefully, they hadn't obtained vital information about the underground compound. It would be harder to locate if they didn't know precisely how to enter. Saron did. However, she was a little fuzzy on the protective barrier they'd established to keep their enemies away. Saron didn't relish getting her ass blown to bits as a result of tripping one of those wires. Nasty booby trap but quite effective.

Glancing at her Universal Temporal Watch, she sighed in relief, noting how close she was to the underground compound. Saron grabbed the phaser gun and stuffed it in her pants. That little death device could not land in the wrong hands. Although she hated the destructive tech and adhered to the rule not to bring one on the mission, she was secretly glad she had one now. Her opponents would not hesitate to use the weapon, nor would she, if it meant protecting Avery.

Cringing, she glanced at the bloody penis on the forest floor and debated whether a predator might gobble up the evidence. Deciding it was more prudent to turn the disgusting body part into a small pile of dust, she retrieved the phaser and aimed, sending a short burst of energy directly at the warrior's vile appendage.

Chapter Two

Avery Simpson seemed to have a sixth sense of danger. Her closest friends, Gloria and Jordan, had learned to trust whatever special gift alerted her to peril. It had saved their bacon on more than one occasion.

A few days ago, the small group of women tasked with keeping their hidden compound stocked, had narrowly escaped a violent attack while on a normal supply run. The local authorities had been less than sympathetic but managed to detain the group of angry men. Avery had endured taunting from the locals before, but the unwelcome attention had never escalated to violence. She was used to having a target on her back, but the growing group of queer women who sought sanctuary with her were not.

Frowning, she looked up from her microscope and announced to her colleague, “Something feels off. I’m going to our surveillance monitors.”

"Do you want me to check it out instead?" Gloria asked. "Security is my expertise. I still can't believe you roped me into coming into the lab this morning. Before the ass crack of dawn, I might add. Only for my best friend."

"Sorry about that, but Jordan gets a little grumpy when I wake her before six. No, I need you to finish what you started with the incubators," Avery answered.

What would I do without Gloria? Gloria preferred the high-tech security room she'd built practically from scratch, but she knew her way around Avery's lab and was an early riser like Avery. She had to admit that, after tossing and turning all night, rising before dawn was a tad earlier than usual. A brainstorm had come to her in the middle of the night, though, and she'd felt an intense desire to follow that instinct.

†

Scurrying to the room containing a wall of monitors covering every inch of the perimeter of their hidden compound, Avery caught movement in one and watched in fascination as an unknown woman cautiously stepped through the forest, occasionally squatting to poke around in the dense foliage. She stepped over the first trip wire. Her straight, nearly black hair framed a strong jawline and prominent cheekbones. The woman was a modern-day Amazon.

"What the hell?" Avery whispered.

Avery allowed herself to feel a couple of things at once—panic that someone was poking around and grudging respect for the stranger's ability to find their traps. Movement in another monitor caught her attention as the woman turned her head toward the man approaching her. Avery held her breath as the Amazon quickly moved to a section of the forest, providing greater cover while adeptly avoiding their traps.

The man, who looked a bit like a grizzly bear, was not as delicate in his approach and tripped one of the wires. Avery grimaced when the explosion hit. Usually, the traps were not enough to kill someone, but they would give their enemies something to consider before attempting to cause the women harm.

The strange woman grinned and made her way quickly to the man. Avery couldn't read lips, but she didn't need that particular skill to understand that the interaction between the two was not polite or respectful. A strange weapon in the woman's hand was pointed at his head. The man was surprisingly agile and rolled away while grabbing a similar weapon. Her movement was almost too fast for Avery to catch before a blast of bright light passed inches from her body, and her answering fire caused the man to vaporize before Avery's eyes.

Wide-eyed, Avery exclaimed, "Holy shit."

Avery didn't need to be a lip reader to recognize the expletive from the woman who swiveled her head, looking for what, Avery had no clue.

Without thinking, Avery deactivated the traps and activated the mechanism to unlock the hatch for the underground tunnel. Hurrying to the ladder, she climbed quickly to the opening and pushed against the camouflaged door. She probably looked like a groundhog popping her head above the forest floor as she called out, "Over here, hurry."

The woman squinted in her direction and yelled, "Get back down in that hole right now!"

The sureness in her voice and commanding presence had Avery following her orders as if she were a subordinate in the military, following an edict. Breathing heavily, she pulled the hatch shut and waited.

†

Damn it all to hell. If the Traditionalists didn't know the entrance to the hideout location before, they knew it now. By Saron's count, there were three additional men on the hunt. Certainly, it was a long shot for her to simply remove this first wave of opposition. They would definitely send more until the Ministry, in collaboration with the World Council, finally took appropriate action against the Traditionalists' colonies. The wheels of justice, when powered by diplomacy, took a bit longer than advisable in Saron's humble opinion.

No, this had always been an extended mission. Things just got a lot more complicated, was all. The Sapphites would need to find a new location for their operations. Who was she kidding? That was always the plan, whether her superiors articulated it or not, because the Traditionalists had the technology to find their hideout. She wondered how this might affect the timeline. Would Avery stay on track with her medical breakthrough, securing the Sapphite revolution? If that movement fell apart, there was no telling how things would ultimately turn out.

Indecision had never been an issue for Saron, but she took a beat to consider her options. Sighing, she jogged to where she'd vaporized the second man, then quickly made her way through the gauntlet, avoiding the rest of the traps. If she were lucky, her opponents wouldn't overcome the obstacles quite as well as Saron, buying her time.

Feeling around the soft moss, she located the handle and pulled. Coming face-to-face with Avery Simpson, Saron wasn't prepared for her reaction. Avery was far more beautiful in real life. Those eyes were so familiar, yet slightly different. The warm, chocolate brown eyes stared at her with open curiosity. Of course, they were the same color and identical shape, but this woman was a stranger to Saron. She didn't have time to categorize the other differences, which, from this fleeting glance, weren't many. They could have been nearly identical twins. Saron shook her head, returning to one of her greatest assets—unparalleled focus.

Avery stood on one of the ladder rungs built into the solid wall of rock and clay, blinking in the dim light. "Who the hell are you?"

"Please tell me there's another entrance," Saron replied.

"Why?"

"Because we need to make this one inaccessible, and we don't have much time to do it. May I?" Saron gestured to the open tunnel. "I'd really rather not have my ass vaporized."

Avery began a slow descent, leaving enough room for Saron to start her journey into the hole after shutting the hatch. Saron met Avery's inquisitive gaze as she reached the bottom. *Good, she isn't panicking.* There was nothing worse than a hysterical woman.

"I'm afraid I didn't do much research on explosives available during this time period. Any chance you have dynamite or something else to blow up this entrance?" Saron inquired.

Avery quirked an eyebrow. "We have explosives, yes, but I'm going to need a full explanation before we do anything so crazy as what you're suggesting."

"Look, I know you believe you're protected with your little booby traps, but I'm telling you, the men sent to take you out have already regrouped, and they have no compunction against using technology to identify and eliminate those obstacles. You're going to need to abandon this lab." Saron knew she was being particularly harsh, but she'd lost any softness over the last ten years and couldn't flip a switch no matter how much Avery threatened to unravel her emotions.

"Are you out of your mind? Do you have any idea how much is invested in my research? Not to mention a safe space for over twenty-five women. We're not giving that up. Let them send their knuckle-dragging assholes. We are well-equipped to protect ourselves." Avery glared at Saron and folded her arms across her chest.

So much like those in her lineage, Saron thought.

"I don't think you comprehend the situation," Saron patiently explained. "Those men are not of your time. They will possess advanced technology that is beyond comprehension. I don't mean to be rude, but you are no match for them." Saron flinched. That *was* rude, she recognized.

Avery's eyes roamed up and down Saron's body. "And little old you are a match?"

"Yes, I am," Saron insisted. "I'm trained for these missions."

"Figures. You have a military presence. Thanks, but no thanks. The military is not our friend. All they want is the ability to use our research for less than noble causes. I told

General Thompson I have no intention of helping them create a super soldier. He probably thinks that sending one measly woman is going to change my mind, although ordering an attractive lesbian to convince me was a nice touch."

Saron shook her head and muttered, "Figures they would give me incomplete details on the mission."

"So, the general didn't tell you about our previous interactions?" Avery smirked.

"Look, we don't have time to squabble over this. I am not from the military. In fact, there isn't really a military in my time. At least not in the sense that you are familiar with."

Avery stared wide-eyed at Saron. "In my time?" she parroted. Her eyes moved to the phaser Saron had stuck in the band of her pants, and she pointed. "Was that thing responsible for what I saw?"

Something in Avery's expression suggested she was struggling with what she'd seen. However, Saron didn't know if it was because the weapon was so foreign to her or the fact that she'd witnessed Saron taking a life in self-defense. *Frak.* Saron supposed it wasn't necessary to blend into the 21st century anymore. At least she wouldn't need to depend on the primitive weapons of this time period.

Saron nodded. "I didn't have a choice. We can get into the details later. I'm a Time Enforcer from the 26th century, and you are my mission. I've been sent to protect you. Avery Simpson, you are an extraordinary woman who will ultimately be responsible for saving the lives of millions. Failure is not an option. Now, can you help me rig up your explosives to block this entrance? They will keep sending men until you're dead. Hopefully, that will give us enough time to escape and make other plans for you to continue your research."

Avery hesitated for a beat before apparently making a decision. "This way. There's a member of the group who is more suited for this task. She'll know where to set the charges. What's your name? It's only fair I know the name of the person I'm trusting to lead into our sanctuary, especially since you know so much about me."

"I am Saron, and I *will* protect you," Saron declared, leaving no room for disagreement.

†

Avery's head was spinning after Saron provided a condensed explanation of her presence in the forest. The woman's cool gray eyes, flecked with violet, seemed to stall for a fraction of a second the moment their eyes locked together. Avery had never seen such an unusual shade. Dark violet, like the famed Elizabeth Taylor, sure, but not the light, almost sparkling pale purple. Yet this was not the most astounding thing she'd witnessed today.

If she hadn't seen with her own eyes how the man had vaporized into nothing but a pile of ash, she probably would have thought Saron suffered from some kind of mental illness. Honestly, she'd made a split-second decision to trust the woman the minute she popped open the hatch and called to her from the opening to their compound. Good thing Gloria had insisted on more than one entrance into the compound. It was their strategic protector, Gloria, who met them midway through the tunnel to the south entrance, breathing heavily.

"Three men are waving some device over the ground close to the south entrance. If I didn't know better, I'd think they landed from that old *Star Trek* show."

"Shit. We're almost out of time," Saron exclaimed as she scrutinized Gloria. Her eyes appeared to soften for such a brief time, Avery almost missed it, before they returned to the steely, disciplined focus of someone used to complicated situations requiring precise training.

"Gloria, help Saron blow up the south entrance enough to block that off from the rest of the compound," Avery directed. "Hopefully, that will give us time to evacuate."

"Evacuate? Why?" Gloria asked.

"It's only a matter of time before they find the other entrances," Saron explained. "And now that they know there are traps, they'll be more cautious in their approach."

Gloria nodded. "Come with me."

†

Avery's life's work was in the lab. She could not afford to lose any of it. She was on the cusp of the breakthrough needed to change the world. No more would women be beholden to men. Not only would she be able to create life without sperm, but that life would be stronger, more resilient to disease, and far more intelligent. The children of the future would be leaders and healers. The women would raise them in an environment of love and compassion.

While Gloria assisted the strange woman, Avery would pack her lab. Her gut told her the woman was correct. But where would they go? Avery sighed. That would be a dilemma for another day.

While packing a piece of very delicate equipment, Avery thought she heard the distinctive sound of gunfire from their security hub. Was the compound being attacked? Although she wanted desperately to close her eyes and pray this was some sort of nightmare she'd wake from any minute, she knew she had to make her way to where Gloria had taken Saron.

†

Now that Saron had met Gloria, she realized her mission had already undergone a slight alteration. Self-preservation dictated that she now had two women to protect. The historical photos she'd studied, though taken from a distance, made the identification easy. Digital photography was in its relative infancy at this time. However, it seemed that both Gloria and Avery were overly camera-shy, and very few close-ups existed of these founding members of the Sapphites.

Gloria led Saron through the dank tunnel until they reached a large room filled with the 21st-century version of Dynamic Surface Displays. She slid into a chair and began punching keys on a panel. "Don't let Avery know about this, but I think I have another way to buy us more time without blowing up the south entrance. She's a bit more of a pacifist than I am. Those men aren't some kind of indestructible robots, are they? I mean, they're flesh and bone, right?"

"The first wave, yes. The Traditionalists prefer to get their hands dirty." Saron shrugged. "Some macho thing, I think. Plus, they have trust issues. The latest weapons technology works for them. Besides, I suspect the Traditionalists realize that robots are too easy to disable, even though I did not bring the tech necessary to make them inoperable. Fortunately, they don't know that."

"Right, then." Gloria continued, letting her fingers fly over the touchpad with the strange symbols as Saron's eyes shifted to the Dynamic Surface Displays.

Gloria's ingenuity impressed Saron, although she did not entirely favor this option. This was another thing that hadn't been shared in her inadequate infosync on the mission. Six automatic weapons attached to a solid metal platform slowly rose from the ground. It took a matter of seconds for the bullets to mow down the three men. A ghastly scene of blood and destruction remained. The weapons were primitive but effective. Saron regretted answering Gloria's question about the vulnerabilities of these men.

"Let's hope they only sent five men in the first wave. You did buy us time," Saron reluctantly admitted. "It's enough to evacuate. I'd estimate we have not more than twenty-four hours, probably less. You seem capable of protecting my flank while I collect their gear and vaporize the bodies. I trust your aim is good enough to avoid hitting me. I would prefer you not hit them either in the unlikely event there are still more men in the forest."

The woman tilted her head and shrugged. "Only if you duck."

†

Saron began her trek to the entrance, retracing her steps and calling over her shoulder, "I guess I'll need to take my chances."

She climbed the ladder and pushed open the hatch. Moving quickly over the ground, hoping Gloria had deactivated the other traps, she came across the first body. It wasn't a pretty sight. Sure, Saron had seen this level of violence before. After all, she was a Time Enforcer, and every time she had to travel to a more primitive and aggressive era, violence was a possibility. She never grew accustomed to it.

Saron lived in a more peaceful time and only occasionally succumbed to her darker side. There was a part of her that might never shed that angry young woman, no matter how hard she worked at it. That had certainly been in evidence by her earlier, impulsive actions. She hadn't needed to mutilate the man, but he'd really pissed her off at a moment when her irritation was at its highest.

In general, Saron appreciated living in the Age of Enlightenment. Unless the Traditionalists were involved, everyone lived in harmony.

Fortunately, the rebel assaults on their peace and tranquility were decreasing every year, and some of the women in the settlements found their way to the outside world. Perhaps it was not the best decision to simply let them live unchecked in those remote settlements, but that decision was made much higher up the food chain. For frak's sake, it wasn't like they were the Amish of old, a protected, peace-loving culture.

Saron suspected it wouldn't be long before the omni-tolerance philosophy lost favor, and they were forced to consider a more permanent solution to the Traditionalists' unfettered autonomy.

Retrieving the future technology, Saron needed to hold it together enough to secure the tech in her ModuPak before aiming the phaser at the body and vaporizing it. The bullet-riddled bodies affected her more than she was willing to admit. They were human beings, too. She rushed to finish this grisly task. She stuffed her ModuPak to the brim with tech before returning to the entrance and finding her way to the security room.

Saron would need to remember to power down each phaser while they traveled to their new destination. Phasers in the ready state emitted a small energy signature that might be enough to track, and she couldn't give the Traditionalists any advantage. The Ministry of Time Politics never thought the Traditionalists capable of obtaining time-travel technology. *What else had they underestimated? Clearly, they had the latest weapons. Did they also have the latest tracking tech? And how had they gotten their hands on something the Ministry believed they had tightly regulated?*

CHAPTER THREE

"We always have a choice," Avery exclaimed.

Gloria shook her head. "I love you like a sister, but no, we did not."

Avery felt a wave of sadness. "That is the second time today I've heard those words. As if stating, 'I didn't have a choice,' absolves you."

"I'm sorry, Avery, but I cannot adopt your pacifist ways. Yes, I went behind your back and developed a little insurance."

"That wasn't insurance, Gloria. That was murder. You killed those men. Now, our time-traveling friend is methodically getting rid of the evidence."

"Time-traveling?" Gloria questioned. "Hmm. I guess that makes sense. The strange weapons and other tech." Gloria nodded as if everything made perfect sense, which it did not to Avery. "I just thought our separatist ways for the last few years maintained our isolation so much that we haven't kept up with the new ways the human race has found to destroy one another. Haven't you ever heard the phrase, 'you can't bring a knife to a gunfight?' All the more reason for my solution to ensure our safety."

"I won't be party to any of this. My work is all about creating life for those who no longer have that option. Warnings are one thing. You promised no one would be seriously hurt, and you'd only set traps to discourage anyone from nosing around."

Thunk. Avery turned her head to the sound. The imposing time traveler stood before them, her bloated backpack lying on the ground, a grim expression on her face.

"We can debate the ethics of the choices that Gloria and I have made, or we can continue to pack all that is needed for you to advance your work, Avery. Nothing else matters if you desire to help us evolve to a more peaceful existence. Unfortunately, I'll need to bend a few more rules to achieve a successful mission. While I cannot allow these weapons," Saron pointed to her bag, "to fall into the hands of men of this time, I won't destroy something that may help me achieve my mission. It would not be prudent to leave evidence of the arrival of time travelers. I'll do my best to return the men to our time to face the consequences versus reverting to their crude elimination methods."

Gloria grinned. "Any chance you can teach me how to use one of those guns?"

Saron glared at Gloria. "No. I must insist that you refrain from using your automatic weapons again. How may I assist you with your packing?"

Avery thought that at least Saron would keep Gloria in check. "Packing the equipment and supplies is not the issue.

Finding another location to work and transporting everyone is a problem without a solution."

"The mission infosync provided a new location, should that be necessary. How many other members are required for you to complete your work?" Saron asked.

Avery felt a pit in her stomach. "You aren't suggesting we can only relocate the women helping with my research? There are twenty-five women in this compound. I won't leave without them."

Saron sighed, and Avery thought she was about to say something before Gloria raised her hand as if she were in school, waiting to be called upon by a teacher. Saron shifted her gaze to Gloria.

"I know of an abandoned bus in a junkyard not too far from here. Obviously, it isn't running anymore, and more likely than not, someone stripped it of the useful parts, but maybe with your knowledge of future technology and all…"

Saron grabbed the backpack she'd dropped on the floor. "How far?"

Gloria grimaced. "A few miles, maybe. Not more than five, I think. Although we might want to wait a little while. The owner isn't exactly an early riser like me." She grinned.

Saron pointed to Gloria. "You will show me. Now. Avery, complete your packing and gather the women. Be ready for transport to the new location upon our return."

"Okay, but don't blame me if we receive less than a warm welcome," Gloria answered.

Saron failed to respond to Gloria. Avery had an inkling about what kind of welcome they would receive. Poor Gloria was now forced to whack that hornet's nest. Mavis was prickly at the best of times, but with their current off-again status, Avery presumed Saron and Gloria would face outright hostility from the junkyard owner.

Avery simply nodded her agreement. She didn't believe she had a choice. It was either remain at the compound and continue to let Gloria wreak hell on any men who approached, or she could put her faith in Saron to keep her word about returning the men to their time, versus killing them.

†

Saron had a grudging respect for Gloria. She smiled at the knowledge that this woman was her close familial connection. Her ancestor reminded Saron of herself at an earlier age—before she mostly learned to control her emotions. She supposed the old saying, "the apple does not fall far from the tree," was particularly apropos in this instance. The rules made it abundantly clear that under no circumstances should Saron reveal her relationship to Gloria, no matter how tempting it would be to have a long conversation with whom she now knew to be her direct familial ancestor.

Saron reflected on how she had been an angry young woman after a small band of rebel Traditionalists had torn her community apart. *Did Gloria have a similar story to tell?* Some of her own anger still rose to the surface occasionally, like whenever she came face to face with one of the Traditionalists.

The terrorist attack had resulted in multiple deaths, including her beloved best friend. At first, she disagreed with the Peacekeeper's method of maintaining order. She had wanted revenge. However, her mother, a prominent council member at the Ministry of Time Politics and a close family friend who was also an officer at the Ministry of Peace, had recognized her anger and steered her in another direction.

Saron supposed she hadn't completely bought into all their beliefs, but she'd adopted the majority of them. She was always headed for the elite Time Travel Enforcement Unit because of her mother's influence, but the extra push from her mother's friend didn't hurt. Although her supervisors had reprimanded her on more than one occasion.

Mostly, she would avoid killing her opponent. However, Saron drew the line at self-defense or ensuring nothing happened to anyone the Ministry sent her to protect. Yes, breaking the cycle of violence was necessary, she supposed, but that didn't mean she would let her opponent vaporize her with outlawed weapons. Nor would she allow harm to a critical individual in the historical timeline. Saron admitted she was like an alcoholic with a tendency toward violence if she didn't actively manage her dark side. She ruminated again about how she'd let that dark side take over when she'd liberated the Traditionalist's pitiful manhood.

Gloria had indicated a need to collect something from her room. Saron's instincts were spot on as she glanced at the slight bulge underneath her jacket, barely noticeable to most, but Saron was a trained professional.

"I understand your instinct to eliminate all threats, but I must insist on restraint," Saron reluctantly directed. "I'd prefer it if you would not carry a weapon." It felt so strange to give direction to her technical elder, but once again, she had no choice but to maintain authority for the sake of their survival.

Gloria poked Saron's vest, landing on the gun attached to the shoulder harness, and sneered. "I don't see you exercising any restraint."

"My weapons are intended to neutralize opponents, not eliminate them, unless I have no other options," Saron insisted, even though she knew deep down she could have made a different choice earlier. She recognized the fact that she hadn't entirely made the final turn to nonviolence since she'd chosen to point a phaser at the second man versus one of the ancient weapons. Although, to be fair, she'd only had a split-second to react and had failed to change the setting on the phaser. Then, there was her choice of information retrieval. She cringed. Yes, she was definitely the pot calling the kettle black. Wasn't that the old saying?

"Sorry, no can do," Gloria asserted. "Those futuristic asswipes aren't the only ones I need my little companion for." She patted her side. "We have our version of dicknobs in this timeframe. Why do you think I jerry-rigged those automatic weapons? I like to call them my equalizers."

Saron shrugged. "I will not be the one to defend your actions."

"Never asked you to. Avery's bark is much worse than her bite."

"We should go now. It will take time to adapt the power source to your crippled bus. I trust you are whole enough to run the five miles."

Gloria squinted at Saron in confusion. "Whole enough? Are you asking if I'm fit enough to run five miles? Uh, that would be a big fat no. Take a look at where we live. Exercise isn't exactly a priority. However, you're in luck because we have a hidden Land Cruiser in a cleverly disguised rock formation. We'll drive there." Grabbing a tablet, Gloria ordered, "Well, come on, sexy time traveler, time's a-wasting. Let's go."

Ew, Saron thought. If only she knew who I was, she'd refrain from referring to me as sexy.

†

Saron liked her ancestor. She would be an adequate ally. Perhaps she wouldn't need to expend as much effort to protect her as she'd initially thought. Avery would remain her primary focus because she clearly possessed no fighting skills.

Saron and Gloria bumped along the forest as Gloria adeptly avoided fallen trees and other debris, making the journey longer than if they had traveled on a paved road. Finally, they approached a gravel road leading to the junkyard. Gloria skidded to a stop in front of the imposing metal gate. A large dog snarled behind the gate, then barked loudly.

Gloria held up one finger. "Wait here," she directed. "I'll need to smooth things over before we barter for the bus. Mavis isn't exactly her best in the morning."

Opening the door, Saron heard the unmistakable sound of a shotgun racking a shell into the chamber. The metallic clank prefaced the blast that came a little too close for Saron's comfort, hitting the gravel inches from Gloria's feet.

Gloria held up her hands. "Aw, come on, Mavis, that was close. You're not still mad about that misunderstanding we had a couple of months ago?"

The metallic clank repeated, and another blast hit an inch closer, sending rocks flying. One hit Gloria's cheek, leaving a small cut as a trickle of blood leaked down her face.

Gloria swiped the blood from her cheek. "Now look what you've done."

†

A small woman emerged from behind a rusty old truck, holding a shotgun against her shoulder. She gave a slight pat on the dog's head. "What do you want, Gloria? Jesus fucking Christ, it's six-thirty in the goddamn morning. I haven't even had my coffee yet. And who do you have with you? Another girlfriend?" She sneered.

"Goddess, no. Besides, we're not together anymore, so why do you care? You're the one who ended things, not me."

Saron rolled her eyes. Of course, lesbian drama survived in any period. She didn't have time for this. Saron emerged from the Cruiser, holding her hands in the air.

"I assure you, I have not had a divine connection with this woman. We've only just met. Important lives are in danger. We do not have time for petty lesbian squabbles. Please show me to this bus. I have ample currency to purchase the item. Diamonds are still valuable as currency, is that correct? Or would you prefer the paper version?"

Saron took a few tentative steps forward and assessed the small woman. When her eyes landed on Mavis' cool gray eyes, it took all of Saron's training not to gasp. *Shit. Now I have another woman I need to ensure lives through this volatile time.* Mavis was Gloria's future fusion partner. Saron recognized her from the slightly out-of-focus pictures of the original Sapphites. If something happened to Mavis, it might alter her ancestry. Saron would need to maintain every ounce of professionalism to make it through this mission unscathed, both personally and professionally.

Mavis smirked. "Got yourself a real winner this time. Who is this nutjob?"

"Allow me to retrieve the needed currency without you unnecessarily testing this ancient vest. I am unsure of its effectiveness with a shotgun at close range. I'd prefer not to harm you." Saron reached for one of the straps on her ModuPak. The woman racked her shotgun again.

"Stop posturing, Mavis. You know you aren't going to shoot us. Saron is a time traveler sent to protect Avery. Unfortunately, we have to relocate our operations and need that bus. Some very nasty dudes are after us."

Mavis looked skeptical. "Right, and I'm the reincarnation of Princess Di. You just want an excuse to run again."

Digging into her ModuPak, Saron pulled out the wad of cash and pouch of diamonds, emptying the precious jewels into her hand.

"Holy shit. Are those real?" Gloria asked.

Saron nodded. "I have emeralds, rubies, and sapphires if you prefer. How much for the bus?"

The woman's eyes widened. "You're serious. Well, since I have no way of knowing if those gems are real, I'd prefer cash. Three thousand."

Saron began peeling bills from her wad of cash.

Gloria arched an eyebrow. "That's rotten, even for you, Mavis. That bus has been sitting in your yard for years. I doubt it has any engine parts left. I suppose if you threw in the parts Saron needs to make it run, that price is fair."

"Fine." Swinging the gate open, Mavis lowered her gun and gestured for the women to come inside. "You can search the yard for anything you need to make it run." Mavis smirked. "Good luck with that. But a deal is a deal. All sales are final. Don't come crying to me if you don't find the right parts."

"I am confident I will make your ancient vehicle work. Whatever I don't find in your yard, I will replicate." Saron strode confidently to the woman, handing her the bills needed to complete the transaction.

Mavis held her outstretched hand to Saron. "Pleasure doing business with you."

"No need to escort us. I know where you keep the bus. There better be a path to drive that white elephant from the lot."

"Oh, there is." Mavis grinned after pocketing the money.

When they reached the bus, Saron sighed, noticing four missing tires. Only two tires remained, looking well-worn but hopefully adequate for the trip to the new location.

"You vengeful bitch," Gloria exclaimed.

"That'll be another thousand for the tires. Hopefully, you'll find some that fit."

CHAPTER FOUR

Saron was becoming increasingly agitated that securing the old bus was taking so long. She would have to remember to ask about the camera she'd noticed hanging on a pole above the fence. Sometimes, businesses installed dummy cameras intended to create the appearance of security. Still, if this camera had recorded their interaction, she would need to ask Mavis to erase any footage of their presence at the junkyard.

Saron would worry about how to get the prickly Mavis to join their group after she'd cleared the first hurdle. The added complication of finding tires somewhere in the massive junkyard exponentially amplified her foul mood. At the moment, Gloria's presence was another worry. Gloria was a curious woman. She wanted to remain by Saron's side to observe how she intended to fix the bus with so many missing parts.

The class in Ancient Machinery and Engine Adaptation taken at the academy came in handy now that Saron needed to adapt one of the ancient transports. Fortunately for her, most of the missing parts weren't required to make the vehicle run. It was a good thing she had no moral obligation to forgo utilizing the replicator and power cells she'd pilfered from the Traditionalists. However, without a decent supply of power cells, her replications were limited. She wasn't sure she had enough energy to replicate four tires. Time was the one commodity she could not replicate.

With the hood open, Saron declared, "I recognize this design. I will work on this while you search for tires."

Gloria's brow furrowed. "I'm not much of an engine mechanic, but even I know several crucial parts are missing. Don't you want to roam around the yard, looking for parts you can adapt to get the bus running?"

Saron shook her head. "No, I only need to replicate parts to attach the power cell. The missing parts are not crucial to generating the energy needed to run the bus. Perhaps you can make amends with your former fusion partner, and she might assist you in locating tires for the bus."

"I assume by former fusion partner, you mean my ex. Uh, no, not happening. The only reason Mavis hasn't blown off my important bits is her curiosity. It's possible she wants to change any first impressions she might have left with her overzealous protection of the junkyard. It certainly doesn't hurt that you're rich and attractive." Gloria pointed to the office where the blinds parted. "She's spying on you right now. Can't I watch what you're doing? I need to understand more about engines, anyway. We don't have anyone with that particular expertise. I'm the obvious choice."

Saron shook her head. "I'm sorry, but what I am about to do will not be an option for you. When I return to my time, the technology will travel with me. Time-traveling rules require us to leave no future technology behind. We must let you discover these things on your own. Speeding up the timeline could have disastrous consequences, especially when the technology lands in the wrong hands."

Gloria grinned. "It was worth a try. All right, I'll search for the tires and something to lift the bus so we can put the new ones on." Gloria sighed. "Shit, I probably need to ask Mavis for that. She undoubtedly allowed whoever bought the tires to use a portable lift, which she'll have in a secure location. The damn woman loves to have all the power and control. Wish me luck." Gloria stalked off.

†

Saron chuckled. Gloria was quickly winning a special, though unconventional, place in her heart. Clearly, she was a player, something Saron never gravitated to, but she had spunk, and Saron might need to tap into that later if things got intense with the Traditionalists.

Saron glanced at Mavis, who was still watching her from inside her office. She grinned and offered a small wave before moving to the other side of the bus and out of Mavis's direct line of sight. She didn't need another person learning about the replicator. It was bad enough that Gloria and Avery had knowledge of phasers. She'd need to limit use of the replicator and get this right the first time. Her eyesight would have to be enough to locate the correct casing to connect with the engine components and allow the energy to flow through the power cell. At least the bus ran on the old electrical current rather than a combustion engine. That made everything much less complicated.

In her time, the cell would simply plug into whatever machinery this clean power source required. Everything needing energy had universal connectors because that was the most efficient means of making all modern technology function. Greed no longer had a place in her world. Nor did competition. However, in this time, different manufacturers used slightly different components, and she couldn't be sure she would select the correct one on her first try. She'd also need to replicate a universal tool if she couldn't find a toolbox within the luggage compartments.

Finally, things went her way as she replicated the casing and connectors and engineered a method to secure the valuable power cell. She doubted the bus had an old key fob to start the engine. Even if she miraculously found the key, she didn't believe the battery was still functional. Skills in old-school hot wiring, although admittedly she was a bit rusty, would come in handy. This was another elective at the academy that she'd only had to use once on a mission set in the late 1990s. Would the same principles apply several decades later?

With the hood still open, Saron climbed into the bus, pried open the area where she suspected the wires connected to the ignition, and secured them to the small, replicated device that would work like a key. Pressing the button on the device, the bus roared to life.

†

"Holy shit! You did it," Gloria exclaimed as she rolled a large tire, letting it fall to the ground when she peeked under the hood.

Saron emerged quickly from inside the bus and slammed the hood, hiding the pulsing blue light emanating from the power cell. "Did you find four tires for us?"

She frowned. "I found three. Two of them are spares, though, that have obviously been in use before. So, um, any chance you can replicate a fourth? You know, like you did with that gadget with the pulsing blue light. Maybe all four because these tires aren't in the best condition."

"I did not replicate a power cell," Saron answered. "Tires may require more energy than I currently possess. I don't have an extra power cell lying around to..." She paused, trying to come up with a way to explain how things worked. Replicators required vast amounts of energy to replicate large items.

Gloria interrupted. "I used to watch *Star Trek* religiously. While I didn't understand the nuts and bolts of how replicators worked, I understood they required an energy source to operate. Is that what your power cells are designed to do? Allow energy to flow into whatever futuristic gadget you use?"

"Yes."

"All right. I'll keep searching for another tire while you sweet-talk Mavis into letting you use the lift. Have you ever changed a tire? Do future automobiles even have tires, or do they hover in the air?"

Saron chuckled. "I believe I can manage to attach a tire. How hard can it be?"

†

Saron marched purposefully to the combination home/office and noticed how Mavis quickly let the blinds fall back into place. Before she could open the door, Mavis met her with a guarded look. The dog sat beside its owner, and Saron sensed both intelligence and affection from the animal. She focused on sending out calm and nonthreatening vibes.

"What was that blue light I saw?" Mavis demanded. "I don't need any trouble here. It's bad enough that some bearded misogynistic asswipes have harassed me almost daily ever since Gloria and Avery moved into the neighborhood. Although I'm not exactly sure where they live." Mavis cocked her head to the side and furrowed her brow. "They're in some kind of cult, and I don't want any part of that. Don't get me wrong, I love women. Probably wouldn't mind living in a community with just women, but something isn't right about them. Besides, they've attracted far too much attention. The men who run this county don't take too kindly to ultra-feminists."

"They are not a cult. The work that Avery is doing will have a profound impact on the world. For the better," Saron added serenely. "I require your lift to replace the tires. I'm willing to pay a rental fee. That is the correct terminology, is it not?"

Mavis narrowed her gaze. "You are a strange one. Sure, why not? I don't need any additional cash. I already feel bad enough for taking you for a ride."

Saron tilted her head to the side, staring at Mavis, trying to figure out what she imagined was 21st-century slang. "I have not ridden in a vehicle with you. Do you wish to come with us? Are you also in danger? You are not my mission, but I don't believe Avery would mind if you joined us."

Saron was proud of herself for finding a nonthreatening way to encourage Mavis to at least consider joining them.

Mavis shook her head. "You *are* a strange one. Come with me. I'll get the lift." She glanced at the dog and ordered, "To your mat." The canine promptly obeyed, curling on top of a large lambskin mat in the corner of the office. "Good girl." Mavis plucked a bone from the cabinet above the bed and set it in front of the dog. Grabbing the bone in her massive jaws, she began happily gnawing on the treat.

†

Saron followed Mavis to a locked shed where she moved several items until grabbing a mechanical device with a solid steel plate attached to a hydraulic apparatus on wheels. Mavis rolled the lift through the path she created. Saron was unsure whether she should offer to take the device from the prickly woman.

Saron's curiosity got the better of her, and she decided this might be her best option to further her objective to convince Mavis she'd be a lot safer if she abandoned her junkyard and joined the fledgling Sapphites. "Why do you believe Gloria is in a cult? Is that why the two of you are no longer a mated pair?"

She intended to use a term that Mavis might understand. Saron realized that fusion partners seemed a totally foreign concept to those living in the 21st century.

Mavis threw her head back and laughed. "Mated pair? Where are you from? Did you come from another cult or something? One that is still living in the 19th century?"

Mavis frowned. "Although that makes no sense since you seem quite proficient with technology. I honestly didn't believe you could get that bus running, especially without collecting missing parts from other vehicles." She continued to roll the lift to the bus while Saron followed.

†

When they reached the bus, Saron approached the lift, examining the primitive device. She assumed the metal plate lifted the frame enough to allow clearance to attach the tires. Perhaps the red switch caused the metal plate to rise. They hadn't covered changing or adding tires in her Ancient Machinery and Engine Adaptation class. She'd vaguely recalled one of her colleagues talking about electric jacks, but this device must be a newer version.

Pushing the device under the front of the bus between the two missing front tires, she tried the red switch and smiled when the steel plate began to rise. Grinning, she glanced at Mavis, proud of her accomplishment.

Nodding, she mumbled, "Yes, not that hard at all."

Huffing, Gloria approached, rolling a second tire and letting it drop on the ground next to the first one. "I'm going to need that lift to take off the other tires. The good news is that I found the fourth tire." Gloria shifted her focus to Mavis. "I don't suppose the stingy bitch gave you a cordless impact wrench we can use on stubborn lug nuts? I doubt they'll be easy to remove with a basic lug wrench." She scanned the area. "Never mind. Maybe the bus has one in one of its luggage compartments."

Saron reached into her memory and plucked out the correct terminology. "Ah, yes, for the connectors to attach the tire. Lug nuts."

Gloria furrowed her brow, then grinned. "Cars don't use tires anymore, do they? Do they hover over the ground, or maybe everything just flies in the future? Wicked."

"That is correct. Tires are inefficient and unnecessary for vehicles of the future," Saron explained. *Damn, I hope revealing that small detail about the future is acceptable.* Saron wasn't sure why she was more open with these women. She'd need to gain greater control of the information. Having personal ties to the Sapphites was a liability if she continued to divulge more than she should to accomplish the mission.

Mavis looked between the two women. "You two are serious. What the hell is going on? How much trouble are you in, Gloria?"

Saron believed that Mavis's initial reaction to Gloria was all an act. She still cared. It made perfect sense now. The two were destined to reignite their past relationship. The fire clearly remained. Unfortunately, coming to the junkyard had likely put Mavis in danger. Saron could not afford to allow anything to happen to Mavis.

Gloria shrugged. "Avery is the one they want. We're just collateral damage, I suppose. I may not see you again until things settle. I can't tell you where we're going. That might put you at risk, but I'll be in touch when this is all over. Or…you could come with us."

Yes! Thank the Goddess for Gloria and her lingering feelings. Saron would add to the plea in the hope that this might push Mavis in the right direction.

"It's possible we've placed you in danger. When the Traditionalists find the compound empty, they will assume we acquired the necessary transportation to relocate. I apologize for involving you. I should have considered the consequences, but we don't have another option in the limited time. Any knowledge you have of a new location will be valuable to them. Enhanced interrogation is not a tactic we use, but these men do not have the same rules to guide their missions."

"Enhanced interrogation," Mavis choked out. "That means torture. Don't sugarcoat it."

Saron grimaced.

"Come with us," Gloria pleaded. "I know you didn't want to move to the compound, and I'm sorry I acted out. But I was so hurt that you wouldn't even consider it. I took a colossal risk even telling you about us. You never even visited, making all kinds of assumptions…"

"All right," Mavis agreed. "I'm tired of running this place, anyway. Besides, the harassment is getting untenable."

Things were going her way. Saron was glad she'd efficiently resolved this new dilemma. She hadn't wanted to share the gritty reality of what Mavis might endure, but the tactic appeared to have worked.

"Really? You'll come." Gloria looked so hopeful. Saron thought that, yes, these two were far from done with one another. That would have been clear even if she hadn't had the knowledge of future events that suggested the two would take their relationship to the next level.

"Yes, as long as you also have room for Buttercup. She is very protective and the best alarm system a person could hope for."

Saron bent her head in agreement. "A canine does have special skills that might prove useful. They will not anticipate this advantage. May I ask about your security cameras?"

Mavis waved her hand in the air. "Oh, they're all for show."

Saron nodded. "Good."

"I'd better help you remove those tires if time is of the essence," Mavis grunted. "We can check to see if the bus has a lug wrench. If not, I have a couple lying around the office."

"I found tools. I did not put them away. Perhaps you can point out the tool required to attach these two tires."

Gloria chuckled. "I guess this is a tad bit more difficult than you anticipated. Should we show you how to attach the tire?"

Finding the solid metal cross, Saron smiled at the tool's simplicity and how easy it was to attach the tire. She'd secured both tires well before Gloria and Mavis returned with the cordless impact wrench and other tires.

CHAPTER FIVE

Avery tried to focus on packing her delicate equipment, but her concern was getting the best of her as the minutes ticked by. She hoped they could secure a large enough bus to transport all members of their tight community. She didn't want to leave anyone behind.

Fortunately, they had prepared for ultimate survival in an increasingly hostile environment and had stored enough freeze-dried food to last for weeks. Would the bus have enough space for all her equipment and the survival containers? Hopefully, the new location would enable them to set up new hydroponic chambers to grow food to support the compound. They might even have time to make multiple trips if the location was close.

A nervous energy filled the compound, but none of the women questioned the need to leave. They'd been through so much. Many had already found solace in being a part of the community and believed in their mission. If Avery said they needed to relocate, no one questioned her leadership.

†

Avery moved to the security hub. Surely, they would need this equipment to maintain, at a minimum, the appearance of safety. She started to unmantle the monitors and computers and gasped when she saw the bus roll to a stop a few feet from the south entrance.

"They actually did it," she announced, though no one was in the room to hear her. She wasn't all that surprised if she really thought about it. Gloria was resourceful, and Saron had an air about her that screamed confidence and competence.

Nora, the expert in hydroponics, entered the room and announced, "Everyone has packed according to your directions. There are primary, secondary, and nice-to-have supplies neatly stacked and ready to go. We've limited personal belongings, including clothing, to make room for the more important items. Are we taking all of the equipment in this room?"

"I hope so," Avery answered. "Unfortunately, security has to be a priority."

Nora nodded. "Agreed." Fidgeting, Nora finally revealed her trepidation. "Are you one hundred percent positive this relocation is required?"

Avery felt sadness and anxiety rush to the surface as she responded, "Yes, I can't explain it, but I trust the stranger. Plus, the technology I saw in action led me to believe that we are no match for this new threat without her help. However, all of you have the choice not to follow me and set up in a new location. I can do this on my own. It might take a little longer to accomplish, but it isn't necessary for all of you to follow me into the unknown belly of the beast."

"Absolutely not. Everyone is committed. We won't abandon you," Nora insisted.

Avery glanced at the monitor and caught Saron emerging from the bus, heading for the south entrance.

"I can see why you trust this woman. She has an imposing presence. Plus, she's very easy on the eyes." Nora winked at Avery. "It's been a long time for you, hasn't it? You know, you could have your pick of women here. Every person at the compound would jump at the chance, even those who have selected a companion. Shit, is that Mavis?"

Avery returned her attention to the monitors. Mavis and Gloria opened the doors to the Land Cruiser as Buttercup bounded out, wagging her tail and sticking close to her owner.

"It is. I wonder if they are on again?" Avery shrugged. "Not the worst outcome. They are a good match for one another. Gloria hasn't been the same since they split this last time around." Watching Buttercup trot next to her owner, Avery added, "If Buttercup is with her, that must mean she's joining us."

"Let's just hope they keep the drama to a minimum," Nora noted. "I should warn Brenda."

Avery raised an eyebrow. "Brenda? You ought to consider giving Mavis a wide berth."

Nora shrugged. "Ancient history. Brenda's more recent. She probably forgot all about our very short dalliance."

"I wouldn't be too sure of that."

"Yeah, I suppose I should have known better than to mess with Gloria," Nora ruefully noted.

"Ya think?" Avery chuckled. "I love Gloria, but she's prone to play with fire."

†

Saron descended the rungs of the built-in ladder into the compound and met Avery halfway down the tunnel. Mavis had decided to remain topside with her dog while Saron and Gloria assisted with the evacuation process.

"We have most items packed and ready to go," Avery announced. "I've asked everyone to separate items into three categories. I'll show you the equipment and bags that are our first priority. We haven't completed boxing the security equipment because it all needs to be dismantled carefully and packed to ensure nothing is damaged. I've been debating how to categorize everything. It's not my area of expertise. Gloria will need to weigh in on this. I'm not even sure it belongs in what we've designated as first priority."

"It does," Gloria insisted.

"I agree," Saron noted. "Besides, from my brief inspection of that room, there is technology that can be adapted. I may need that for other purposes. You packed the entire lab, correct?"

Avery nodded. "Although I am conflicted about all of that being categorized as first priority. I should have evaluated the equipment with more prudence, especially since it will take up considerable space." Avery shifted uncomfortably on her feet.

"No, there is nothing more important than continuing your research," Saron insisted. "You must trust me on this. We've emptied the luggage compartments on the bus of everything but the tools I found. We will also take the Land

Cruiser. Shall we begin to load the bus? Put the more delicate equipment in the Land Cruiser. Gloria, perhaps you can finish packing the room with your security equipment."

"Avery, I know you aren't crazy about the automatic weapons, but I'm planning to dismantle them to take with us. I'd rather be transparent. Sorry I didn't tell you about them before." Gloria looked away, not meeting Avery's eyes.

"When I get the chance, I'll look into modifying those weapons. Instead of killing the men, I might be able to alter the firing mechanism and adapt it to phaser technology. A stun mode will provide enough time for me to send them back."

Gloria grinned. "Awesome. Can I watch you work on that?"

Saron shook her head. "No, I am sorry. I cannot provide you with the knowledge to adapt your current technology. That is against the rules."

Gloria shrugged. "It was worth a try."

"We are wasting valuable time discussing things," Saron stated.

Gloria saluted Saron. "Rightio, Chief. I'm on it."

"The women were waiting for you to return. Follow me. I believe the old saying, 'many hands make light work,' applies here."

†

Saron walked behind Avery to a large room with stacks of boxes and bags. Several of the women were still bringing bags and luggage into the space.

Avery pointed at Saron. "This is Saron. She's going to take us to our new home. I trust her. The bus is here. Those who have completed their packing can carry items to load onto the bus. We'll start with our first priority. Thank you for your sacrifice." She frowned. "We'll need to figure out how to bring the items to the surface, especially the heavier luggage and boxes. For now, set them at the bottom of the ladder at the south entrance."

The women were eerily quiet as they openly assessed Saron. A few gave her an appraising look, but none seemed hostile. Saron took that as a good sign. At least there would not be an internal rebellion.

Without another word, several women lifted items from a section of the room where the fledgling Sapphites had neatly stacked a significant number of boxes and bags. Saron assumed this was the first-priority pile. She would do her best to ensure these women did not have to sacrifice too much, even if that meant returning for a second or third load and placing her own life at risk. She only hoped the second wave would not arrive for another day or two. By then, they would be long gone.

The Ministry of Time had prepared for this alternate plan, and if the Time Agents had done their job, the new location would not only be remote but also a place she could easily defend. If not, she would have to rely on a third and final option to separate Avery and create a rolling lab. Maybe she should have suggested that to begin with, but Avery seemed very attached to her small community.

Saron smiled reassuringly at Avery. "I will engineer a pulley system to lift the baggage through the hole. Do you have rope or cable?"

Avery nodded. "I'll get that for you."

CHAPTER SIX

The small caravan, if it could be called that since there were only two vehicles, rolled slowly down a dirt road. Avery worried the bus wouldn't make it. The Land Cruiser had four-wheel drive, but the old bus was not intended for off-road adventures.

Saron directed Avery to stop in the middle of the dirt road and scrambled from the Cruiser. Avery saw her climb onto the bus, and Gloria nodded obediently from the front after standing and obviously listening to whatever Saron was saying. Jogging to their vehicle, Saron motioned for Avery to roll down the window.

"Give me a few minutes to scan the area. I need to make sure this location is safe," Saron directed.

"We're in the middle of nowhere. I doubt the boogeyman is going to jump out at us. When you said remote, I didn't think you meant this! Where will we get supplies? I'm skeptical about a store close by to meet our restocking needs." Avery wondered what could possibly be in these woods that would house nearly thirty women. Would they be expected to camp out? Sure, she had solar panels to run critical equipment, but she didn't believe the panels would be efficient enough for their needs in the dense foliage.

Saron shot Avery a cocky smile. "I thought you trusted me."

"I, uh, do, but…" Avery began. "Never mind, do whatever you need to do. I'll just wait here and see if one of the women will give me a manicure. I've been meaning to do that," she replied sarcastically.

†

Saron chuckled and bounded away. Avery tried very hard not to focus on her backside, but she couldn't help noticing how her sinewy muscles moved fluidly. Every flex was a symphony of efficiency and grace. Yes, she had to admit that Saron was extremely attractive, even with that military presence she had clocked when they first met. Usually, Avery wasn't prone to getting lost in the affairs of the heart because she had important work to accomplish, but she was only human and a lesbian. She imagined she wasn't the only one to notice Saron's numerous assets. It had been a long time since she'd been intimate with another. Surely, that was affecting her ability to resist the intriguing woman.

She'd have to be careful not to be distracted from her primary mission. She was so close to accomplishing her ultimate achievement. New life without the need for sperm would be world-altering. The imposing woman had insinuated that this work was critical to saving millions of lives. She hadn't quite worked out how the two things tied together but had stored that tidbit away for when they had a moment to discuss her role in history. Avery frowned. Maybe this had nothing to do with her work on spontaneous ova fertilization. Perhaps it was her work with genetic manipulation that saved lives. Well, that was unfortunate. She really hoped it was the former.

†

Saron used the dial to scroll through the tools on her Universal Temporal Watch until she found the locator option. She smiled as she thought of the band of women who had abandoned the complex and set up a new location in another part of the country. Fortunately, this was the perfect location to retrofit the underground compound that would now serve the founding members of the Sapphites.

She hoped this slight change to the timeline would not have an adverse effect on the future. Obviously, it was more than a real possibility for Saron to relocate the Sapphites, or Captain Grimes would not have shared the ciphered directive. Since history had not noted a new location, she had to factor the change into her mission. Fortunately, Saron was a savvy Time Enforcer who often needed to adapt and utilize the specialized resources that the Time Agents had prepared as a contingency.

In the ciphered directive, Captain Grimes detailed how the Time Agents had arrived a year earlier to adapt the new Haven Sphere in the event a rogue group compromised the historical compound. Saron wondered what the compound looked like now. It had always been a revered landmark, visited by millions over the years. The historical attractions in the eastern portion of Old America, marking the country's independence, paled in comparison.

The Sapphites were a critical piece of the Enlightened Age. Even before the blip on the time map indicated a problem, the Ministry sent Time Agents to ensure that a backup plan was in place, providing the Time Enforcers with every possible resource for a successful mission should that be needed. Surely, those much smarter than herself would have accounted for this change. She was still alive and well, so at least there was that.

Trees camouflaged the rickety old cabin, making it nearly invisible unless a person knew exactly where it was located. The wood had clearly seen better days. Saron wondered if the Time Agents had basically kept it intact but used modern technology to ensure the cabin remained standing for another hundred years. Would they have also needed to shore up the stone fireplace, or would stone fare better over time? They needed the cabin to access the underground compound below.

Saron stepped on the creaking wooden stairs, which groaned as if to announce their age and displeasure at being disturbed in their well-earned retirement. The handle on the door turned easily, revealing that the cabin was unlocked. That made sense, she supposed. Why would they lock it? It was literally in the middle of nowhere and hidden from view.

Saron's eyes locked onto the well-crafted stone fireplace, and she glanced at her Universal Temporal Watch to find the instructions for the correct stone to access the invisible panel. None of the stones revealed any indication of a button or discoloring. Without inside information, no one would ever discover how to access the compound below. But then, they hadn't known how the Traditionalists had gotten their hands on time-travel technology. She wouldn't put it past them to have researched history and learned of The Organization. If she were in their place, this would be the first location she would check. Fortunately, very few individuals knew of this compound's existence.

There were only vague references in the history books of a covert organization of primarily women, who had affected a great many shifts in the divisive politics in the 21st century. Saron had read everything she could get her hands on regarding the mysterious group, yet she didn't have all the details of what the Ministry knew about them.

Finding the stone, she pressed hard, and the invisible panel shifted, revealing a cement stairway leading to a tunnel below. Although she really wanted to check out the compound, she resisted the urge. The longer the bus and land cruiser remained visible, the more at risk they would be. Saron touched the stone again to shut the panel.

†

Jogging to the bus, Saron directed, "Gloria, I need you to follow me and park as close as you can to the Land Cruiser. It will make it easier to unload. We need to make quick work of emptying the bus and the Land Cruiser. It's hard to know how much time we have to create a safety perimeter."

Gloria saluted and said, "Ay-ay, Captain Time."

Mavis rolled her eyes before lightly smacking Gloria on the arm.

"How many times do I need to say I am not in the military and am far from the rank of captain?" Saron grunted but without much bite. She controlled the smile that threatened to erupt.

"Rightio."

Avery had kept the window open, so when Saron approached, she announced, "Everything appears intact. I'll direct you to the spot."

Saron climbed into the seat next to Avery and guided her, suggesting that Avery move forward several feet to allow the bus enough space to park in front of the cabin. One arched eyebrow from Avery was enough to show her displeasure in what felt vaguely familiar to Saron.

After parking the Land Cruiser where Saron had directed, Avery exited the vehicle and stretched. Saron sidled next to Avery as she stood staring at the old cabin. "This is your idea of a safe place to reside? I doubt twenty-five women would fit inside that decrepit cabin, all standing upright, let alone the vast cache of equipment we have. We are not sardines," Avery said with just a hint of frustration lacing her smooth voice.

Saron couldn't help herself. The smile slipped into place before she could rein it in. "I thought we had established trust. Have a little faith. Come. I'll show you. Make sure you grab a box or two. It's best to be as efficient as possible so we can get rid of the bus and hide the Cruiser once we've settled into this compound."

"Compound? Aren't you being a bit generous? I've heard about houses appearing deceptively small from the outside, but one cabin does not make a compound."

The chuckle escaped, and Saron decided not to stifle it. Instead, she grabbed a heavy box and made her way to the door. Shifting the box to her left hip while holding it steady with her hand, Saron reached for the door and pushed it wide open.

Saron looked over her shoulder and noted that while Avery remained quiet, she had listened to her directive and grabbed a large box. A mix of curiosity, fright, displeasure, and sadness played on the faces of the women emerging from the bus. To their credit, or rather Gloria's, each woman selected a box from the storage area and followed Gloria in an orderly line. They stayed a respectable distance from the cabin, presumably waiting for Saron to lead them inside.

†

Finding the stone quickly, Saron almost dropped the heavy box before pressing the stone and revealing the invisible panel. The gasp echoed in the small cabin.

"I will never question your authority again," Avery declared with genuine awe. "I suspect the bunker below is similar to our previous complex."

"I've not yet inspected it," Saron admitted. "Time is not on our side, so the priority is to unload and settle quickly. But I trust our Time Agents. They will have done everything possible to make the space livable."

Avery nodded, and Saron began her descent. Saron tried not to get discouraged as the long stairway leading into the depths of the earth ended with a brightly lit, relatively narrow tunnel that seemed to go on forever but was probably not more than three hundred feet. The tunnel ended in a Y, and Saron wasn't sure whether to turn left or right.

Apparently sensing her indecision, Gloria said, "You and Avery go to the right, and I'll take a few of the women to the left. How about we meet back at the Y and regroup after checking things out?"

"Will fifteen minutes be enough time?" Saron asked. "I'd like us unloaded within the hour. We can do a more thorough exploration after dumping the bus."

"Yup. Should be plenty of time," Gloria answered.

†

As they continued down the passageway another two hundred feet, Saron approached a solid oak door. She set down her hefty box and opened the door. Her arms were tiring, and she didn't want to drop the delicate equipment while trying to open the heavy oak door.

This time, she didn't even attempt to hold back her smile as she took in the room that she was sure would make a fine control center. Computers, Dynamic Surface Displays, and other equipment she couldn't identify, but that she was sure would be top of the line for the 21st century, neatly occupied the enormous room. There would be ample space for Avery's lab equipment. Several Dynamic Surface Displays revealed a broad swath of the grounds around the cabin. A blinking red light caught her attention when an alarm began to beep from a biometric panel.

"Shit," Saron exclaimed. "I sure hope they assumed I would be the one to shut off whatever booby trap this panel is alerting us to." Saron placed her hand on the panel, and the light turned yellow. Recognizing the old technology, she shifted her gaze and placed her eye against the crystal-shaped orb, slightly off to the side of the panel. She breathed a sigh of relief when the light turned green. "How in the hell did they know for sure I would be on this mission?" she mumbled to herself. "Oh, frak." Saron took off on a dead run. *What if the other tunnel has similar security?*

†

Saron barely heard Avery remark, "Well, this is impressive," as she ran as fast as her legs would take her down the tunnel.

Several doors were open, leading to what appeared to be staff quarters. Gloria turned her head and remarked. "What's lit your ass on fire?"

Breathing heavily, Saron answered, "The other tunnel has security measures that might have proven problematic. I wasn't sure if you all had come across the same obstacles."

Gloria frowned. "Oh. You mean like a booby trap?"

Saron nodded. "Probably."

"Did you use your fancy tech to disable it?" Mavis asked.

"No. It's biometric. I know I have access, but given the Ministry's nature, several of you may also possess the biometric keys to disable the security protocols. Avery will undoubtedly be one, and I suspect that you, Gloria, will be another. Possibly Mavis as well."

"Why me?" Mavis asked.

"I cannot reveal that to you," Saron answered. "Sorry. Time rules prohibit me from revealing information about your future."

"Well, that's bloody convenient. What the hell have I gotten myself into?" Mavis muttered.

Gloria waggled her eyebrows. "Clearly, you're some kind of VIP. Me too, I guess."

"I can tell you that I have a vested interest in keeping all three of you safe. It would be my honor to ensure your safety in addition to Avery's," Saron declared with all the solemn promise of her duty as a Time Enforcer.

"Now, that's settled." Gloria brushed her hands together, gesturing finality. "It looks like this tunnel goes on forever. We only opened a few doors, but this fork appears to be where everyone can live comfortably. They aren't mansions, but someone equipped these pods with everything we'll need. They were thoughtful enough to put in these little fake windows. Press a button, and presto, a new scene. There are even sounds that accompany the sights. It's bloody ingenious. I'll bet whoever designed these was a clever little scientist. It will keep the claustrophobia at bay in this techno dungeon."

"All right. Can you keep your exploration to a minimum and get the bus unloaded as soon as possible? Take the personal effects to the left and the lab equipment, computers, security devices, etcetera, to the right."

†

Avery ran her hands along the computers, lovingly stroking them. She opened one of the cabinets and found lab equipment she'd dreamed of owning. Although she had managed with her second-hand equipment, this was top-of-the-line stuff that would make her job faster and easier to accomplish. She felt like an angel was watching over her. Maybe that angel was Saron and her time-traveling colleagues. She wasn't about to look a gift horse in the mouth.

She hadn't heard any screaming, so she suspected all was well on the other side. Her suspicions were verified when her guardian angel strolled into what she was now referring to as her lab, though it was also clearly some kind of control center. She supposed she should explore this section of the compound a little more. Perhaps another room could serve as her lab.

"I know it's tempting to check out this room more thoroughly, but our priority is to unload and secure the compound before further exploration." Saron's quiet command broke Avery from her dreaming.

"Right, sorry. You said that already. I'm ready. I'll follow you out and join the assembly line," Avery quipped.

"Before we go topside. I want to test a theory." Saron walked to the biometric panel and reset the security measure, then proceeded to the other side of the door. Avery followed Saron, who shut the heavy oak door after leaving the room. Saron opened the door and quickly returned to the control room. It didn't take long for the alarm and blinking red light to activate.

Saron pointed to the panel and instructed, "Place your hand on the access panel."

Avery did as directed, and the yellow light appeared.

"Now, bring your eye to the retinal scanner just like I did before."

Avery followed Saron's instructions, and the light turned green.

Saron nodded. "As I suspected. You should have access to whatever technology is present in the complex. We'll check to see if Gloria and Mavis also have access, but later. We have a bus and a land vehicle to unload."

"How did you know I could access the security system?"

"Time-travel secret that I'm unable to share, other than you are an important person to protect. It would make sense for you to have all the necessary access to accomplish your goals and set humanity on a course to enlightenment."

"Why would Gloria and Mavis have access? Especially Mavis? She all but spat on our notion of peaceful living separate from others. Called us a cult," Avery said with a note of sadness.

"I cannot provide a full explanation, but humans are capable of change and more enlightened perspectives," Saron answered. "Give Mavis a chance to unlock her full potential. She may surprise you."

Suddenly, Avery was very keen to know what Saron thought of their all-women society. She felt like she needed to explain why there weren't any men. At least not cisgender men.

"It's not like we hate men. We simply see no reason to add them to the mix, especially after I am successful with my research. Many of us have discovered there is a tendency for cisgender men to take over as if they're the natural leaders. We've found it works better without their mansplaining and aggression."

Saron cocked her head, and those arresting pale eyes seemed to assess Avery. "Do you believe you need to explain your life choices?"

Avery considered her response. Normally, she would never feel the need to justify her choice with anyone, but for some reason, Saron's opinion of her mattered. "Um, no. I suppose you might find us odd—being from the future, where it seems you don't even need any military. Are the men of your time…different? Was my split-second assessment that you're a lesbian incorrect?" Avery probably should not have blurted out her assumption that Saron was a lesbian when they first met, but her gaydar had been finely tuned over the years, and she was never wrong.

Saron chuckled, and Avery quite enjoyed that sound. "Ah, you are clever, Avery. Are you trying to weasel information out of me about the future? I suppose I can answer some of your questions in a general sense. All genders live in harmony, and most cisgender men differ from what you are used to. As I shared previously, the group that is determined to wipe out your existence are called the Traditionalists. Ironically, their roots are of this time. They are a separate society that does not share the same views as most of the world. First, they believe there are only two genders; the rest of the world accepts a wider view. Their numbers have greatly diminished over time, and there are some who question the decision to allow the Traditionalists to exist outside the bounds of society with their own rules and governing structure, especially with this latest threat."

"You didn't answer my second question. Is that a time-travel secret?"

Saron smiled. "No. I suppose lesbian would be an accurate label in your time. Although I have not had a divine connection with another for over ten years. Some might consider me asexual because of my disinterest in anything beyond my missions."

"Oh." Avery failed to keep the disappointment from her voice, and Saron cocked one eyebrow in response.

"We can talk more later, and I will answer whatever questions remain inside the boundaries of our rules, especially those that will help you survive. However, we do need to keep moving." Saron gestured for Avery to exit the control room, and she hit the reset button for the security system.

Avery nodded in approval. Making a habit of setting the security system, even when returning in scant minutes, seemed a good thing to do. Forgetting to do that at a crucial moment could have disastrous consequences.

†

Saron tried not to be too unsettled by the conversation she'd had with Avery. She rarely engaged in banter, especially of a personal nature. Although banter might be the wrong word. Getting too intimate with Avery was a perilous path to tread for so many reasons. She tried to push from her mind the motives behind her eager acceptance of this particular mission. She only hoped that Captain Grimes had assumed it was due to her familial ties to the Sapphites, rather than the eerie resemblance that was hard for her to ignore.

She'd caught Avery watching her as they carried the many boxes into the compound. It felt familiar, yet different. She couldn't deny that it felt good to have Avery clearly admire her physical form. For the first time in over ten years, she not only noticed but welcomed the attention.

Saron was pleased it had only taken one hour to unload. She frowned as she considered what would be the safest next step. Her primary mission was Avery, but what if something happened to Gloria or Mavis in her absence? Dumping the bus at the junkyard and removing all evidence that it had been used in the relocation was the smartest move, but that would require too many hours of travel, leaving one or both women vulnerable to attack. She could have Gloria drive the bus while Avery accompanied her in the Land Cruiser. They would need to be extra cautious. By the time they made it to the junkyard, a new set of Traditionalists would surely be canvassing the area. The other option was to leave all three at the secure compound and handle the bus on her own. Using a power cell for individual emergency transport was an option, but it would only cut the journey time in half.

"What are you ruminating about over there?" Avery interrupted Saron's contemplations on the best way to proceed. "I can see the concern," Avery approached Saron and touched her forehead, "right here, in this tiny wrinkle in your brow."

"I'm trying to decide the best course of action for returning the bus to the junkyard."

"I can follow you in the Land Cruiser. You'll need another person to go with. Since I am your primary mission, I don't suppose you feel comfortable letting me out of your sight." Avery smirked at Saron.

Saron sighed. She realized Avery was teasing her, but this was no laughing matter. "That's the problem. Having you join me may put you in the middle of danger. Something I am keen to avoid."

Avery scowled at Saron. "You think I can't take care of myself. I'll have you know, I've dealt with more than my fair share of assholes who've done everything in their power to shut us down, including various half-hearted attempts on my life. I will not be intimidated by a bunch of backward-thinking, straight, white men."

Patience and a finely developed ability to remain emotionless over the past ten years had served Saron well. She hoped her measured response might settle the fiery woman. "I've no doubt about your capabilities in your time. But please remember that the adversaries we will likely encounter are not of this time. Their weapons, tools for tracking, travel capabilities, and other technologies far exceed what we have at our disposal. While Time Enforcers, such as myself, generally adhere to established rules designed to manage the timeline, the Traditionalists have no such limitations."

"Perfect. We'll have many hours for you to explain everything to me, including what kind of technology we might encounter and how to counteract those limitations. Perhaps I'll have suggestions to assist you in your mission. I've been told I have a creative approach to tackling challenging problems. I know what we have available for you to adapt for optimal use. I doubt your mission briefings were as thorough as actually speaking to someone who lives in this time."

Saron quickly shuffled her options, and with Avery the likely target, she decided that keeping her close was the best decision. Perhaps if they encountered any of the rogue time travelers, she could dispatch them to the Ministry minus their weapons, power cells, and any other technology she might find useful. It was bending the rules just a smidgeon, but Saron was particularly good at justifying her actions in the field, and this mission was too critical for the Ministry to squabble over minor rules.

"All right. You win. May I borrow one of your communication devices so that we stay connected on the journey to the junkyard? I would feel better if I had a way to contact you should we need to make a detour. Give me a few moments to study your equipment and see if there's a way to jerry-rig a device for energy detection. Jerry-rig is the correct term, right? Or is it MacGyver? I took a class in 21st-century slang."

Avery chuckled. "So much to unpack here. First, by communication devices, I assume you mean smartphones. Walkie-talkies went out of fashion decades ago. As for your understanding of slang, either works, but I prefer 'modify.' There is no need for slang. I'm delighted you decided to allow me to accompany you. I have so many questions."

Avery gestured for Saron to lead the way. "I'm sure you'll find something of use in the control room. Just don't abscond with any of my lab equipment. I need every piece for my research."

Chapter Seven

"Fraking idiots. If you want something done right, I suppose you have to do it yourself," Commander Joseph Banks grumbled.

When his Heritage Warriors failed to report back within the eight-hour timeframe, he had no choice but to assemble a new team. This time, he would lead a smaller team of three. Five men with individual personalities were harder to control, especially since one of the prerequisites of living separately from the rest of the world was a tendency to be an ultra-alpha male. He would personally lead this mission. With his head turned toward the large three-dimensional hologram of their target, he failed to notice Captain Rob Carson's unusual interest in the woman despised by all those in his leadership circle.

"Any chance we can breed her before elimination? She's a looker. Seems a shame to waste good genes," a man called out.

"Nah, too intelligent," a young man with bulging muscles interjected. "What if she has a girl? The last thing we need is an uppity woman leading other women into some half-assed attempt at revolution. Every time that happens, we put ourselves at risk when we go on the hunt for new breeders to replace the ones we were forced to euthanize."

Captain Carson scoffed. "Right, Morehouse. You're such an expert on this. How old are you again? If I'm not mistaken, you were still shitting your pants when that occurred. We've made significant progress with our rehabilitation program. I believe it might be worth pursuing."

Commander Banks' booming voice filled the room. "I don't want to waste time arguing about the mission. No fraking around. We'll take her out the first chance we get. None of you are authorized to play with her. Do I make myself clear? I'll be there to ensure nothing goes wrong this time." He narrowed his eyes at Captain Carson when he noticed the subtle shake of his head. "Something else you want to say, Carson?"

"No, sir. Other than I volunteer to be on the team. I believe my dedication to past missions makes me an ideal candidate."

Banks turned his head, noticing that General Robert Carson Senior had entered the room. The man was the very definition of stealth. *Shit*. He did not need this. Of course, the general had most likely caught the last exchange, and now he would have to accept the general's son for the mission. With respect to genes, in his opinion, the young captain must have inherited more than his fair share from his mother. At least he would be easier to control.

Junior was far too soft on women, treating them almost as equals and with a respect the commander did not believe they deserved, especially when they acted out. No, a firm hand was what was required to keep women in place.

"Carson and Morehouse," he pointed to the young man who'd spoken earlier, "be ready to leave at 14:00." The kid was young, but he had the right attitude and physical presence. At least he would have another like-minded man on the mission. And, his youth, along with an almost hero worship of those in command, made Morehouse another perfect choice of someone easy to control.

General Carson nodded. "I'll expect an update in no less than four hours. If my son believes this woman is salvageable, I'd prefer you take her alive. I may wish to offer my seed to her, or perhaps she would make a good wife for my son. It's time he remarried. Make elimination a last resort."

The commander hated politics. This wrinkle would make his job ten times more challenging. If the general's son, accompanied by this woman, did not return, then his career, and possibly his life, were as good as gone. None of the general's ruthlessness had transferred to his son. He almost wished Junior were his superior rather than the man whom many revered but all feared.

†

Saron often forgot to eat at the appropriate times while on a mission. Avery reminded her of that basic need when she insisted they ask Nora if the hydroponics expert had something for them to take on the road. The rolled-up veggie and cheese sandwich was surprisingly tasty, and Saron scarfed it down as she drove on the relatively empty highway. As soon as she'd taken her last bite, Avery's voice interrupted her moment of peace.

For such ancient technology, Saron had to admit that the small communication devices that linked seamlessly with smartphones sat comfortably in her ear, completely shutting out all ambient noise while leaving Avery's melodious, slightly raspy voice to fill the void.

Saron had mounted the small tablet she'd modified to track any unusual energy bursts onto the large dashboard. Setting the device to monitor a five-hundred-mile radius was probably overkill, but Saron was nothing if not thorough. Although she might not hear the sound alarm while she talked with Avery, she wouldn't miss the blinking red lights.

She could picture Avery's beautiful face as she asked carefully worded questions. Saron had laid the ground rules. Everything was fair game except for detailed descriptors of 26th-century technology and major events in the future, including the historic milestones directly attributed to Avery Simpson. She was skating the edges by revealing even the basics of what was possible in the future. Still, she wanted to ensure that Avery knew her research was the linchpin of a peaceful tomorrow.

"So, there really are no wars?" Avery's question came out with a fair amount of disbelief. "Not just in the United States, but all over the world? I can't believe the Middle East finally resolved its differences."

Saron took a breath to answer her question. It was a little complicated, but she vowed to be as honest as possible. "Scarcity of resources to meet the needs of the masses no longer exists. There is now universal agreement that individual wealth is not a concept worth fighting or dying for."

Skepticism bubbled into Avery's response. "That can't be entirely accurate, or there wouldn't be men from your time sent to kill me."

"Very astute of you. Yes, it is slightly more complicated. There are still squabbles. Those will always exist when men are in charge. This is why the Traditionalists exist in pockets of the world where they maintain their own form of government, but are not allowed to impact or exercise authority over the rest of the territories or nations controlled by the World Council, which has remained under the leadership of women for over two hundred years. Technology, invented by a woman, exists to neutralize any and all weapons of mass destruction. Without those weapons, no nation could exercise domination over another. Limited use of small arms is authorized by the council for select individuals. The Ministry of Time Politics, of which I am a member, holds such an exemption."

"I can't be the woman who invents this technology. I'm a geneticist."

"Now you are entering territory, I cannot fully answer. I can reveal that your research plays a crucial role in the ultimate breakthrough development. Think of a stone tossed into a pond. The impact of the stone on the bottom of the pond is not the only thing of consequence. It's the ripples caused by the stone that are just as important."

"Cryptic. I will figure things out given enough time, but for right now, let's talk about something else as we travel this long, boring road to the junkyard. Do couples still marry?"

"Of course. We now have a more enlightened view of love and family. There are an unlimited number of combinations of people defined as family. Some choose to fuse with one person, while others believe they are better suited to more than one individual. And some are perfectly happy existing in solitude. Families are more than genetics. Although we don't discriminate against families consisting of a man, a woman, and children. Nor do we ostracize those who choose to live in tightly knit biological communities. However, found families are as popular as biological families."

"Fuse. That's an interesting way of describing a committed relationship. Hmmm. I suppose you don't blink an eye at two women raising children together."

Saron chuckled. "That is actually the most common type of family."

"Do you have a family, or do you live alone?" Avery asked. "Sorry, that's personal, but you did share the assumption by others that you are asexual. I am simply curious."

"Perhaps we could table this line of questioning. I would much rather have this conversation face-to-face." *What the frak am I doing? I shouldn't be talking with Avery, of all people, about my reasoning behind celibacy or the related decision to volunteer for this mission.*

"Fair enough, Saron. I will hold you to your offer to talk more about yourself."

Saron couldn't help the chuckle that escaped. "That was not exactly what I said."

"We're almost there. Two more miles to the road leading to the junkyard."

"Yes, I am aware of the location. This electronic map is quite detailed."

Three blinking red lights appeared on the tablet. They were a short distance from the old compound but several miles from the junkyard. That was still far too close for Saron's comfort.

"Avery, I need you to listen very carefully to me…"

†

"So much for pacifism," Commander Banks barked as he pointed to the pile of ash on the ground. "Now do you see what we're dealing with? I doubt very much we will rehabilitate those men-hating shrews. We should not only eliminate our primary target but take out the whole damn unnatural coven of women as well."

Captain Carson figured dealing with Banks would be difficult, especially with the sack of muscles he'd brought along to support his viewpoint. He would have to tread carefully if he wanted to bring the woman back alive.

The minute he'd seen the hologram, he'd known she would be worth it. Rob Carson had never seen a more beautiful woman. She was even more stunning than his late wife, although the resemblance to her was remarkable. The loss had devastated him. Not only had he lost his wife, but he'd lost his only child.

At first, he'd been angry. Maybe if they'd found their way to one of the medical units in the territories controlled by the World Council, both his wife and daughter would have survived. Nadine had almost convinced him to leave. They would have a good life outside of the crushing autocracy, she'd argued. Nadine feared for the kind of life they could offer their daughter, especially after she'd learned that the baby had a genetic condition, making the child inferior in the eyes of most of the Traditionalists. They would have to argue for her life.

After a few heated discussions, Rob had convinced his wife he was making inroads to change. His philosophy of treating women with kindness and respect was gaining ground with some of the newer generation. He still believed the man was the head of the house, but that didn't mean it was necessary to beat women into submission. It was like breaking a horse. Some did it with a whip, while others gentled the horse in different ways. Didn't women deserve the same gentle treatment as a beloved pet? Unfortunately, things had not worked out because his wife bled out, and his premature daughter did not survive the hour. He refused to admit he'd been wrong not to leave with his wife. Didn't the man always know better? Certainly, his father thought so.

"What the hell are you doing over there, Carson?" the commander barked. "Off on one of your daydreams? Let's move out. Their compound is this way. Use the detectors provided to locate any trip wires. And keep your eyes peeled for other booby traps. These women have teeth," he admitted, with almost grudging respect in his voice from what Carson could hear.

†

Saron jumped from the bus and waved Avery over. She'd made quick work of unlocking the gate and vibrated with energy as she held the tablet out for Avery. She'd noticed the three red dots moving toward the old compound.

Handing the tablet to Avery, she directed, "I need you to keep an eye on those three dots. The minute you see them move closer to our location, let me know. It seems I'll have less time to dismantle the enhancements to the bus than I originally calculated."

"So, watching you work is out of the question, then?"

"It would have been inadvisable without the recent threat."

"Oh, you're no fun," Avery teased.

"Avery, this is not a game. Those men are not here to pay you a social visit."

"I know. Sorry. Sometimes, I make inappropriate jokes to ease the tension. Of which there is a considerable amount emanating from your body."

Saron sighed. This woman would be the death of her yet. Taking a quick scan of the area to make sure no one was around, she moved to the storage bin to retrieve the ancient tools.

As she bent to undo the lock, she turned her head to address Avery. "Would you mind pulling the lever inside the bus to open the hood?"

"You're sure I can take my eyes off the tablet?"

Saron was tempted to call her out for already doing just that as she caught her checking out her backside. She smiled to herself. She supposed she still had it if the woman was intent on blatantly showing her interest.

"I don't believe they will have made their way to this location in less time than it takes for you to flip the hood," Saron remarked as she unlocked the bin and searched for the universal tool she'd replicated earlier. She would have to take that with her as well.

Avery chuckled. "Ooh, look at you trying out 21st-century slang again."

As Saron rummaged around in the toolbox, she answered, "Perhaps we can save the witty repertoire for when we are in the Land Cruiser heading to the Haven Sphere."

"Haven Sphere? What the hell is that? Do you mean the safe house?"

Saron crinkled her brow. "But it is not a house. The house is merely a front for the underground complex."

"All right, safe complex, then."

"In my time, locations intended to keep important persons safe are called Haven Spheres. I forgot the old lingo of the safe house. Apologies."

"Never mind." Avery shook her head and moved quickly to the bus, pressing the lever to pop the hood. Saron knew they wouldn't have time to remove the tires and return the bus to its original condition prior to her modifications, but at least there wouldn't be evidence of 26th-century technology.

She worried about the weak electronic signature that might cling to the connecting parts after removal. There wasn't enough time or the necessary technical resources to ensure she wiped it clean. She wasn't even convinced there was enough power in the cell to replicate an energy power vaporizer, but she had to try. Even after nearly depleting the cell, it would be necessary to mask the signature of the power cell as they returned to the Haven Sphere. But she couldn't leave the cell for people to find. That was a strict rule that no Time Enforcer had ever violated. The Traditionalists would know a Time Enforcer had done something to the bus. It wouldn't take a genius to presume they had used the bus to relocate all the women at the compound.

After removing the power cell, Saron replicated the energy power vaporizer, hoping the device would eliminate most, if not all, of the residual energy signature. The last thing she needed was a trail that might lead them to their new location. Waving the device over the engine block, the nearly depleted power cell, and the universal tool, she waited until it blinked green, then she moved to the Land Cruiser and repeated the process until the green light appeared again. She sighed in relief, noting she'd done her best to eliminate this latest hazard. She scanned the yard for new license plates.

"What was that you just did? And where did that device come from?"

"No time for an explanation." Saron continued her perusal of the yard. "We need to find a similar vehicle with license plates and swap them out."

"Good luck with that. These large tour buses use specialized plates. The old school buses might have plates, but they won't be the same."

"We'll have to take our chances," Saron answered.

After switching the plates with an ancient yellow bus, barely still in one piece with rust covering ninety percent of the shell, Saron noted the time. It had taken longer than she'd planned for.

†

"Why didn't you just use your fancy technology to alter the license plates?" Avery asked. "Problem solved."

"Get in." Saron motioned to the Land Cruiser. "I can answer your question once we are well on our way."

"Well, at least we won't run out of things to talk about on the way back. You owe me a whole lot of answers and further conversations that you promised we would have face-to-face. I'm looking forward to that." Avery grinned before climbing into the driver's side. "I'm driving. I doubt you have a driver's license. Not sure how we would explain that if we're pulled over."

"I did just fine on the way over." Saron activated the electric seat belt. "I'm an excellent driver. These antiques are a piece of cake. I also took a class in Operating Ancient Machinery."

"Of course you did." Avery smiled. "Let's go, Rainman." Avery pressed the power button to start the Cruiser after activating her seat belt.

Saron tilted her head and looked at Avery in confusion. "Why do you call me that? I am not a man, nor have I demonstrated an ability to produce rain."

"What? You didn't take a class in 20th-century classic film?" Easing from the gravel road leading to the junkyard, Avery made her way to the paved road that connected to the highway.

"No, I did not," Saron answered. "That seemed somewhat frivolous. Although many still watch the old *Star Trek* movies and serial episodes. We find them entertaining." Saron frowned. "It was a favorite pastime at the Academy. It's been years…"

"You really are all work and no play. I'm going to make it my mission to change that. Sometimes, Saron, a woman needs balance in her life. I'm going to introduce you to that concept."

"I've had balance in my life and play…" Saron's words trailed off as she remembered her time with Jasmine. Had it really been that long since she'd enjoyed anything in life enough to relax and play?

"Sounds like that is something in your distant past. How sad for you." Avery slammed on the gas pedal, accelerating to well beyond the speed limit, and laughed. "You wanted to get back to the Haven Sphere quickly, right? Good thing this vehicle has sufficient power to make this a fun ride."

"I don't believe exceeding the speed limit by," Saron craned her neck to look at the dashboard, "twenty miles per hour is a prudent thing to do. I remember reading about your officials, and they do not appreciate rule breakers."

"Rule-breaking can be a lot of fun. Consider this your first lesson," Avery said as she pressed harder on the gas pedal. "Don't you have any special gadgets to detect the police?"

"Replicating anything that would be helpful in avoiding the authorities would be a waste of precious resources."

"Oh, Saron, if it's the last thing I do, I'm going to get you to loosen up. Now, let's return to the topic of love and marriage, specifically why you aren't married."

†

"Frak!" Saron watched as the dots moved on the tablet. "It's taken them less time than I thought to discover the trail to the junkyard."

"That's the second time I've heard you say frak. What is that? Some kind of futuristic curse word? Whatever happened to fuck?"

Saron absently responded, "Fuck lost its impact sometime in the 22nd century. It was a very overused expletive, more than all the others, which is why shit, damn, hell, bloody, bitch, bastard, asshole, prick, and bugger remain in most people's vocabulary when expressing displeasure. Frak became the preferred word when things really went sideways. I believe a popular entertainer used the word during an extraordinarily aggressive meltdown, and it caught on." Saron shrugged.

"Good to know that people still swear in the 26th century, despite what you describe as a near utopian society devoid of war. I've always believed that swearing can have a beneficial impact on one's psyche."

Saron frowned as the alarm notified her of a large burst of energy preceding the dots moving quickly on the screen. Obviously, they were on the move. Saron suspected they were attempting to overtake a moving vehicle, and it did not fare well for whoever occupied the ancient form of transportation. "I support your need for acceleration to maximum velocity. The quicker we return to the Haven Sphere, the better. I believe I can modify this tablet to include a feature that detects officials. I'd rather not use the FlexiPad I found in the Traditionalist's ModuPak."

"Now we're talking!" Avery exclaimed with an almost maniacal enthusiasm.

Saron failed to mask the anguished sigh as the alarm beeped again, accompanied by a second large burst of energy. Avery glanced in her direction, curiosity written all over her face.

"What the hell are those alarms? And why are you so…sad?" Avery asked.

"Indications of large bursts of energy. Those sent to track you have, in all likelihood, just obtained their own transportation. The alarms suggest multiple instances of phaser fire. I suspect they sent a second team with a high-ranking official trained specifically as what you may refer to as a sharpshooter or perhaps a sniper expert. However, the weapons they use are phasers, not guns. Two bursts mean that they likely vaporized two individuals to secure transportation. I am sorry for the senseless loss of life."

Avery slowed the vehicle and jerked the wheel to the right, slamming on the brake as she veered off the highway and onto the exit that curved around. "We have to stop them before they kill anyone else!"

"No, absolutely not. You, and perhaps Gloria and Mavis, are my only concern. I believe you might call this collateral damage. I cannot be troubled with saving others."

"Collateral damage. Are you fucking kidding me? Excuse me for using the old swear word, but it works just fine for me," Avery spat out. "No life is more important than another. Whoever just got vaporized was somebody's son or daughter, mother or father, sister or brother, wife or husband. They matter."

Saron sighed. "Fine. I will direct you, but please follow my instructions exactly. You cannot become involved. I will take care of sending them back to the Ministry of Time Politics." Saron regretted her words almost immediately, but she couldn't wipe the look of disappointment and disgust practically vibrating off Avery from her mind. That would haunt her for the rest of her days on the planet in whatever time she had left.

CHAPTER EIGHT

After thoroughly searching the underground compound, Commander Banks found nothing useful to salvage. He suspected the large group of women would require a big enough vehicle to transport them along with their equipment, probably one of those ancient transport buses. The old junkyard was several miles away, according to his electronic map. They had landed in an especially remote area of the country, so finding a small transport vehicle might be more difficult than he'd planned for.

He was skilled in enhanced interrogation techniques, although he preferred to call it what it was—torture. He would find the owner of the junkyard and torture the information from that person. Even back in the 21st century, there were numerous means of tracking the ancient vehicle, but they would need supplies. He could tap into traffic scanners and potentially utilize the vast government surveillance system, including their popular facial recognition software. Maybe he'd get lucky, and the cameras would catch their target, narrowing the search location.

"Morehouse," Banks barked, "find me an energy signature for a transport vehicle."

"While the electric cars of this time are easier to track, there are limitations on the range," Carson offered.

"I know that," Morehouse answered. "I'm not an idiot."

Carson walked away, grumbling, "We should be focusing on how to find the Sapphites. Transport will do us no good unless we detect an energy signature not from this time. And so far, all we've discovered is the residual energy from the phasers used against our own men."

"Do you have a problem, Carson?" The commander worked hard to control his frustration with Junior. He seethed at the man's dance on the line of blatant insubordination. Perhaps he'd been too hasty when deeming the man easy to control. "It's abundantly clear they've packed up and relocated to a new location. These women are not stupid. The new location will not be walking distance from their old compound," he patiently explained through gritted teeth. "They will require their own transportation. Something large enough to carry all their equipment and around twenty-five women, if our intel is correct. I'd prefer not to walk to the closest location on this map where they likely acquired that transport. It's several miles away. The trail is getting cold. We need to explore this junkyard to pick up any clues to where they may have gone and interrogate the owner."

"Why can't we use our individual transporters?" Morehouse asked.

"Because that would expend too much energy, leaving us inadequate resources to complete the mission, genius," Carson snarked.

While Carson's assessment was accurate, Banks would need to manage the growing hostility between the two men before Morehouse decided he was justified in taking out a weaker man.

"Maybe the timeline has already changed because we chased them from their home," Morehouse offered. "We should send Carson back to check it out." He crossed his arms over his massive chest and glared at Carson.

Banks doubted the timeline had altered. It certainly hadn't happened while they were still preparing to travel to this time, but he rather liked the idea of sending Carson back.

Carson glared at the commander. "Don't even think about it. You may outrank me, but my father still carries considerable influence. There is precedent for ignoring direct orders. I can formally challenge your authority at any time. You know as well as I do that if the timeline had changed as a result of their relocation, we would have known that before leaving for this mission."

Morehouse reached for his phaser. "And there is also precedent for disposing of weak-minded traitors. Just say the word, Commander, and I'll turn this fraking asswipe into dust."

Banks lifted his hand. While he'd like nothing better than to have Morehouse disintegrate the sniveling thorn in his side, his own self-preservation was a guiding principle. Returning from the mission without the general's son was a death sentence.

"The mission is short-staffed enough without making it more difficult. The women have proven far more of a challenge than expected. No doubt they have a seasoned Time Enforcer assisting them. Working together is the only option. You two get your shit together. Our fight is with the Sapphites, not one another."

Banks nearly sighed in relief when Morehouse's attention shifted to his energy signature tracking device. "I got something. A signature moving quickly, coming within a thousand yards of our present location. Looks like there's a forest road or something over there." Morehouse pointed to the left.

"Go, go, go! We need to temporarily disrupt the energy and vaporize the owner," Banks ordered.

†

The three men took off in a dead run, heading toward the location Morehouse had indicated. Banks took aim at the unsuspecting passenger, firing with laser precision. The beam made a perfect hole in the glass, finding its target and turning the young woman into ash in mere seconds. Morehouse focused on the driver. While the shot was slightly off, hitting the man's shoulder, the phaser still did the trick, taking a few seconds longer to do its job, leaving a second hole in the passenger-side glass where a small portion of the beam had landed.

The men continued to chase their target as the car slowed without continued pressure on the gas pedal. As the more agile member of the team, Morehouse managed to grab the driver's side door handle and climb inside the slowly moving vehicle. Once the old truck came to a stop, Carson and Banks joined the commander. Before climbing inside the ancient truck, Banks brushed at the ash until the seat was relatively clean.

"I'm never going to get the stink of these human remains from my pants," Morehouse grumbled.

The commander chose to ignore Morehouse's petty observation as he focused on his map. "Get back on the main road. I'll let you know when to turn."

In the back seat, Carson mumbled something that Banks didn't quite catch but sounded a lot like a dig about Morehouse's manhood. Clearly, Morehouse heard the tone, if not the actual words.

"What was that you just said?" Morehouse barked.

"Enough!" Banks shouted. "I am tired of your petty arguments. I'll personally phaser you both and continue this mission alone if I hear another word."

The commander did not utter these words in an idle threat. It was becoming increasingly apparent that the two might prove a liability rather than a crucial asset in completing the mission. If he left no one alive to report back, he could invent whatever story he wanted. That option sounded better with each passing minute. The short drive to the old junkyard was blessedly silent after his warning.

†

Avery was no coward. It didn't matter what Saron directed. She would not let her face the men alone, nor could she stomach any other innocent person dying because they were after her. *What if one of those phaser blasts killed a child?* She'd never forgive herself if she allowed more carnage.

"I remember a place to park the vehicle close enough to the junkyard but hidden well. I'll have the element of surprise," Saron explained. "No doubt they will assume we've relocated and are looking for evidence or weak energy signatures to follow at the junkyard. I don't believe they realize how advanced the new energy vaporizers have gotten. At least I certainly hope the vaporizer did a thorough job. Please remain with the Land Cruiser until I complete my mission."

To Avery's sensitive ears, Saron didn't sound entirely confident about her fancy energy vaporizer. In fact, it appeared as though she may be relying on some version of blind faith. All the more reason to appease Saron.

"Sure, sure. Whatever you say," Avery answered absently as she thought of ways to help Saron without her knowledge. She gave Saron a side glance and noticed the deep groove on her forehead.

"You are placating me," Saron stated. "I'm serious, Avery. You must promise you will not, under any circumstances, follow. I'll leave you the device used to track energy. If the alarm goes off, I'll need you to use that lead foot of yours to make it to the new Haven Sphere as quickly as possible. Do not stop for any reason. Once you reach the compound, you must destroy the tracking device. I cannot afford to leave any future technology behind. Additionally, please destroy the remaining tech retrieved from the Traditionalists in the ModuPak that I left behind at the compound. The Ministry will send another Time Enforcer should my life force extinguish."

"I'm not leaving you behind on the off chance one of those phasers misses. I've seen your skills. I believe in you."

"If I survive, I can find a way to the compound on my own," Saron insisted. "As you've stated, I have many skills. Pull off to the right and take this dirt road that winds around the back of the junkyard."

Avery eased the car onto the dirt road and followed Saron's directions to an area with overgrown trees and bushes, then scoffed when she put the vehicle in park. "So, I'm just supposed to hide in the back seat or something, while I listen for alarm bells, telling me you're in serious trouble?"

"Yes, that's exactly what I want you to do. Please, Avery. I don't think you understand the significance of remaining unharmed while you continue your research."

"Then perhaps you'd better fill me in because I don't take orders from anyone without good reason."

Saron sighed, appearing to consider her options, before deciding on what might constitute the least damaging piece of information to share with Avery. "One offspring of your fertilized eggs invents the technology that neutralizes the weapons of mass destruction. Absent your breakthrough research on egg fertilization without sperm, this woman would not exist. Another Sapphite ancestor finds the ultimate cure for cancer. These are just two of the examples of how impactful your research was to society."

To Avery, what Saron revealed was huge, far more than a small detail of Avery's future. She considered this additional piece of information, which she was sure Saron was not authorized to reveal. She quickly discarded the justification because she couldn't live with herself if something happened to Saron. Others could take on the mantle and complete the research. She would have to make her acquiescence believable. Saron had a scary ability to read every subtle shift in her facial expressions.

"All right. You win."

Saron carefully opened the door and climbed out, silently moving toward the junkyard with a combination of stealth and grace. She was a vision of magnificence. Avery wanted nothing more than to continue to spend time with the fascinating woman. Not only because she possessed a great deal of knowledge, but there was something about how she controlled her sadness, just below the surface. Avery wanted—correction—needed to know what that was all about.

Chapter Nine

Commander Banks frowned as they approached the junkyard. His handheld scanner indicated there weren't any large life forms, just a few smaller ones that he suspected might be rats. He was looking forward to torturing the owner, and now, not only would he not get the chance, but that left him without their best opportunity at a lead on the Sapphites.

Glancing at the camera mounted on a pole above the gate, he barked at Carson, "Find the security feed attached to that camera." After pointing at the camera, he continued, "Morehouse and I will check out the yard and see if we can pick up a residual energy signature. Maybe we'll get lucky."

Carson appeared to scan the yard before landing on what looked like a combination residence/office. Thankfully, there wasn't any pushback or snarky comments from the captain.

The commander began to walk through the collection of rusted vehicles while checking his tracking device for any residual signature. Morehouse followed along, his nose wrinkling in disgust.

Although the large bus did not contain even the slightest residual signature, the commander would bet his entire fortune that a Time Enforcer had adapted the ancient machine and returned it, erasing all evidence of its use. It was precisely what he would have done.

He climbed into the bus and looked for the mechanism to access the engine compartment. Finding the hood release, he pulled on the lever to pop the hood and proceeded to scrutinize the engine. The commander's focus shifted to a vacant spot where a power cell was likely attached to run the engine. He ran his energy detector over the empty spot and found a very weak signature. Assumptions confirmed.

Morehouse interrupted the commander's inspection of the engine. "This place is a dump. Are you sure those dykes found a working vehicle to transport a group of women?"

"A weak energy signature corroborates my theory that they used this bus and returned it to the junkyard, hoping to throw us off their trail. Leaving a large vehicle that satellite photography can spot in a remote location is like a blinking neon sign of their new site." Leaning down, he took note of the license plate number. "Traffic cameras will help us narrow the search."

"They certainly are clever bitches, but not as cunning as they think they are. We'll always be a step ahead." Morehouse puffed his chest out, displaying the arrogance of youth.

The commander wasn't so sure they were the ones a step ahead, but he wasn't about to admit that to Morehouse, much less to himself. Although the one thing the Time Enforcers hadn't counted on was the cloak agent deep inside their organization. He'd been the one to provide the intel on the location of their compound and the technology to travel back in time. Unfortunately, the Ministry of Time Politics had tightened the flow of information after learning of their new capabilities with time travel.

First, he would try tracking them. However, if they were unable to find their new complex, the team would return only long enough to gather the necessary intel about the strategic relocation. It was not an option to fail. They needed to restore the proper world order with men, not women, in charge. Perhaps then, the Traditionalists could take their rightful place and emerge from their forced isolation.

Carson jogged over to their location and shook his head. "It looks like whoever manages this shithole left in a hurry. I couldn't find any Dynamic Surface Displays attached to the cameras."

"Of course not," Banks grumbled. "Give me a few minutes to do a search of the network of traffic cameras using the license plate number on the bus."

The commander's frustration grew upon discovering that the particular plate number had not shown on any traffic cameras within the last forty-eight hours. Viewing hours of raw video footage would take additional time, something he did not have.

"Nothing?" Carson asked.

"Fraking Time Enforcers. I'll bet the bastards used our stolen power cells to alter this plate after returning the bus to the junkyard." Sensing something was amiss, he moved his focus away from his universal device and scanned the yard, looking for whatever had alerted his senses. He'd taken the enhancement specifically designed to heighten his olfactory senses. He knew that smell. Time enforcers used slightly different technology, but the aroma was unmistakable. That specific odor typically clung to a time traveler for at least twenty-four hours.

Banks grinned. “We might have caught a break,” he whispered. “We aren’t alone in the yard anymore. There’s another time traveler close by.”

Carson and Morehouse both swiveled their heads, looking panicked. He was dealing with cowards. He thought that at least Morehouse had the balls for dangerous work. Apparently, he’d overestimated the younger man’s bravado.

†

Saron was glad she’d saved the remaining energy from the stolen power cell that she’d thought to grab before exiting the Land Cruiser. She’d had just enough to fabricate a climbing apparatus, traverse lines, and a stun gun. People rarely looked up when evaluating the risks of their surroundings. Lucky for her, the small team remained in a tight formation. That would make her approach easier. Granted, it would still be a tricky maneuver, but the Ministry had trained her well in the variety of ways to approach an enemy without revealing your position.

Stealthy as a predator, she climbed the nearest pole to the trio. She needed to act fast because it appeared as though she’d blown her cover. Two of the men nervously scanned the yard after what Saron suspected was the leader’s instruction to watch for her presence.

Setting the traverse line to the sturdy bumper of the bus, she hung on with her left hand while aiming for the group with her dominant right hand. The noise alerted the leader, who moved quickly and avoided her fire. The young man in the middle with the massive physique also managed to evade the powerful beam. At least she'd hit one of her foes. Unfortunately, she wasn't quick enough to fend off the blow from the steroid-enhanced thug. That was going to leave a bruise for sure.

The man quickly reached for his phaser, but the leader yelled, "No, don't kill her! We need information."

Saron was not going down without a fight. Scrambling to her feet, she adopted a fighting stance. The muscles made the young man slow, and she danced outside his reach, landing a roundhouse kick before finishing him off with a well-placed blow to his manhood, causing him to double over in pain before crumbling to the ground. A quick blast from her stun gun kept him on the ground next to his colleague.

And then there was one.

†

Saron stared into the cold, dead eyes of the leader, who now had a phaser aimed at her chest. She scrutinized the leader, and recognition came quickly now that she was up close and personal with him. Commander Banks. They had to be desperate if the Traditionalists sent him on the mission with only two other individuals to back him up. Two rookies, if Saron had to take a guess. She wondered why they kept sending their Heritage Warriors and not the elite Apex Warriors. There had to be a reason why they'd avoided using their strongest fighters, even if they had a tendency toward mass destruction versus precision.

"I would have rather kept you alive, but…"

"Hey, asshole," Avery shouted from the other side of the bus. "Over here."

That wonderful, lying woman. Saron couldn't help but admire Avery's moxie. The distraction gave Saron just enough time to stun Commander Banks.

"I thought I told you to stay in the Land Cruiser."

Avery smirked. "After further consideration of your arguments, I deemed them not a good enough reason to obey your order. What do you plan on doing with them?"

"They've all earned a one-way ticket to the Ministry of Time Politics' main headquarters. The commander will receive fair treatment, but they won't return him to the Traditionalists' camp. We have ways of extracting information without the use of barbaric methods such as enhanced interrogation. Unfortunately, the Traditionalists have zero compunction regarding the use of those out-of-date methods. I would have chosen conscious departure before allowing that man the satisfaction of capturing me."

"Can I watch?"

"Watch what?"

"How you send them back," Avery answered.

Saron shrugged. "You won't understand what I'm doing, but I suppose you've earned that privilege."

†

Before sending the men back, Saron emptied their ModuPaks, consolidating everything she deemed valuable into two ModuPaks. It was a tight fit, but she managed to make it work. She was quickly running out of transport devices. Having more power cells would be crucial to replicate a new supply if they sent additional teams. Pulling three transport devices from her pocket, she carefully attached one to each man's wrist and pressed the button. A faint whirring sound preceded a swirl of blue light before the men disappeared without a trace.

"Wow, that's so impressive. Gloria would be peeing her pants with excitement to watch. This kind of technology is more her thing, but I'm still very delighted to have witnessed this. Can we use one of those devices to transport us to the Haven Sphere?"

"If I utilized my limited supply, yes. I am already concerned I will have an insufficient number. I am hesitant to waste these power cells that I've just commandeered to replicate additional transporters. We will need them if more come after us."

Avery chuckled. "Commandeered. I like that. Much nicer word than stolen."

"How does that old saying go? You say *puhtato*, I say *potahto*."

Avery tossed her head back and belly laughed until tears leaked from the corners of her eyes. "You really need to brush up on 21st-century lingo. You sound like my grandmother."

"I'm anxious to return to the Haven Sphere. Let's go. I hate to squander any energy from these remaining power cells, but by the time we return, I hope to make contact with the Ministry to discover what they learned from this team I sent back." Saron cringed. "The first man I sent to the Ministry may not have been in a talking mood. I suppose I let my emotions get the best of me and returned him minus his manhood."

"Yikes. That doesn't sound like you at all. I thought Time Enforcers didn't torture anyone for information. Remind me not to piss you off."

"I have my moments. Some men should not be able to reproduce. I was doing our world a favor. Besides, they'll give him a new one. More than he deserves," she said with derision.

"So, you aren't perfect, after all," Avery noted.

"Far from it. You should have seen me in my youth. I've actually gained more patience and restraint over the past ten years. It was worth the demotion I'll receive after returning from this mission."

Avery frowned. "I forgot that you'll be returning to your time. How long will you stay with us?"

"Until I'm sure you've successfully completed your research."

"I don't suppose you're going to give me a more specific timeframe since you know the details of my future."

Saron shook her head. "No, sorry, it's against the rules."

"And you're so careful to abide by all of them," she replied sarcastically.

"Some rules are far more important than others. If I gave you the details of your future, that would most certainly impact the timeline in ways we cannot predict." Saron gestured for Avery to start walking. "We have several hours to continue this discussion in the car."

Chapter Ten

Once they'd reached the highway, Avery noticed how Saron seemed to relax. Perhaps this would be the perfect time to get Saron to reveal more about herself. The woman fascinated Avery.

"So, tell me about young and stupid Saron."

Saron turned her head and lifted one eyebrow. "Who said I was ever stupid? Breaking the rules doesn't necessarily equate to stupid."

"We're all a little stupid in our youth, thinking ourselves indestructible. Come to think of it, I don't believe you ever lost that touch of arrogance so common in young adults."

"Nor have you," Saron quipped. "Need I remind you of your earlier decision not to heed my warning and stay in the car?"

"Touché. You're not answering my question. What were you like? Did you have a great love that caused you to do unhinged shit?"

Avery noted the sadness in Saron's eyes before she masked that second of vulnerability. "Mmm, yes. I still haven't figured out whether it is better to have loved and lost than never to have loved at all."

"Surely, you haven't given up on love. Have you?" Avery asked.

"You don't appear to have a special person in your life," Saron redirected. "Have you loved and lost as well?"

Avery chuckled. "Seems like I fell in and out of love quite often in my younger years, but none are worth agonizing over. Perhaps that means I was never truly in love. Hormones can do that to you. And good sex," she added. "I suppose lately I've been so focused on my work that I haven't even had time for sex with no strings. I'm so close to a breakthrough. This trip has been an exhilarating distraction. I needed that. Sometimes, it's good to walk away and gain a new perspective before returning to the task at hand with renewed vigor. I should have agreed to those offers of a healthy diversion when I had the chance. It might have allowed me to refocus on my work."

Saron's brow crinkled. "Are you referring to recreational sex when you speak of sex without strings attached, or healthy diversions?"

Avery chuckled. "Surely, they still do this in the 26th century. If not, I'd rather stay in my time despite the leap to evolutionary utopia."

"Oh, yes, it's quite common, actually. I'm just not one to partake in this form of recreation."

"Well, why the hell not?"

"I have my reasons," Saron answered cryptically.

"Is your love and sex life a state secret?" Avery asked. "Come on, you're giving me breadcrumbs here, and I'm starving. Before you redirect me again, spill it. What happened ten years ago to turn you into this serious, duty-bound ghost of your previous self? I get the sense that you were a lot more fun in your youth."

"You remind me so much of her, and not just in looks, either. Perhaps genetics plays a larger role in personality traits than we've thought. Surely, after so many generations, this would not be the case." Saron's gaze lingered, almost reflecting an acute longing. A longing for what, Avery didn't know.

Although the confession, because that's what it sounded like to Avery, seemed one of the most honest things Saron had revealed, she wasn't sure exactly what Saron was talking about. "Come again?"

"Never mind. I wish to avoid talking about my misspent youth. Can we move on to another topic?"

"Fine, let's talk about your opposition to friends with benefits."

Saron breathed out a long-suffering sigh. "You are like a dog with a bone. I believe that's the correct 21st-century saying."

"I call it tenacity," Avery quipped. "It's what makes me so effective with research."

"All right, I'll respond to your query. I suppose I believe that divine connection without the depth of emotion is not as satisfying. My Vibesync is perfectly capable of scratching that itch."

"Really? What's a Vibesync? A futuristic version of a vibrator?" Avery guessed, stifling a fit of laughter.

"Yes, exactly. The new and improved version of a 21st-century vibrator. It adapts to the personal preferences of the user automatically."

Avery grinned. "Hmm, I'd like to get my hands on one of those. Any chance you can replicate one for me?" She held up her hand. "I know. It would be a waste of your precious power cell. By the way, no one says 'scratching that itch' anymore. It's sort of disturbing if you think about it, comparing sex to scratching an itch, especially since most itches mean there is an underlying health issue. You do know that several sexually transmitted diseases can cause itching—chlamydia, genital herpes, pubic lice, and gonorrhea, just to name a few. Seems a bit ironic that the thing causing the itch might be used to offer relief. Don't you think?"

"That is a good point, Avery."

"That's all you're going to say about this? All right, let's get at this from another angle. Do you mean to say that if I literally threw myself at you, offering one night of passion, you'd turn me down?"

Saron began coughing and stuttering, "I…I…"

For the first time, Avery knew she had finally rattled the woman to her core. That was enough for her to know this was possible. She decided to give the woman a break. "Didn't realize you'd be so easy to unravel." She smirked. "I'll keep that in mind. But for now, I have questions of a less personal nature. You don't need to answer the question I just posed."

Avery smiled to herself and wondered how easy it would be to unravel Saron if she ever got a chance to settle comfortably between her thighs. Now, that was a delicious thought.

†

Commander Banks was sure he would be able to resist whatever tactics the Ministry used to tease information from his steel-trapped mind. He wouldn't need to follow protocol. Although he hoped the others would activate the covert release device. The cloak agent they'd embedded into the Ministry hadn't been able to discover much about the Neuro Analysis Unit commonly used when they captured the Traditionalists who broke their fraking rules. There were rumors of how invasive the neuro-analysis process could be, where they would dig around in a person's brain using a kind of electric cap.

The commander wasn't worried because he knew the bloody pacifists didn't use torture to obtain intel. *Pussies wouldn't even call it torture.* The term enhanced interrogation had endured the test of time with the World Council and a handful of prominent Traditionalists. He didn't much care for the watered-down phrase. *Just call it what it is, for frak's sake.* But for some reason, although his ancestors had tried and failed to sell it to most of their constituents, a few prominent Traditionalists insisted on the antiquated phrase. They hadn't learned from history how much the expression turned out to be as retroactive as the uranium used in the smaller targeted bombs that eventually became obsolete due to that damn woman who had invented a way to neutralize them.

Wars helped eradicate the weak. How did the people not realize this? The meek were never intended to inherit the earth. That was a bunch of liberal bullshit.

"Commander," the smooth voice of the statuesque woman began, "I regret to inform you that Captain Carson chose conscious departure. Although, before his departure, he revealed the name of one of your cloak agents. We've detained the agent, and he is awaiting neuro-analysis. Additionally, Captain Carson conceded that two, not one cloak agent, are embedded in the Ministry of Time Politics. The third member of the team did not possess any useful information."

Two? Banks thought. He was unaware of this. *How dare the general tell his pissant, weaktit son and not bring me into the loop? At least the coward chose to activate his covert release device, knowing he'd succumb to their interrogation.* Banks seethed with anger at being left out, failing to appreciate that they had an additional cloak agent able to provide valuable intel.

"Frak you." The commander spat at the woman, who gracefully side-stepped the viscous glob.

"I regret we had to restrain you, but it makes it easier to fit your head for neuro-analysis. I assure you, the procedure is not painful or permanently harmful to you. The effects last only as long as the device remains attached to your head. After the procedure, I'm afraid we are unable to return you home. In the past, this has proven an egregious mistake. I will personally accompany you to our Automated Luxury Restorative Justice Facility. While it is unfortunate that you will lose your freedom, the accommodations are quite comfortable. It is more than I can say for how the Traditionalists choose to treat prisoners. We no longer use the term prisoner, but I suspect justice participant is not an easily recognizable term for you."

They'll send more once our cloak agent uncovers the location of the new Haven Sphere. The commander wasn't worried because the Traditionalists had committed to changing the course of history. They wouldn't stop sending more loyal servants until they captured or killed the woman.

Then time would right itself, and he'd find himself in a world where strong men prevailed. When that occurred, he'd no longer be a prisoner in their fancy jail, no matter what luxuries it offered. Perhaps the Ministry of Time Politics wouldn't even exist anymore in this new time.

Chapter Eleven

By the time they reached the Haven Sphere, Saron was exhausted, and she hadn't even driven. It had been a long time since she'd answered this many questions, especially ones that ventured into territory she wasn't eager to explore.

"I'm starved. Aren't you hungry?" Avery asked. "It's been over six hours since we've had a proper meal. Do you have any MREs in that pack of yours? I know you said you aren't military, but you sure present like someone in the military."

Saron scrunched her face in confusion until she remembered the terminology used by the military of the 21st century. "Meals ready to eat. No, but we do have sustenance packs that keep us nourished. I admit to preferring your veggie wrap."

"Please tell me you still enjoy a fine meal in the 26th century. I don't think it would be a lot of fun to savor a sustenance cube over candlelight."

Saron choked on Avery's words. "Candlelight? That's a romance tradition in your time? Surely, you're not suggesting we have a 'proper meal' by candlelight?"

Avery smiled. "And what if I were to suggest that? Would you be offended? Flattered? Disgusted? I'm having trouble getting an accurate read on you. Sometimes, that intensity I've grown accustomed to hints at interest. It's the way you occasionally look at me. It was the first thing I noticed after you descended into the old complex, and we faced each other in the confined space. Granted, that was under stressful circumstances, and I don't believe I made a very good first impression. I've been trying ever since to tease it out of you. Am I wrong?"

"I shouldn't answer that."

"Oh, you most definitely should." Avery left no room for debate.

"It is far more complicated than I am able to divulge. You remind me of someone very special in my life. Let's leave it at that."

"A girlfriend? Partner? Wife? You're very sketchy on the details of your past romances. Is she no longer special? Or no longer in your life?"

Saron growled. "You aren't going to let this go, are you?"

Avery grinned. "Not when I am so close to unlocking the mystery of Saron…I don't even know your last name."

Saron smiled. "Now, that is a question I can answer. Bahl."

"Back to my questions about your lady love, Saron Bahl. Who was she?"

Saron thought about her time with Jasmine. Although it was still painful to remember, over the years, that pain had dulled, like the blunt edge of a knife that had once been razor sharp. "The love of my life."

"And she broke your heart?"

"In a manner of speaking, though she can't really be held responsible for that," Saron answered.

"So, you drove her away? Made a huge mistake, huh? Tell me you didn't cheat on her."

Saron was sure her expression looked completely horrified at the notion that she would have ever cheated on Jasmine. "No, of course not," she asserted. "I would never. To me, a commitment to another is sacred. I've no judgment of other notions of love and commitment," she quickly added.

"What happened?" Avery's voice softened.

Saron knew it was a mistake to reveal her greatest pain, but for whatever reason she couldn't explain at the moment, Saron felt a compulsive need to confess to the woman who looked at her right now with such empathy and care. "She didn't make it back from her first mission as a Time Enforcer."

"Oh, I'm so sorry." Avery reached out to Saron, taking her hand in comfort. "That happened ten years ago," she guessed.

Saron nodded and swallowed hard to keep her eyes from welling. Certainly, she'd cried a lot at the time, but then, after diving into work, she hadn't shed a single tear in nearly ten years. She wasn't about to show weakness in front of Avery, of all people. Straightening her shoulders, she blurted, "You promised a meal. I *am* rather hungry."

"All right." Avery took her hand. "Let's go find Nora."

†

It nearly broke Avery's heart to watch the commanding woman on the verge of losing her composure. She was sure Saron was so close to releasing the tears that had briefly collected in her eyes before she gathered her strength and visibly stood taller, as if the conversation had never taken place.

Avery regretted goading Saron into answering her very personal questions. *Why did I do that?* It was one of her greatest weaknesses. She always had to push the envelope beyond what people were comfortable with. *No wonder I'm still single*, she thought.

To Saron's credit, she was acting as though Avery hadn't put her finger in an old wound and pressed until she screamed, *Uncle!* Avery racked her brain for a way to make it up to her. On their way to where Nora had decided to set up her hydroponics, they ran into Gloria and Mavis.

"Saw you enter, but it looked like you were in the middle of a very intense conversation, and we didn't want to interrupt." Gloria shifted her feet and wouldn't meet Avery's eyes.

Tactless as ever, Mavis quipped, "Have a lover's spat, did you? Looks like you kissed and made up, though. Not literally, because we didn't see any kissing or good stuff."

"What?" Saron responded. "We are not fusion partners. Nor have we engaged in divine connection. Sorry, I must remember to use your terms. We are not a couple, nor have we had sex with one another." Saron sounded so flustered, Avery almost forgot her own discomfort while Mavis roared with laughter, and Gloria stifled a giggle.

Avery came to Saron's defense. "I kind of like your terminology, divine connections and fusion partners."

Gloria playfully smacked Mavis. "Cut it out, Mavis. Look what you've done to the poor woman. It's none of our business."

Mavis shrugged. "What? You can see the sexual tension from a mile away. Besides, you were the one who told me that Avery—"

Gloria placed her hand over Mavis's mouth. "Do not finish that sentence. Sorry, Avery."

Avery loved her best friend, but damn, she should have known that Gloria would pick up on her attraction to Saron. She probably hadn't been all that subtle. *How many of the others knew?* Avery sighed. She and Saron were undoubtedly the talk of the compound or Haven Sphere, as Saron had referred to their new location.

There was only one way to deal with this. She'd tackle it head-on. "It's okay, Gloria. I mean, can you blame me? Just look at her. We were just heading to Nora to see about dinner. Care to join us?" Avery caught the surprise on Saron's face before focusing on her best friend again.

"Well," Gloria hedged. "I wouldn't want to interrupt anything, but we've been dying to get an update on your road trip. Anything we need to know? Please tell me you didn't run into those assholes on the way."

Saron finally regained composure and responded, "Unfortunately, we did. I am concerned about the possibility of a cloak agent. I have a suspicion that was how the Traditionalists obtained time-travel capabilities. I'm sure the Ministry has come to the same conclusion. We were able to send them back, and the Ministry will conduct neuro-analysis on the men to learn more about what they know and how they obtained time-travel technology. I suspect it would be prudent to remain diligent. Will you be able to assign someone to the Dynamic Surface Displays at all times?"

"I've already created a schedule," Gloria answered. "We've got that covered. One thing you will learn is that we are a very collaborative bunch of women, willing to do whatever it takes to protect our way of life and right to exist."

Saron nodded. "I'm afraid more trouble will come. They've been surprisingly clever. I worry that one of their cloak agents has already discovered this location. You have proven yourselves to be a resourceful and competent bunch. I should have recognized this earlier. It was, after all, reflected in our history books. However, I am used to working alone on missions. Old habits." Saron shook her head. "Perhaps it would be more prudent for me to be open to other ways of protecting you."

Gloria raised her fist in the air. "Now we're talking."

"I'm not sure I'm really cut out for all this Amazonian Warrior stuff," Mavis grumbled.

Gloria kissed Mavis's cheek. "Yes, you are. What happened to that shotgun-toting badass?"

Mavis smirked. "I do love my shotgun."

"A strategy session over dinner," Avery suggested.

"We took it upon ourselves to claim the unit next to ours for the two of you." Gloria grinned. "Not everyone can have their own pod or whatever we're going to call them, so we agreed to double up, and I've put your personal belongings in the pod for you and Saron." She winked. "Sorry, neither of you can claim your own space, but they're surprisingly roomy. The only communal spaces we've discovered don't have working kitchens, so you're hosting, Avery."

"Why am I hosting?" Avery asked.

"Because you're a better cook than I am," Gloria responded as if the answer was obvious.

"I am proficient with meal preparations," Saron offered. "My grandmothers taught me this skill."

"Good to know," Avery noted. "You can be my sous chef. Let's see about gathering whatever fresh vegetables Norah has in her hydroponics lab."

"Katy already distributed the meat and cheese she insisted we transport. You know how she hates to waste food. It was a tight fit in the bus, but I'm glad she persevered. We need those stores until we find a way to retrofit the lovely garden we discovered. I can't wait to show you. It's amazing. Nora is already eyeing it for expansion, but most of us believe we should use the space to raise chickens and goats. We'll still have to find a source for beef, but that should reduce how often we need to leave the compound for provisions."

Avery noted the momentary scowl from Mavis when Gloria mentioned Nora, but to Mavis's credit, she seemed to move on quickly. Hopefully, Gloria and Mavis had an opportunity to talk and smooth over their past misunderstandings.

"Good thing we found the garden, I wasn't sure how I was going to deal with Buttercup's bathroom needs," Mavis interjected.

Saron nodded. "Yes, I hadn't thought of that. We have other ways of dealing with that in the 26th century, but limiting time on the outside of the Safe Haven is advisable."

"Did you already stock whatever pantry is in this pod?" Avery asked.

"What are besties for? But I can't really take all the credit." Gloria visibly vibrated with energy. "Here's the really amazing thing we found while unpacking—someone or something already stocked the pantries. Maybe Saron waved her magic device, and poof, everyone has the basics. I can't wait to take both of you on a proper tour. The women made quick work of unpacking and setting everything up while you were gone."

"I would not waste energy from the power cell on spices and pantry items," Saron scoffed. "I suspect the Time Agents handled that minor detail."

"Whoever stocked the pantries deserves our undying gratitude," Gloria noted. "By the way, I hope you don't mind that I relocated your lab. I found an empty room and thought it might be too crowded in the control room."

Avery's stomach grumbled in response, punctuating her need to stop talking and get to it. "The sooner you show us to our pod, the better. I'm starved, and it'll take at least thirty minutes to prepare the meal."

Murmurs of agreement followed as the women made their way through the tunnels.

CHAPTER TWELVE

After collecting fresh vegetables from Nora, the small group traveled the corridor to the section of the compound designated as individual dwellings. Saron noted some underlying tension between Mavis and Nora and wondered about Gloria's relationship with the hydroponics expert. She absolutely wanted no part of that lesbian drama. Saron had many skills, but acting as fusion partner counselor was not one of them.

On the journey to what would be their pod for an undetermined period, Saron repressed the urge to close her eyes and engage in the recall retrieval technique often used to bring forth information that hovered just beyond consciousness. Something was niggling at a memory that she knew was important. If only she could remember the details. She knew, as sure as her own name, it might reveal more clues to the identity of the cloak agent hiding among the Time Enforcers and Time Agents. She shook her head. No, the Information Retrieval Agents who monitored and administered neuro-analysis were experts. They would learn the necessary intelligence, and if it was something Saron needed to know, they'd access the Safeguard Broadcast Network for an event horizon transmission. The transmission had a distinct auto-looping beep that would not subside until she retrieved the information. Saron had the utmost trust in the competency of the Ministry of Time Politics. Except for the rare loss of a Time Enforcer, they had a flawless record in protecting time.

†

When they reached the pod, Saron looked around appreciatively until she noted the single bedroom. She groaned, remembering Jasmine's affinity for those lesbian holo-novels. Jasmine had often cited one of her favorite tropes—the single bed. There must be something to this trope if it had endured over countless centuries. Avery, on the other hand, appeared to take the single bed in stride.

Gloria seemed to watch with interest and a bit of mirth as Saron and Avery explored the pod, especially when Saron's eyes landed on the single bed. Gloria's eyes locked onto Mavis, and she gestured with her head to move to the central living area.

"We'll just relax over here so we're out of the way," Gloria announced. "Unless you need more help."

"No, I think we can handle this just fine," Avery responded. "I'm going to throw together a simple grilled chicken salad if that's okay with everyone."

Avery retrieved a package of chicken from the compact refrigerator and set it on the counter next to the vegetables.

Opening several drawers, she seemed to find what she was looking for, placing the cutting board in front of Saron. Then, she selected a knife from the wooden block and handed it to Saron.

"If you wouldn't mind cutting the green onions, bell peppers, and tomatoes, I'll prepare the chicken. Hopefully, there is an electric grill in one of these cabinets. It would be better than using the oven," she mumbled to herself.

Saron looked to Avery in confusion. "The 21st century has many notable gadgets that would perform the slicing more quickly and efficiently. Why do you require me to cut them by hand?"

Avery continued rummaging through the cabinets, pulling out various spices and setting them on the counter. She resumed her search. "I suspect if this complex is anything like the one we're used to, energy is a treasured commodity. No sense in using a fancy Cuisinart when a knife will do just fine. Surely, you understand, seeing as how you hoard those precious power cells."

"I do not hoard, but your point is well made," Saron responded.

As Saron carefully chopped the vegetables, something compelled her to ask, "Does it not bother you that there is only one bed in this living chamber?"

"Are you afraid I'll try to ravage your body?" Avery teased. After searching in several additional cabinets, Avery discovered an electric appliance that Saron believed was the grill Avery had been looking for. "Yes! I think I'm going to love living here." Her eyes traveled to Saron, and she winked. "This pod has absolutely everything I want and need."

As Saron felt the warm tingle inch up her face and neck, she couldn't believe she was actually blushing. Saron did not blush, nor did she act like a biofluxscent going on their first vibradate. *What the frak is wrong with me?* Avery had asked a question. She needed to answer her, but what would she say?

"I'm familiar with the lesbian holo-novels that feature the one-bed trope. I have always wondered if the trope was entirely fictional or if there was any basis for some truth behind it. Regardless, women who are not fusion partners do not share the same bed, unless engaging in recreational divine connections."

Avery burst into laughter. "I've somehow flustered the immovable, duty-bound officer. Your blush is charming, Saron. If you hate the idea of sharing a bed with me," her eyes drifted to the couch where Gloria and Mavis sat as their heads bent in whispered conversation, "there's always that couch over there. It looks comfortable."

"I did not state I hated the idea of sharing a bed. I simply noted what was common in my time."

"Oh, it's the same in this time as well," Avery explained. "Although occasionally, best friends will share a bed, especially when we're younger. And what about your rigid time rules? Are you even allowed to share a bed with someone you're obligated to protect?"

Saron frowned and tried to think about the guidelines set forth for missions. She could not recall any rule specifically forbidding her to share the bed with Avery, but there were certainly warnings. Everyone knew that developing friendships or divine connections with those not of their time could be dangerous and problematic for everyone involved.

Saron decided to stick with the most straightforward answer without getting into details. "No, there are no rules that would prohibit sharing a bed."

"Good. That's settled. The bed appears large enough to comfortably accommodate two adults. I promise nothing will take place in that bed that you don't want to happen." Avery pointed at Saron, who had temporarily stopped chopping vegetables during the conversation. "Now, chop chop. Literally. I'm pretty sure everyone would like to eat before midnight."

†

Captain Grimes wasn't sure why they'd summoned her to the Neuro Analysis Unit. Her unease increased when she noted the most esteemed Information Retrieval Agent waiting inside the Classified Operations Chamber. She'd heard rumors of a cloak agent. Surely, they did not believe she was the traitor sent to infiltrate the Ministry of Time Politics. She was a decorated officer who had been with the Time Travel Enforcement Unit for over twenty years.

Dr. Evelyn Wise waved Captain Grimes inside and directed her to an open chair before activating the SecureSound barrier. "Thank you for coming, Captain."

Captain Grimes nodded, thinking, *not that I had a choice.*

"I see your discomfort, Captain. Please let me allay your fears. You are not in trouble. I won't be putting you through neuro-analysis."

The captain felt her body relax. "Thank you for clarifying that. I admit, that was my first thought. Although I am not opposed to undergoing neuro-analysis, if you believe that will produce useful information. I assume this is a top priority if they've engaged your talents."

Dr. Wise inclined her head. "Let me get right to the point. We've suspected that a cloak agent has been at work for some time now. Recently, we've had a break in our efforts to uncover the identity of this person. Thanks to Officer Bahl, I've personally conducted neuro-analysis on several of the Traditionalists she sent to us. We've detained Officer Graves as a result of what we learned. Unfortunately, we also discovered there are not one but two cloak agents operating in the Ministry. I've been made aware of the fact that you've attempted to schedule a meeting with Minister Barnes shortly after deploying Officer Bahl. May I inquire about the nature of that request? You've rarely petitioned meetings with ministers in the past."

"I thought it strange when Jude Dodd offered to provide administrative support in an infosync with Officer Bahl based on a suggestion from Minister Barnes. I wanted to confirm that with the minister. Unfortunately, Jude informed me the minister was not available until next week because she's away on Ministry business."

"Ah, good instincts. That is very strange, indeed. I happen to know Minister Barnes is not away on business. The minister and I shared a midmeal earlier today." Dr. Wise smiled. "Thank you, Captain Grimes. I may have more questions after I've had a chance to talk with Jude Dodd."

"Is there any chance Jude could have discovered the location of the Haven Sphere?"

Dr. Wise frowned. "It's possible. We found a breach in a Collaboration Nexus typically used by the Time Travel Enforcement Unit. I assume this is where you conducted the infosync with Officer Bahl."

"Frak!" Grimes exclaimed before apologizing for her expletive.

"No need to apologize, Captain. That same word entered my mind."

Captain Grimes frantically searched her memory of the infosync. If someone managed to reactivate the recording, she might have inadvertently shown the map of Old America, pointing to both locations and the roads Saron would need to travel should the original complex become compromised. Fortunately, Saron was particularly skilled at spatial awareness and operating from memory. They wouldn't even take the chance of retaining the map or providing a copy to Saron. After the infosync, the captain had destroyed any evidence that the map even existed.

"I made sure the audio and visual recording equipment was turned off prior to entering the nexus and used my FlexiPad versus a holomap. Did your discovery of the breach include tampering with the recording devices?"

"I'm afraid it did. Our experts uncovered the removal of three terabytes of data during the approximate time of what you assumed was a secure infosync. I suspect someone managed to reactivate both audio and video recording of the meeting."

The captain tried to visualize the room, attempting to recreate in her mind's eye where she was standing and the angle of the built-in capture lens. She nodded to herself. Yes, it was possible that at least parts of the map were visible.

"We need to send an event horizon transmission. Saron needs to know that the Haven Sphere is potentially compromised. Fortunately, I kept the infosync concise and hand-delivered the ciphered directive on how to access the underground complex. Knowing Saron's ability to adapt, I believed she would figure out how to access the central control unit in the compound. The biometric access will make it hard for the Traditionalists to penetrate."

"Brilliant of you, Captain," Dr. Wise praised. "However, you are correct. We'll send a transmission after speaking with Jude."

Captain Grimes sighed. "Sometimes I wish we were less benevolent. An Automated Luxury Restorative Justice Facility is far too generous for those little worms."

Dr. Wise allowed a slight smile to appear on her face, transforming her beauty into something more. Two could read nonverbals, not only had she interpreted the good doctor's agreement on her assessment of the overly generous treatment of justice participants, but if the captain was not mistaken, something was going on between Dr. Wise and Minister Barnes. The minister was a lucky woman.

"Is there anything else you're able to share that might assist us? I'm sure you recognize the importance of Officer Bahl's mission."

Captain Grimes hesitated to reveal her knowledge of Saron's link to not only the Sapphites, but specifically the woman she was sent to protect. Her gut told her the connection would not be a problem and might even increase the likelihood of success. Which was why she'd sent the troubled officer. Better to reveal this now than have another meeting with the impressive doctor, when she'd have to admit she'd kept the information hidden.

"Avery Simpson is the spitting image of Saron's former fusion partner. Jasmine died ten years ago on her first mission. Saron has never gotten over her death. I'm sure Saron has already traced the connection Jasmine had to

Avery. In addition, her matrilineage is tied directly to the founding Sapphites."

"Aren't we all tied to them in some way?" Dr. Wise appeared unfazed by this information. "I suspect that will make Officer Bahl more, not less, effective. Still, an event horizon transmission is the prudent course of action."

Captain Grimes breathed a sigh of relief. "Thank you."

"You care about Officer Bahl," Dr. Wise stated.

"I do. Saron is as close to a daughter as I've ever had."

Dr. Wise quirked her eyebrow. "No children of your own, Captain?"

The captain offered a sad smile. "I haven't found the right fusion partner to raise a child with. I still hold out hope. Although my years on the planet suggest I'd better get my butt in gear, or I'll be chasing them around in an adaptive mobility unit."

Dr. Wise chuckled. "I believe you have a fair number of years ahead of you. I wouldn't worry about finding the right fusion partner immediately. I've taken up enough of your time, Captain. Enjoy the rest of your evening."

†

Saron had to admit that sharing a meal with the three women was an enjoyable experience in many respects. The meal itself tantalized her taste buds with the freshness of the food. Saron hadn't shared food or drink with others for many years, preferring solitude. As such, it wasn't worthwhile to prepare meals using fresh ingredients. Her eco-dwelling sphere was equipped with the latest technology, including the luxury food replicator. Meals materialized in seconds rather than minutes or hours. Yet, she had to admit her food replicator didn't match the level of freshness of food picked from the garden or meat freshly butchered. She fondly remembered all those times in the culinary hub with her beloved grandmothers.

Surprisingly, the term farm-to-table, first used in the early 20th century, remained popular among elite restaurateurs. Saron hadn't been to one in over ten years, though she could easily afford the luxury. It was the company she found lacking. Her fellow Time Enforcers stopped asking if she wanted to join them after the first dozen refusals. Even the new ones avoided extending an invitation. Whether that was due to a specific energy emanating from her or they'd been warned she was a lost cause, Saron didn't know. And she hadn't really cared. But now that she was sharing a meal with Avery, Gloria, and Mavis, she had to wonder if she had missed out.

Saron remained mostly quiet during the meal, preferring to listen to the friends talk about how the other Sapphites were adapting to their new space and what they'd discovered as the women had scoured nearly every inch of the Haven Sphere.

Gloria finished chewing her last bite of salad. "You may have to call together the council, Avery. Katy and Nora were already engaged in an enthusiastic debate over the use of the manufactured garden."

"Looked to me like they should just fuck and get it over with," Mavis declared. "Maybe then Nora would stop pining for you."

Gloria chuckled. "Nah. That isn't sexual tension; they're more like sisters who fight about who gets to use the hair dryer next. For the last time, I told you there is absolutely nothing between Nora and me but friendship. Now, Nora and

Jordan—those two have been circling one another for nearly a year. I was merely a distraction for Nora."

"I agree," Avery said. "We all see it, but neither of them is brave enough to make the first move. Back to the storm brewing regarding the garden. Your thoughts?"

"Nora will claim the space is already set up like a garden, but I don't think you can argue that having fresh chicken, eggs, goat milk, and cheese isn't a higher priority. Especially since Nora already has the space for her hydroponic garden. She mentioned something about not having some stinky goat trample or gnaw on her vegetables. That really got Katy's goat. Pun intended." Gloria laughed.

Avery sighed. "I love them both, but Goddess, they're so damn stubborn. I suppose I should check out the space after dinner. I assume everyone else on the council has been to the garden."

"Yes, they have. I'm not sure it's large enough to satisfy both of their needs, but maybe you and the council can find a way to equitably assign the space. If I didn't know better, I'd believe the sun was shining down on us. No wonder Nora was practically drooling at the lush greenery. Everything is powered by generators that somehow gather solar energy. I was hesitant to explore above ground, but there must be solar panels somewhere close to the rickety old cabin."

†

Saron's ears perked up at the mention of exploring the area around the cabin. "I'd prefer that no one travel to the surface unless absolutely necessary. I will evaluate the energy source and how vulnerable that would make us should the Traditionalists find this new location."

"Saron, I understand your concern, but at some point, we will need to restock," Avery patiently explained. "We'll be fine for several weeks. If the council approves using any part of the garden for animals, which I suspect it will, I imagine Katy will want to purchase chickens and goats sooner rather than later. She's always wanted to raise chickens, but the setup at our last location made that virtually impossible, so we had to make do with provision runs."

Mavis snickered. "That's not all she wants to bring down into this hole. I heard her say she'd love to raise a few ducks. I do enjoy duck eggs. I vote to support Katy. Goat cheese, duck eggs, chickens, what's not to love about all that?"

"Too bad we can't have fresh fish, too," Gloria lamented. "Like stocking a pond for walleye or trout. I'd even eat a catfish as long as it's covered in yummy batter."

Saron wondered whether the women truly understood the danger they now faced and was about to respond when her Universal Temporal Watch announced an event horizon transmission. The loud staccato beeps caused the three women to look around.

"Is that the alarm? I need to go to the control room and see what's happening on the outside," Gloria announced.

Saron held up her hand. "No need. It's not the alarm. Please excuse me while I answer the event horizon transmission."

†

Saron didn't waste time noting their reactions. Since the pod was too compact for Saron to have a private conversation, she stepped out into the tunnel and shut the door behind her. Rotating the wheel, she activated the transmission.

"Officer Saron Bahl, authorization 6257634, ready to receive the transmission."

"Officer Bahl, thank you for your authorization. We haven't had the pleasure of meeting in person yet. I am Dr. Evelyn Wise, Senior Information Retrieval Agent. We uncovered two cloak agents and were able to expose certain intel suggesting the location of your Haven Sphere may be compromised."

"May I ask the names of the traitors?"

"Officer Paul Graves and Jude Dodd. They've been dealt with," Dr. Wise answered.

Saron thought about her meeting with Captain Grimes. She should have known those two were involved. Something was off about how interested Graves had been in their conversation after the meeting. He had leaned in as if to overhear some juicy gossip. Then there was Jude's attempt to provide administrative support, but the captain had declined his offer; so, how did the Traditionalists obtain the intel? Maybe the Ministry was being overly cautious. She needed more information to adjust her strategy to keep Avery, Gloria, Mavis, and the rest of the Sapphites safe.

"How? I presume only the highest level had access to this information, and when the captain briefed me in the Collaboration Nexus, we were alone."

"There was a breach in the Collaboration Nexus," Dr. Wise admitted.

"Frak. All right. Thank you. I won't share the details over this transmission in case there is another breach, but the Haven Sphere has adequate safety guards."

"I assumed that fact, and it isn't necessary to share those. May your trajectory of success unfold without disruption. Just so you know, the World Council authorized an ultimate expedient. This should resolve any future conflicts with the Traditionalists. We afforded them every opportunity to abide by the Accordium. We have no choice. Unfortunately, we weren't able to accomplish this before the breach. Expect a final barrier to success. End transmission."

Saron did not relish relaying this new information to the Sapphites. They would not appreciate her restricting them to the underground Haven Sphere for the foreseeable future. She would be the only one allowed to venture outside. The above-ground solar panels might be a beacon marking their exact location, and there were plenty of tactics the Traditionalists could use to smoke them out. *Frak. Frak. Frak.*

CHAPTER THIRTEEN

Avery hadn't known Saron very long, but she recognized the concern written all over the woman's face. The deep wrinkle in her forehead, along with the slight downturn of her generous mouth, were the two tell-tale signs. Her movement into their pod seemed cautious. Their pod. She had to get used to that now. They would be living together. Sharing a bed. The closest thing to domestic bliss she'd ever known in her life. Tonight had been surprisingly nice as they worked side by side to prepare dinner for friends. It had seemed almost normal.

Except, things were far from normal because there was a group of right-wing fascist pricks determined to wipe the Sapphites off the face of the earth. It would be the ultimate erasure—as if they never existed. The future's version of complete genocide—ensure those who would make a difference were never born. Avery scoffed. The Traditionalists' mission was the exact opposite of hers. She sought new ways to bring forth life, and the Traditionalists, who were so opposed to abortion, ironically sought a form of sterilization.

"While the transmission was not a complete surprise, the news is concerning and will dictate how we move forward." Saron slowly paced the compact space.

"How bad?" Avery asked. "I like our chances here with the additional biometric security and the clever way this bunker was designed."

An anemic smile appeared on Saron's face. "That is in our favor. My main concern is the solar panels, which will serve as a beacon for this site. There was a breach in the Collaboration Nexus. We have to assume they possess a general idea of our location. I've got to go topside to find those panels. Gloria, I may need your help in engineering a few surprises for when they arrive. Perhaps between the two of us, we can organize undetectable traps."

"Are there ways to hide the panels?" Avery inquired.

Saron considered Avery's suggestion. "I won't know until I inspect the number of panels and their location. To power a Haven Sphere this large, with the technology already here, and the additional equipment vital to your research, I suspect there are too many to hide."

Gloria grinned. "Oh, don't be so sure about that. I've been working on a way to supercharge solar energy. Technology has come a long way since the days of needing an entire field of solar panels to provide enough energy for a complex of this size. For now, we can swap a few of my test panels with several of the ones currently powering this place. That will likely reduce the footprint above. Then, I can work on adapting those we've swapped out."

"What do you need me to do?" Avery asked.

"Continue your research," Saron stated as if this were self-evident. "There is nothing more important than your breakthrough technique with ova."

Avery felt a rush of joy. She'd been working so long on this. She knew that was the primary purpose for Saron's mission, but for whatever reason, it had finally registered with Avery. She would be the pioneer of the ultimate triumph for women. Her colleagues had scoffed at her radical theories, but she would ensure that the impossible was possible.

"Thank you," she whispered. "It won't be me the world owes a debt of gratitude to. It'll be you."

†

Gloria led Saron to the control room, where one of the Sapphites sat focused on the Dynamic Surface Displays, only briefly glancing up to acknowledge Gloria and Saron.

"How's it going?" Gloria asked.

The woman shrugged. "Boring. But I suppose boring is better than the alternative. Everything has been clear. A few deer, that's all."

Gloria frowned. "Damn. We'll have to get creative again with our traps. I'd hate to inadvertently hurt the local wildlife."

"I might be able to help with that," Saron added absently while scouring the room.

Someone had neatly stacked the smaller, more portable panels they'd carried from their previous complex. Saron had noted their size when the Sapphites were packing up and hadn't given them much thought. All her readings of the mid-21st century led her to believe solar energy would be an inefficient source because of the massive amount of silicon, glass, metal, and plastic polymers that comprised one panel. Yet, this was the time in history when they were touted as the answer to the world's energy problems.

Gloria must have noticed Saron cataloging the equipment and proceeded to pick up a panel, grinning like a madwoman. "Mini panels. My personal invention that I've recently improved upon." She pointed at the next panel. "Grab that one."

†

Saron had an idea. It might just be the answer to their current dilemma. Although it would require bending the rules. She still had the stolen power cells. If, somehow, these mini panels could recharge the power cells, they might have enough energy to keep the Haven Sphere running without a massive field of solar panels marking their location.

She led Gloria away from the woman who was watching the Dynamic Surface Displays, hoping to have a private conversation. Nothing in the woman's demeanor made her untrustworthy in Saron's eyes, but the less she involved other Sapphites in her plans, the better.

"Do you think one of your mini panels can serve as a source of energy to recharge a power cell?"

Gloria's eyes sparkled with delight. "Maybe. I've been meaning to get my hands on your tech. This is so exciting. I'm willing to give it a try. You may need to educate me on the basics."

Saron frowned. This was not merely bending the rules but outright breaking them. Providing any detailed explanations, not that she was able to, anyway, because

Saron was not an engineer, was strictly prohibited. That would lead to inventions occurring well before their time, which in turn would change the timeline.

Saron shook her head. "I'm sorry, I cannot allow you access to future tech. Instead, I will need to learn everything I can about your solar panels. Who knew that elective on early 21st-century solar power would come in handy now," she grumbled.

Gloria shrugged. "It was worth a try. Just call me Professor Gloria. I always wanted to teach."

"You've thoroughly explored this Haven Sphere, correct?"

"Yes. Why?"

"Do you know the construction of the walls and ceilings?" Saron asked.

"I can take an educated guess. However, to be sure, I would need to conduct tests," Gloria answered.

"Lead would be preferable if memory serves accurately from my course on The Basics of Quantum Energy," Saron absently revealed.

"Why?"

"Using the power cells instead of a field of solar panels creates a different risk," Saron explained.

"How? I didn't get a good look, but they're minuscule compared to solar panels, and they don't even have to be in the open, right? We can hook them up to a mini panel, and we can use whatever cable runs down into the complex."

"Power cells emit a very specific energy signature. One that can be tracked easily. We would need to use energy from the power cell to mask the signature, and that would defeat the purpose of connecting the solar panels to the power cells. If we're able to place them in a location that naturally masks the signature, that is the ideal set-up. Lead, though not an organic compound, is a natural masking agent."

Gloria nodded. "Well, we may be in luck. If the Goddess is shining down on us, the walls in this control room are probably made of lead or steel. I don't know if I have a magnet to test, but I can look for one."

Saron walked to the one wall, closely inspecting it. She remembered a class where the instructor taught her students the differences between lead and steel in early manufacturing. Looking around the room for a sharp object, she finally found a pen and scraped the wall, leaving a noticeable scratch that uncovered the shiny metallic surface beneath the oxidized outer layer. Smiling, Saron announced, "I'll have to remember to buy the Time Agents a drink when I return. I am confident that at least the outer casing is lead. Steel is much harder and retains a shiny, blue-gray, reflective appearance over time."

"Well, aren't you a walking encyclopedia?" Gloria teased.

"I will need your word that you will not touch the power cells, take them apart, or in any way try to understand the technology. We will house the cells in this room. In a location known only to you and me," she added.

"Seriously?"

"Yes, I must insist."

"I can't even take a quick peek?" Gloria pleaded.

"No," Saron answered with finality.

"All right. You have my word."

CHAPTER FOURTEEN

General Robert Carson Senior relaxed in his study, enjoying a rare cigar. After the Unified World Leaders had relegated the Traditionalists to remote areas across the globe, it was virtually impossible to obtain fine Cuban cigars. The general wasn't sure if that was because trade was limited or the market had simply dried up. The use of tobacco products had fallen out of fashion worldwide long ago.

At the buzz to his inner sanctum, the general turned his head and scowled at the interruption. Things were not going as planned with the mission to reset the balance of power, but sticking one's head in the sand did not win the war. Senior stood to receive the latest update, sensing it would not be good news. The doors slid open, and a tall, well-muscled man stood at attention, his eyes facing forward.

"Sir, I have an update."

The general's coal-black eyes narrowed as he looked at the man. "Be concise, Major. I've no time for superfluous intelligence."

"Commander Banks, Paul Graves, Jude Dodd, and Private Morehouse were apprehended and sent to an Automated Luxury Restorative Justice Facility. Your son acted honorably and chose conscious departure. Prior to his capture, Agent Dodd obtained critical intelligence on the general location of a Haven Sphere and transmitted the information to central command." The major remained rigid, awaiting the general's order.

The death of his son was unfortunate, but unlike the others who chose a cowardly path, his son had acted with honor. The general knew he'd made the right decision to keep Commander Banks out of the loop on the presence of a second cloak agent, but then, how had they discovered Jude's identity? Even his son was not provided the name of the second cloak agent, only that there were now two, not one. The Ministry was not stupid; they would have easily figured out there was a cloak agent within their ranks. Sending two had been the general's brilliant strategy. At least that tactic had paid off. The location of the new Haven Sphere was invaluable to the mission.

"I want the names and files on every Apex Warrior in the Spector Corp. It's time we stopped fraking about. I should have sent them to begin with, but how difficult is it to capture or kill one fraking woman?"

The general knew full well why he hadn't chosen to use the Apex Warriors, but he certainly wasn't about to admit this to anyone. Commander Donovan O'Rourke led the elite Spector Corp. The general knew the shitbird had designs on his job. He was an arrogant, scheming prick, not known for precision or maintaining a small footprint. Instead, the Apex Warriors were a blunt tool intended for mass destruction.

"She is protected by a Time Enforcer, sir."

"That was a rhetorical question, Major," the general barked. "I know all about the Time Enforcer. Another incompetent woman," he spat. But the words didn't ring true because that incompetent woman had evaded both teams and managed to secure the safety of not only their primary target but every single one of those founding Sapphites.

"Sir." The major nodded. "You'll have those files within the hour." Crisply pivoting, the hiss of the doors closing marked the end of the infosync.

His wife would be hysterical at the news. He might need to lay a hand on her to get her calm. There was nothing more irritating than a crying woman. A backhand to her face often did the trick. At least she'd given him a son and not a daughter. A dead son now.

The general would have liked to try for more sons, but his pathetic wife lost the ability to bear more children after giving him a son. Perhaps his biggest mistake was his benevolent treatment of her. It would have been well within his rights to replace her. A barren woman was not valuable. But he'd been a new father, delighted with the fact that she bore him a son, and he'd kept the wretched woman.

The commander had chosen to lead a team, believing his competence would ensure a successful mission. While it was tempting to lead the team of elite Apex Warriors, the general was intelligent enough to stop fraking around and have the commander over the Spector Corp lead the mission. His warriors were blindingly loyal to their commander.

Perhaps it was time for that blunt tool. He sure hoped this would not result in unintended consequences. Fraking around with time was always a risk, he supposed. He only hoped this risk would be worth the rewards. The general would authorize a larger team. Taking only a modest team of five, or the even smaller team of three that the commander insisted on, was a huge mistake.

†

The cavernous, stark white room contained rows of virtual reality machines and the latest smart resistance trainers, but Commander Donovan O'Rourke preferred the old-school rack of weights. As a small boy, he'd been enamored by the old footage of the bodybuilders training for the Mr. Olympia competition, and he had insisted on equipping the Spector Corp's ExoGym with several sets of weights.

O'Rourke was in the middle of his exercise routine when General Robert Carson Senior entered the empty space. It took everything in his power not to snarl at the general. The fraking idiots had sent Heritage Warriors on the most crucial mission of his lifetime. *What did they expect?*

O'Rourke took his time to finish his set before turning to face the general. In his opinion, the general was not worthy of respect. He knew protocol dictated that he stand at attention, but he also recognized that the general needed him and his warriors.

"Sir?" he snarled as he remained in a sitting position on the bench.

The general glared at him. "Stand up, Commander."

O'Rourke took his time and rose, stepping close to the general and towering above him. He watched as the general's jaw tightened, and he appeared to grind his teeth in irritation.

"I could have you executed for insubordination, Commander."

"Sir, I believe both you and I know how unwise that would be. My Apex Warriors would never follow your lead."

The general removed a phaser from his holster and pointed the weapon at the commander's head. "Son, you've no idea what I'm capable of."

Commander O'Rourke remained unflinching as his steely gaze met the general's. "I am not your weaktit son." The hiss of the doors caused him to glance at the imposing man who entered the ExoGym.

"What the frak is going on here. General, holster your phaser."

The commander smirked at General Carson. The Supreme Exarch's appearance confirmed his suspicions. Not only would he be taking over all aspects of the mission, but that arrogant piece-of-shit general would likely be demoted or executed. The Supreme Exarch needed a scapegoat.

"Commander O'Rourke, you will lead the mission and have responsibility for all details going forward. General, you've been relieved of your obligation for the mission. Please return to your domicile until you're summoned."

"As you wish," the general snapped, shooting daggers at O'Rourke before exiting.

"I am sure you are aware that two teams have failed to achieve success. I regret not intervening sooner. We should have sent your unit to begin with."

"I agree, Exarch Ritter. The Spector Corp is always ready to serve." The commander smirked.

"You have complete control over the mission, Commander. Every available resource will be at your disposal, including the prototype for a new phaser with an additional wide-beam setting. Judicious use of this prototype is highly recommended as it requires considerable energy, and only three are cleared for use. I would appreciate receiving frequent transmissions regarding your progress. We've obtained event horizon transmission technology, which the infidels utilize, making it possible to communicate between different time periods. Can you be ready for a full infosync within the hour?"

"Yes, I can."

"I will see you at Central Intelligence in precisely one hour." Supreme Exarch Ritter left as abruptly as he'd arrived.

†

Sitting calmly in the Command Chamber at Central Intelligence, the Supreme Exarch stared blankly ahead. He needed a few minutes to grapple with the absolute shitstorm the two failed missions had stirred under his leadership.

The general didn't know it, but he was already a dead man, and Ritter suspected he was next if the Apex Warriors failed. Throughout his illustrious career, he'd managed to shift any failure of his leadership onto his appointed leaders. Learning the tactics of an early 21st-century president had been his secret to avoiding responsibility in the past, but this situation was different. He should have known. Eventually, the masses had grown weary of the MAGA leader's continued failures and had turned against him, especially after his ICE agents had started to engage in more aggressive tactics against United States citizens.

Ritter understood he was on the brink of disaster for the same reasons. Too many were asking uncomfortable questions. Unlike the 21st century, the masses would not be satisfied with his removal as the Supreme Exarch. No, they would demand a public execution. Commander O'Rourke was the answer to all his problems. The man was ruthlessly effective in the field.

Ritter cursed his decision to delegate responsibility to General Carson, who had made the grave error of sending Heritage Warriors versus the elite Spector Corp. Both Commander Banks and General Carson had severely underestimated the enemy, blinded by their views on the capabilities of women.

The Supreme Exarch would never admit this to anyone, but he was not as naïve as his fellow compatriots. The Unified World Leaders had begrudgingly allowed small pockets of Traditionalists to struggle in remote areas of the country, while the rest of the world prospered under the leadership of both men and women. He understood the many contributions the women had made over the centuries to that progress. Unfortunately, his brand of leadership appealed to a particular type of fanatic. He would never hold a prominent role in world leadership.

†

A beep preceded the barely audible hiss of the door, and Commander O'Rourke entered, his arrogance on full display as he captured a seat across from Ritter without waiting for an invitation. The smug son of a bitch knew he had the upper hand. The Supreme Exarch needed him more than the commander needed the Supreme Exarch. He didn't even have the good grace to wait for Ritter to speak first.

"I'll expect a promotion to general after the successful completion of the mission. And, of course, appointment to your cabinet as your new Chief Strategic Director of War. I assume General Carson no longer serves in that role."

Ritter needed to do something to regain control. He was willing to ignore certain indiscretions, but blatant defiance would not keep him in power. Leaning forward, with quiet fury, he spat out, "You listen to me, you little pissant. I'll tell the masses that you personally refused to engage your elite Spector Corp in their patriotic duty. You'll be hung up by the balls, and I'll simply appoint a new commander. Do I make myself clear?"

The commander glared at Ritter. "Crystal. Might I remind you that both our careers depend on a successful mission? I work best when there are rewards at the completion of important missions. Threats might work on the masses but have little to no value to me personally." He shrugged. "I'm not afraid of dying. My men know that. Your lies won't so easily persuade them. Expect a revolt if the masses string me up by the balls."

"You will get your promotion, but you will behave with deference to me. I demand complete loyalty. You may be correct, or as evidenced in the past, those masses will come together to protect me against your band of traitors. That's how I will spin it. I'd prefer we work together toward mutual benefit."

O'Rourke leaned back in his chair. "All right. I can be a reasonable man. You have a deal. But if you renege on that deal, nothing will stop me from coming for you. Now, shall we get to the details?"

"We weren't able to pinpoint an exact location for the Haven Sphere but could extrapolate the position within a fifty-mile radius." Ritter pressed a button on the console of his chair, and a holographic recording showed two women studying a partial view of a map.

The commander frowned. "That's unfortunate." O'Rourke leaned in for a better look. Although both women had their backs to the lens, he recognized the one on the left.

Once he'd learned about the Traditionalists' new capability with time travel, he'd made contact with his old mercenary buddies who'd managed to escape capture. They were still in complete disarray after the World Council had forced them into hiding and stripped them of the crucial time-travel technology they had illegally obtained, but that didn't mean his former colleagues didn't possess critical intel on the Time Enforcers. He'd sought to learn everything he could about their personnel and their capabilities.

The only time-travel mission he'd been a part of ten years prior had not exactly gone as planned, but at least he'd taken out one of their officers. Now, he was surc he was looking at Officer Saron Bahl, the dead officer's mate. Unnatural women. He shook his head. But she would be a formidable opponent. O'Rourke would not underestimate the woman, unlike his predecessors, because he didn't particularly believe all the crap they spewed.

"Did the general have a confidential file on Saron Bahl with more information than I've had access to?" he asked.

"Who is Saron Bahl?" Ritter asked.

O'Rourke pointed to the tall woman on the left. "The Time Enforcement Officer the Ministry sent to protect the Sapphites."

"Yes, we likely have an in-depth file on her. I'll see to it that a Central Intelligence Officer provides that to you. Are you familiar with this officer?"

"I am. Saron Bahl is formidable."

Ritter arched his eyebrow. “A woman?”

O’Rourke sneered. “Don’t insult my intelligence. You don’t believe the crap you spew any more than I do. You are well aware of the competence of women. They’ve been controlling how much power you have for several hundred years.”

“Why did you re-join the Traditionalists if you have such disdain for our beliefs?”

“I don’t disdain the core beliefs that men should retain all the power. Or that two women should not be allowed to procreate and raise that child together. I am simply a realist. Women have proved repeatedly that they are not the weaker sex. That is simply a fact both you and I recognize, even if neither of us dares to publicly admit it.”

Ritter took a second to appraise the arrogant man before him. “Despite your insolence, I am confident I’ve chosen the right man for the job. Perhaps this partnership will reap the rewards we both desire.”

“Count on it.”

CHAPTER FIFTEEN

Avery wasn't sure when or if Saron would return. It was starting to seem like she might choose to work all night. She seemed the type to do that. When would Saron sleep or rest? Avery supposed she got very little time for relaxation with her job. It was now well past midnight.

Sitting in the dim light, Avery glanced about the room. It was cozy enough. She emptied her mind and thought about her breakthrough research. Saron had told her it was the most important thing to accomplish for humanity's future. Millions would die if the Traditionalists succeeded, Saron had emphasized. Avery wasn't so sure that was the answer. So, what if Avery completed the research? What would keep the Traditionalists from returning again and again? Maybe they'd decide to go back in time even further and kill her mother or father? Saron wouldn't let that happen. There must be more to this time travel than Saron revealed. Was it like that old legal saying, "you only get one bite out of the apple?"

She stood, ready to go to her lab and continue with the new batch of eggs. Her eggs. Although many of the women donated their own eggs for the research, Avery wanted to save them as a last resort. She knew the early trials would not be successful, and with each failure, she keenly felt the loss. It wasn't fair to subject the others to the same anguish she felt every time an egg failed to begin cell division. Another wasted egg. They were so precious.

†

The doors to the pod slid open, and Saron stepped inside. "You're still up?"

Avery smiled. "As are you. I was about to go to my lab. My work is the highest priority. Isn't that what you said? I'm really only useful or important until that's completed. Then you can be on your way."

Saron held out her hand, and Avery took it. "Come on. It's time to rest. Gloria and I engineered a temporary solution, even though I didn't find any large panels close to the cabin. Four mini panels on the roof will not draw unnecessary attention. Tomorrow, I'll look for the power source. We assumed they were solar panels, but maybe it's something else entirely." Saron paused as if measuring her words. "For the record, you are important to me, not just your research." Saron continued holding Avery's hand, reaching for her other one and holding both of her hands as she looked directly at Avery in what appeared to be a desperate plea for her to understand.

"But you'll still return to your time as soon as I have the breakthrough and the masses are able to replicate the results." Avery felt her eyes fill with unshed tears and realized with stunning clarity that she didn't want Saron to leave.

"I don't belong in your time," Saron whispered as she led Avery into the bedroom. "You can use the bathroom first, and then you may have to show me how things work." She let go of Avery's hand and stood awkwardly beside the bed.

"What? No classes on 21st-century living quarters?" Avery offered an impertinent grin. "I suppose you have something like sonic showers and laser toothbrushes. The water here is surprisingly clear. I won't drink it without using my Steri-Pen, but I think it's pretty safe to shower or wash with. Probably okay to rinse with after brushing your teeth, too."

Before entering the bathroom, Avery studied Saron carefully and found the dark purple half-moons beneath her eyes. The woman seemed to run on fumes. Or was the expression, "nearly depleted power cells," more in line with 26th-century lingo? She stifled a laugh. Hopefully, Saron would join her in bed and allow her body a much-needed rest.

†

Avery was surprised to find Saron on the other side of the bathroom door in a tight black tank top and snug black briefs. She'd laid her outer garments neatly folded on top of the dresser. *Holy shit, she's gorgeous.* The outline of her small breasts was readily visible through the fabric of her tank top. Well-defined muscles revealed Saron's dedication to keeping her body in top form. That was evident to Avery on the few occasions she'd seen her fight. It was also why she'd mistaken Saron for someone from the military.

"My base layer can serve as a sleeping garment. There are clothes inside the drawer that might work for you. I, uh, am aware of the discomfort of wearing a bra to bed."

"Are you now? You own a lot of lacy bras, do you?"

Saron blushed. "Oh, no, not me. I don't need the support. My undergarment works well." Setting her gaze on Avery's ample breasts, she continued, "You require the support."

"Some women choose to wear sexy bras and underwear, even if their breasts aren't large enough to need the support. And that choice is not to satisfy some sexist view of what a woman should wear." Avery grinned at Saron's discomfort.

The corner of one side of Saron's mouth turned up in a crooked grin. "I am aware of that. That is one thing that hasn't changed in my time. I am not one of those women, though. I hope that doesn't disappoint you."

It took every ounce of willpower not to let her eyes roam over Saron's body, but she'd seen enough already with a simple glance. "Not in the slightest." She pointed to the bathroom. "Your turn. Let me know if you have problems with anything."

Saron nodded once and moved with determined grace into the bathroom.

†

Avery let out a sigh and began her search for appropriate sleepwear. Finding loose T-shirts and soft gym shorts in one of the drawers, she plucked them out and began removing her clothes. She heard the water running and assumed that Saron had figured out the faucets.

Just as Avery prepared to slip the T-shirt over her head, Saron emerged from the bathroom and hesitated before turning away. Avery continued pulling the T-shirt down over her bare breasts.

"They're breasts, Saron. Surely, you've seen them before," she chided. "I've covered them, so you can turn back around now."

"I'm sorry. I didn't mean to offend you. I was trying to be respectful. I understand the men of this time are not always courteous. Perhaps some women as well?"

"True. Mostly the men." Avery shrugged before approaching the bed and turning down the covers on one side. "I suppose I should have asked if you have a preference?"

"A preference? I thought I already revealed I am a lesbian."

Avery laughed. "Oh, yes, I'm well aware of your preference for women. I meant which side of the bed you like to sleep on."

"Oh." Saron smiled. "I have no preference. I'm used to making do with whatever is presented to me while out in the field. A bed is a luxury." She pulled her own side down and slipped under the sheets.

"Good to know." Avery crawled under the bedcovers and turned to face Saron. "Can I ask you a question?"

Saron rolled on her side to face Avery. "Yes, of course."

"Say you're able to defeat this next set of Traditionalists, and I complete my research, what's to stop them from going back further in time and taking out my mother or father? Or simply repeating their assault at this approximate time. Can't they just continue until they've succeeded?"

"My unit is responsible for the immediate time blips. Another specialized unit will handle the removal of time-travel technology from those who have demonstrated a reckless disregard for the rules. Although that is above my pay grade, I believe we've been far too lenient with the extremists. While it is always preferable to search for peaceful means of dealing with gross violations of time travel, that specialized unit will do whatever is required to prevent future abuse. You don't need to worry about that. The World Council authorized the ultimate expedient, which means rounding up everyone in the last of the Traditionalists' settlements."

"Aren't there women and children in those settlements?"

"There are. We will offer them a better life," Saron answered.

"According to whom? You and your benevolent Ministry?" Avery challenged.

"We were not the ones who broke the Accordium," Saron argued.

"What's an Accordium?" Avery asked.

"I suppose it's what you might call a treaty. We agreed to allow self-governance and to refrain from interfering in their internal affairs. In exchange, they agreed to cease all violent attacks on places outside their settlements. When the Traditionalists acquired time-travel technology and decided to use it to eliminate or capture you, the Ministry considered this a gross violation of the Accordium. It would be perfectly within our right to disband the Traditionalists."

"Did you say capture?"

"A woman of childbearing age is a commodity to them," Saron spat out. "Before the Accordium, the Traditionalists captured many of our citizens. A bloody battle ensued. As part of the Accordium, we exchanged technology and resources for the release of our kidnapped citizens. I wanted them to negotiate for any woman or child who wished to leave the settlement, but that didn't happen. It was the best they could get in the negotiations. Sometimes diplomacy is unfortunate, especially when the other side has no intention of sticking to the Accordium."

"So, there are still wars?"

"Battles or skirmishes are not the same as war. Weapons of mass destruction, such as missiles or bombs, are a far cry from phasers and other small-scale weapons. There are too many ways to harm another. It's impossible to eliminate all of them. We've done the best we could."

Avery couldn't help herself when she reached out to touch Saron's cheek. She looked so sad, explaining that even in the 26th century, they couldn't eliminate every threat to a peaceful existence.

"I know you did, correction, *are* doing the best you can. And if I haven't been properly grateful, I'm sorry."

"You aren't obligated to thank me for anything. I haven't completed my mission. You'll get sick of me soon enough."

"Never." With Saron so close and no indication of pulling away, Avery closed the distance and brought their lips together. It wasn't a ten on the spice scale, but she felt the thrill of connecting with another in a way she hadn't for a long time. The kiss could have meant anything—a thank you that Saron didn't necessarily want or need. Perhaps it meant that Avery wanted to take advantage of every opportunity to be close to this woman before she had to leave. Or maybe she kissed her because she wanted to—no, needed to experience the intimacy with another woman. It had been too long. "Good night, Saron."

Saron's eyes blinked rapidly before she quietly answered, "Good night, Avery."

†

Saron woke to the sound of birds chirping and a sliver of light that fell across her forehead. "What the frak?"

The light was coming through the fake window, and damned if there wasn't a tree complete with a pair of birds singing their little heads off. The holo-technology of the Safe Haven was certainly an unexpected bonus. She gave a silent salute to that covert organization, primarily composed of women, and thought perhaps they were the true origins of the influential Sapphites.

Somehow, in the middle of the night, her body had gravitated to Avery's, and she'd wrapped an arm around the smaller woman, just like she used to do with Jasmine. Her beloved used to joke with Saron that, even in sleep, there was that protective streak of hers. She would argue that, while she was small, she was mighty, and although waking wrapped in Saron's arms felt wonderful, she didn't need the protection. Saron suspected Avery would share Jasmine's beliefs. She'd already corrected Saron on her ability to take care of herself.

Not wishing to wake Avery, Saron began to carefully remove her arm, but Avery was having none of that as she made adorable sounds of protest while grabbing Saron's hand to keep her snuggled against Avery's back.

"Nooo," Avery mumbled, "too soon. Five more minutes."

Saron smiled, and before she gave her actions too much thought, she tightened her hold and placed her lips gently against Avery's shoulder.

Avery wiggled a little and moaned, "Mmmm. Did you just kiss my shoulder?" she asked groggily.

Shit. Deciding to ignore Avery's question, Saron stated, "I need to search for the panels today. I assume there is sufficient light now if these holo-windows are set to timers." She loosened her arm, and Avery rolled over to face Saron.

"Good morning." Avery offered a quick kiss as if it were the most natural thing. "I suppose you're right. The sooner I complete my research, the more relaxed we'll all be."

Saron thought the words were valid, but the frown at the end of her sentence led Saron to believe that there was something about completing the research that made Avery unhappy. Perhaps she was the type to always need a challenge. Saron could relate to that.

"I would like you to wear one of your communication devices while I'm above ground. If anything unusual shows in the Dynamic Surface Displays, or if you feel unsafe for any reason, you must alert me."

"Maybe it would be better for Gloria or whoever has the morning shift in the control room to do that," Avery suggested. "I'll be so engrossed in my work, I won't notice if the entire compound starts crumbling around me."

"I doubt that very much. You seem to be a woman of many talents, including the ability to multitask. Don't worry, I had planned on asking Gloria and whoever she assigned to the monitors this morning to wear an earbud. That is what they are called, right? I have a hard time getting used to some of your nomenclature. I suppose monitor *is* a much simpler term than Dynamic Surface Display," Saron noted.

"Close enough on the earbuds," Avery answered. "It's a lucrative market, so companies often invent unique names that consumers associate with their brand." Avery rolled on her back and stretched. "How about some breakfast before you leave?"

"That sounds nice. I *am* enjoying the food of this time."

Saron hopped out of bed and crossed the room to gather her clothes. She would need to ask about machines designed to launder clothing or look in the drawers for something she might borrow during this mission. Wearing the same clothes two days in a row was acceptable, but more than that, depending on her activity level, would not be optimal. Typically, if the Ministry expected Saron to remain in a specific time period for more than a few days, the paper money and gems were more than sufficient to purchase additional clothing. More pressing needs took precedence over clean clothing.

"Do we have time for a shower?" Avery sat up in bed and lounged against the backboard.

Saron looked at her Universal Temporal Watch and nodded. "It is just after sunrise."

"No wonder I wanted to smack you as if you were a snooze alarm. I don't normally function well with only four hours of sleep, but for whatever reason, now that I am up, I'm almost raring to go."

"I plan on making a quick trip to the control room while you shower. Then perhaps after you're done, I will try this 21st-century shower to determine for myself its efficiency level." Saron winked before leaving the room.

CHAPTER SIXTEEN

There were the elite soldiers in the Traditionalists' military, such as the Apex Warriors, and then there were Commander O'Rourke's hand-picked cream of the crop. He'd selected ten of his finest men to accompany him on this vital mission. A tiny niggle of uncertainty fluttered in his mind, though. Messing with time could have enormous consequences.

His origins were unknown, as he'd only joined the Traditionalists by circumstance. A story told to him as a teenager hadn't always computed with his early memories. Nightmares of being ripped from his mother's arms haunted him as a young boy. Growing up in the Traditionalist colony was all he knew, but O'Rourke always had a bit of a rebel streak, something he wondered about.

As a young man, he'd sought answers, deciding there must be more to life than the restrictive colony. It wasn't that he didn't have privileges as a man, but he wasn't born into one of the prominent families, and he craved the kind of respect given to them by virtue of their lineage. As soon as he turned twenty-one, he'd ventured out on his own, hoping to make a name for himself, and fell in with the group of ruthless men. Mercenaries. Guns for hire.

That life suited him until he'd done a solo job for the Traditionalists, and they'd enticed him home. The timing could not have been more convenient. The World Council had cracked down on the mercenaries, making it nearly impossible to operate with impunity. The work had quickly dried up. So he'd left the mercenaries, and the only game in town to achieve the money and power he desired was with the Traditionalists. He couldn't argue with his rapid rise in the ranks, and now he'd reach the pinnacle of success.

Having a troop of men to lead had appealed very much to him. He was tired of acting alone, and the Traditionalists were offering a swift elevation in rank. They'd kept their promise as long as he remained successful with the rebel strikes against the "infidels." O'Rourke rolled his eyes at that term. He didn't necessarily buy their crap philosophies, but the skirmishes appealed to his rebel nature. Toppling anyone in power was a good enough reason to go to battle.

Now, in the recesses of his mind, he wondered where he'd come from, and if, by some ironic twist of Karma, he would eliminate the woman ultimately responsible for his very existence. It was possible. He'd been told enough times that he should feel lucky they'd saved him from a wretched life. As a young boy, he'd been the object of disdain. He was an "other." Not born in the colony but taken pity on and raised by a benevolent couple who had been unable to have children of their own.

"Sir?" Major Dawson, his second-in-command, questioned.

Shaken from his thoughts, O'Rourke refocused on the map. "We've a lot of ground to cover. A fifty-mile radius is larger than I would have hoped we would need to search. We'll break into two groups. Dawson, you take four men of your choosing, and I'll lead the rest. As I recall from my earlier studies, this century favors solar energy. A compound supporting a large group will need a field of solar panels to support their energy needs."

"Sir, if solar power is so popular, won't there be fields of panels everywhere?"

"Yes, and we'll need to destroy every single one. Cut off the power, and we'll smoke the women out."

"That's a lot of collateral damage, sir. Not exactly a small footprint."

O'Rourke narrowed his eyes at Dawson. He'd never been one to question an order. "We don't have the time or resources to make a different choice. We are the best of the best. I trust the local authorities will not have the training to put up much of a fight. I'd be more worried about alerting Saron Bahl before we're prepared to deal with the Sapphites. Collateral damage is a necessary evil. I suspect that is the reason they've chosen to outfit us with three prototype phasers. We'll be able to field test the wide-beam setting. From what I'm told, the Ministry has very little knowledge of these weapons, nor a way to neutralize their destructive capability."

"Yes, sir."

O'Rourke pointed to the map. "Take this half of the target area and, after locating and destroying the panels, place our surveillance technology close enough to observe all activity around the panels. When the women surface like pesky groundhogs, we'll strike. Lieutenant Collier will remain here and monitor our surveillance." O'Rourke pointed to the center of the target area. "I'll take one of the new phasers and give the other two to you and Collier. At the first sign of the women, we'll rally to the location and finally end the Sapphites."

Dawson quickly pointed to each man who would be under his temporary command. O'Rourke smiled to himself as Dawson made his selection. Yes, Dawson was a shrewd leader, selecting the very men he would have chosen. No matter, they were all competent men.

†

After a hearty breakfast of the best pancakes and eggs Saron had ever had, she went outside. She moved quickly through the dense forest, tracking the energy signature she'd detected that was large enough to be the likely source of power for the Safe Haven.

Gloria was working on connecting more mini panels to the roof, making it appear as though the cabin was owned by a recluse who intended to live off the grid. They only needed a couple more tied to Saron's power cells for a complete disconnect to the previous source.

However, Saron was worried that the Traditionalists would target the large field of solar panels, causing tremendous harm to the local inhabitants who depended on that source of energy. She should only be concerned about Avery, but it was hard not to consider how Avery would feel if Saron ignored the impending destruction. She could almost see the disappointed look on Avery's face as Saron tried to explain that Avery and the Sapphites were her only priority.

Finally, after following a line of discoloration that she suspected hid the thick cable linked to the cabin's power, Saron reached the massive solar farm. She whistled at the number of panels. Clearly, someone had designed this system to meet the energy needs of a large city.

The Time Agents must have taken months to lay the illegal cable necessary to tap into the energy generated by the panels. This farm was over two miles away. She really needed to buy them all a drink when she returned.

If the Traditionalists destroyed this solar farm, it would cause havoc to millions of homes and businesses, likely affecting hospitals and vulnerable communities of people. Saron couldn't let that happen.

Think. Think. Think. What am I going to do to protect this community? I can't be in two places at once. Even if I install surveillance equipment around the field, it will take too long to reach the solar farm to prevent a catastrophe. Frak.

†

As Saron ruminated over her dilemma, Gloria's calm voice reached her earbud. "Saron, Nora just entered the control room. She was listening to the news, and a town about twenty miles away just lost all its power. It's complete chaos. They're saying that terrorists attacked the solar field, blowing up every single panel."

"How long before your mini panels are ready?" Saron asked.

"Almost done. Maybe another thirty minutes," Gloria answered.

"If whoever is watching the Dynamic Surface Displays sees any movement at all within the perimeter, I need you to return underground immediately. Don't be a hero. Understood?"

"Fuck that. I'm connecting these panels. I suspect we're going to need them. I have my trusty sniper rifle with me. My next task is to install automatic weapons as a welcome mat like we had at our previous compound."

Saron sighed. "I'm heading back now."

There wasn't much she could do for the men, women, and children who had already been the recipients of the Traditionalists' unhealthy obsession with changing the timeline. They would consider it all collateral damage necessary in war. Saron wasn't sure she had the skills or resources to stop what was yet to come. The only positive was the likelihood that the Traditionalists did not have an exact location for the Safe Haven; otherwise, they would not have attacked a solar farm twenty miles away. Perhaps that gave her time to devise a plan. In the meantime, she once again bent the rules and strategically placed tiny surveillance cameras on the perimeter of the solar farm. If anyone discovered this future technology, there would be hell to pay, but she couldn't ignore the ramifications of the Traditionalists' reign of terror just to get to one woman.

†

Avery watched as Saron approached the cabin. Gloria was climbing down from the roof just as Saron neared the almost rotting stairs leading to the front door. Avery could see how animated the conversation was before they moved inside the rickety old cabin. She smiled, thinking the cabin might not look like much, but clearly it was solid enough to install mini solar panels on the roof. Perhaps the rickety appearance was by design, and everything that needed fixing was merely cosmetic, leaving the structure solid enough to remain standing for years to come.

Avery met Gloria and Saron as they entered the control room. She frowned when she saw the rifle slung across Gloria's back.

"No, absolutely not," Saron barked. "I haven't even had a chance to explore potential modifications."

"They came in handy before," Gloria argued.

"We've already pushed the limits of exposure with you installing more panels on the roof," Saron patiently explained.

"What the hell are you two talking about now? If I didn't know any better, I'd assume you crave putting yourselves in danger. I heard about the attack on that town twenty miles away." Avery pierced them both with an angry glare.

"I want to install my automatic weapons system. You may be a total pacifist, but I am not. I'm going to mow down those fuckers," Gloria declared.

"Is there anything we can do besides 'mowing down' human beings to protect the other communities from their destructive actions?" Avery inquired.

"I'm afraid the best I can do is to monitor the solar farm about two miles away. This is the energy source the Time Agents used to power the Safe Haven."

"I've already disconnected us," Gloria noted. "If they destroy those panels, we'll still have power."

"That isn't exactly reassuring to me." Avery felt a sudden weight of sadness overcome her. She was the one responsible for all this destruction.

Saron met Avery's eyes and seemed to understand what she was thinking. "Avery, you are not responsible for the actions of a band of immoral men. I need to link my surveillance equipment to our Dynamic Surface Displays. As soon as they make their presence known, I promise I'll do my best to ensure this solar farm is protected."

"Why can't we alert the local authorities?" Gloria asked.

Saron quirked an eyebrow. "And say what? Terrorists from another time will stop at nothing to change the course of history by hunting down a colony of strong women?"

"It's the truth," Gloria defended.

"Thus far, they've only sent Heritage Warriors. I suspect the ones on the ground now are Apex Warriors, and the local authorities will not easily defeat this elite group of fighters," Saron explained. "These warriors are not known for their restraint. I've embarrassed the Traditionalists. They'll be out for blood. Hopefully, this will be the last group I need to contend with. The World Council has undoubtedly neutralized the problem by now."

"These Apex Warriors are just men, right?" Gloria asked. "I mean, they aren't some kind of indestructible robot, like the Terminator?"

Saron laughed. "I am familiar with that old movie. It is a campy cult classic among Time Enforcers. No, once again, they are flesh and blood, like the men who attacked your old compound. Computers control many things in my time, but they aren't generally used for warfare. As I previously explained, they are too easy to disable. You can thank a brilliant descendant of yours, Gloria, who invented a way to shut down rogue computers and synthesized humans, making it virtually impossible to use that form of technology for destruction."

"Really?" Gloria answered in amazement, then shifted the discussion to her prior idea. "Then all the more reason to install the security perimeter."

"I'd prefer something less gruesome," Avery countered. "Why can't we capture them and send them back, like you did with the others?"

"We can. It is the reason I agreed to bring the automatic weapons system to the Safe Haven. I believe I'll be able to adapt your technology. Prior to this mission, I had not considered automatic weapons as a foundation for the stun setting on a phaser. Show me your cache of weapons and how you planned on installing them on the perimeter."

"I suppose that's a viable alternative," Gloria grumbled. "I'd just as soon blast the fuckers into oblivion. If they don't care about human life, why should we?"

"Because we aren't them," Avery answered. "We're striving to achieve a better life, not destroy it because we stoop to their level."

"It's just so hard not to respond with equal fervor. I'm not as morally pure as you," Gloria declared.

"Nor am I," Saron answered. "I'll try to adhere to your principles as much as I can, but make no mistake, I will do what is necessary to protect you, Avery. If that means ending their life, I won't hesitate to act if I have no choice in the matter."

Avery brushed her hand over Saron's shoulder. "I understand. Thank you for at least considering my perspective."

Saron grabbed Avery's hand and squeezed. "Always. You are an exceptional woman. Why wouldn't I listen to your opinions?"

CHAPTER SEVENTEEN

Raising his optic scanner to his eyes, Commander O'Rourke scrutinized the adjacent road to the solar field. "Fraking military." When Lieutenant Collier had notified him of the unwelcome activity at the first location his team had obliterated, he'd been forced to double back and take care of the situation.

A procession of vehicles bathed in camouflage could only be the military of old. Apparently, destroying a solar farm created a much larger stir than O'Rourke had anticipated. Tapping into the local media revealed the US President's response to a "terrorist" event.

Sighing, he muttered, "I guess there'll be more collateral damage."

The military of this time was no match for his soldiers' advanced weaponry, even if the Traditionalists didn't possess weapons of mass destruction anymore. Their phasers could cause moderate destruction and remain an efficient killing tool for multiple enemy combatants, especially with the new prototype wide-beam phaser. He wouldn't hesitate to use that wide-beam setting. He understood that death to the soldiers would be slower and more painful, but a widened beam affected greater numbers at once. At the highest and widest setting, the phaser could take out nearly an entire troop of men. He couldn't remember if this era included women in their fighting units, but that mattered little to him. They were merely an obstacle to his success. The only downside was the excessive expenditure of energy, requiring the use of precious power cells to recharge his phaser.

O'Rourke hadn't counted on such an immediate response to his plan to smoke out the Sapphites. If the military or other experts picked through the rubble, they might come across the surveillance tech, and he couldn't have them messing with that.

"Major Dawson," he barked into his communicator.

"Sir?"

"We have a situation. Delay my order until we've resolved the issue."

"What situation, sir? If I may ask."

"Old America has assumed this was a terrorist attack and deployed the military," O'Rourke explained. "I suspect they've sent technical experts as well to comb through the debris. We'll need to eliminate this threat before proceeding."

"We've just finished placing surveillance on the perimeter and were about to move on, sir."

"Frak. Expect company, Dawson. Use the wide-beam setting on your phaser and eliminate any threat to our mission."

"Won't they keep sending more troops, sir? This was an especially paranoid time in history, and Old America had vast military resources."

"Then we'll give them reason to pause," O'Rourke growled.

"Sir—"

"Just follow my orders, Major."

A small part of O'Rourke knew this was a losing proposition, but visions of glory upon his return to his time kept getting in the way, causing him to make rash decisions. Perhaps he should have been more strategic in his approach. More cunning and less brutal force. That's how Saron Bahl operated, and that seemed to work well for her.

"Frak," he muttered. "Dawson," he barked into his communication device.

"Sir?"

"Belay that order. For now, I want you to monitor the situation. Our priority is to prevent the military from discovering our surveillance technology."

"Might I suggest using something native to the land to hide the surveillance? Rocks could be useful. Placing the tech far enough from the destruction might work."

"Yes. Proceed. We may have to wait until the military leaves, then look for a less showy means of cutting their energy source. Maybe we'll get lucky and find we've already destroyed the correct solar field connected to their Safe Haven."

"With his might, sir," Dawson answered. "Vengeance is righteous."

"Yes, with his might," O'Rourke absently answered.

He'd never been one to follow the religious teachings of the Traditionalists, who firmly believed God guided every success with might and vengeance. But he would parrot the sayings if it meant he achieved the power he vociferously sought.

†

Connecting the optic capture devices to the Dynamic Surface Displays had been far easier than Saron thought it would be. This was yet another reason to be thankful for the Time Agents. They had anticipated everything. Saron hadn't worried about Avery or Gloria learning too much about future technology as they intently watched her work.

She was about to suggest coming together to form a long-range plan when Nora flew into the control room like her pants were on fire. Saron's head swiveled in her direction as she relayed new information in rapid-fire succession.

"President Whitmer is calling this a terrorist attack, and he sent the military to both locations."

"Slow down, Nora," Gloria soothed. "What do you mean by both locations?"

"There was a second bombing or whatever it was. They can't quite figure out what happened to the solar fields, only that the terrorists completely obliterated them with something." Nora's hands shook as she relayed the information. "Or at least that's what they are saying happened to the solar field. There are rumors of a new weapon, and that's got the politicians really nervous. They're sending scientists along with the military. Both were within twenty miles of the nearest town. They know where we are, don't they?"

Saron needed to reassure the woman who was clearly coming apart at the seams. Walking over to Nora, she clasped her shaking hands. "We're safe, Nora." Smiling and giving Gloria a respectful nod, she stated, "Gloria attached her mini panels to the power cells. We are no longer dependent on the solar fields. This underground facility is secure."

Continuing to tremble despite Saron's reassuring touch, Nora disputed the comfort. "We can't stay down here forever. We'll need to go on a supply run, eventually."

"I'll take care of that," Saron assured. "I promise. I'm here to keep all of you safe. Your only job is to keep growing those delicious vegetables. I've never had such scrumptious meals. I may never leave," she teased.

"You can stay as long as you'd like," Avery commented. "Right, ladies? We would be happy to welcome Saron into our fold."

Everyone in the control room, including the woman watching the Dynamic Surface Displays, whose name escaped Saron, enthusiastically affirmed Avery's declaration.

"A tempting offer." Saron turned to the woman whose eyes never left her station. "I'm sorry, I've forgotten your name."

"It's Rachel," the woman responded without meeting Saron's eyes.

Saron chuckled. "You know you don't have to stare so intently. I doubt you'll miss anything with a fleeting glance in another direction."

Avery crossed the room and placed a hand on Rachel's shoulder. "Rachel has always been one to take any job seriously. It's one of her most endearing qualities."

The young woman beamed but kept her focus on the Dynamic Surface Displays. Saron tracked Avery's gentle hand on Rachel's shoulder and wondered if the two had ever engaged in divine connection. She felt an irrational rush of jealousy. The gesture appeared affectionate. Far too friendly for Saron's liking.

Saron's face must have revealed her displeasure because Avery sidled up next to her, tilting her head as she asked, "Now what's put that concern wrinkle in the middle of your forehead?"

"Nothing for you to worry about," Saron answered.

Avery rolled her eyes. "Oh, sister, I could almost hear the 'your pretty little head' at the end of that sentence."

Saron was genuinely shocked by that comment. "That has never crossed my mind. I am well aware of your brilliance. Those are condescending words I would never use. Yes, the Ministry sent me to protect you, but only as a kind of insurance. I realize how capable you are. All of you," Saron added.

Avery grinned. "And don't you ever forget that."

After shifting the conversation away from the actual reason for the apparent grimace on her face, Saron thought it prudent to move the conversation further away from her uncomfortable and inappropriate feelings of jealousy. "Gloria, what is that saying, 'there is no time like the present?' Perhaps we can work on that automatic weapons system of yours."

Gloria enthusiastically rubbed her hands together. "Now we're talking."

†

Avery should have been in her lab, working on her research, but ever since Saron had arrived, her need to know that Saron was safe trumped her prior obsession with self-fertilizing ova. Recognizing she would be of no assistance to Gloria and Saron, she'd reluctantly entered her lab, pleased to see Jordan bent over a microscope. Scanning the room, she noted that Jordan had managed to unpack everything, and the lab looked completely functional.

"Well, hello, stranger." Jordan's mouth quirked in a teasing half-smile. "I thought I'd never see you drag yourself away from tall, dark, and sexy. Heard the two of you were bunking together. I'd be happy to switch with you anytime you find yourself bored with her."

"Seriously, Jordan? What a disrespectful thing to say. You sound like a man."

Jordan shrugged. "Aw, come on, you know I was teasing. Lighten up. Well, mostly teasing. Honestly, I approve. It's been years since anyone caught your eye like Saron. Your work has always come first. I can't say I blame you. She *is* very eye-catching."

Avery couldn't help but smile. "She is. I'll deny ever admitting to this, but I *am* smitten."

"Good. I'll stop teasing you because I need you to look at this. I followed the notes you left on the next experimental solution to inject into the ova…well, just come see for yourself." Jordan completed her thought with a hint of jubilation in her voice.

Bending to the eyepiece of the powerful light microscope, Avery saw what Jordan was so excited about. It was right there under the lens. The ova had divided into four daughter cells. It was a significant step in the right direction, but Avery knew they still had a long way to go.

Stepping away from the microscope, Avery gathered Jordan in a zealous hug, crushing their bodies together. "We did it!"

"You did it. I just followed your notes." Jordan chuckled. "You know, if I'd known you were going to hug me so passionately, I'd have started on this latest process a lot sooner."

Avery chuckled. "Stop flirting. I know your secret."

"What secret?"

"You have your eye on Nora." Avery shook her head. "You aren't fooling me one bit with your comments about Saron or your incessant flirting. Every time Nora enters the room, your eyes light up, and you practically track her every move. Ask her out already."

Jordan blushed. "She's not ready yet."

"Because of that short-lived thing with Gloria? Oh, please. Ancient history. Gloria's hooked up with several of the women here, including her latest, Brenda. That was never going to turn into anything serious. Gloria was just looking for a distraction after Mavis. And Jordan, Nora is just biding her time until you get your head out of your ass."

"You think so?" Jordan asked with uncharacteristic diffidence.

"I know so," Avery responded.

"Has she said something to you?"

"Oh, no, I am not playing the high school game with you two. You're grown women. Act like it!"

Jordan chuckled. "Okay, I will refrain from asking you to pass a note to Nora with checkboxes to indicate whether she likes me or not."

"I just believe that life is way too short to screw around. Take the plunge," Avery counseled.

"Perhaps you should listen to your own advice," Jordan retorted.

Avery grinned. "Oh, no worries there. I'm working on it. For such an imposing woman, Saron is like a skittish kitten when it comes to matters of the heart. Baby steps…"

"You go, girl!"

"Now, let's get back to work," Avery directed. "I don't know whether to glue my eye to the microscope, or work on alternate experiments when the inevitable cell division process doesn't turn out the way we hope it will. It cannot be this easy."

"Easy? You call all the failed experiments over the past two years easy?" Jordan asked in exasperation.

"I suppose you're right. Nothing worthwhile is ever without considerable effort."

CHAPTER EIGHTEEN

Idle was not something Commander O'Rourke was very good at. It didn't take long for him to get antsy. They needed to find those other solar fields. What he would do when they got there, he didn't know, but he'd figure it out.

"Let's move out," he barked.

"Sir?" a square-jawed man responded. "I thought we were going to lie low, hidden in the forest until there is less scrutiny from Old America?"

"The military of old are not known for expediency. We could be here for weeks. I want to find another way to disrupt the power to other solar fields that's less obvious."

The man frowned. "Won't any disruption to their main power source bring attention to the area?"

"Attention, yes, but the government of this time will likely send one pathetic troop. We can handle that along with a few engineers poking around the site, trying to figure out why the solar panels have failed," O'Rourke answered.

"Yes, sir."

"I've studied the map and believe I've found an open area likely to contain the next solar field. Within this fifty-mile radius, based on the size of the two fields we've destroyed, I estimate there are an additional three or four other fields powered by their inefficient solar panels. We get in, disrupt the source, and get out. Then it is merely a matter of time before the women emerge from their hole."

"Will you be ordering Dawson's team to proceed?"

O'Rourke pointed to the center of his FlexiPad. "Yes, and we'll rendezvous here. The forest will provide sufficient coverage to wait."

"Those military transport carriers are very tempting to steal. It sure would be faster and more efficient to travel in one of those."

O'Rourke grinned. He'd get to engage in hand-to-hand combat today. He missed that. By the time the military sent more men to investigate why none of their men were responding, they'd be long gone, with one or two of their transport machines.

"Yes, it would, Lieutenant. We're going to get up close and personal with a few of those men. Silent and stealth elimination. Once we've commandeered one or two of their vehicles and stolen their clothing, we'll move them far enough away to enable me to use the wide beam on the remainder of their troop. I'm sure they'll send more men, but by then, we'll be long gone. Unfortunately, we'll need to be quick about camouflaging more surveillance tech to replace what we will destroy with our phasers."

The Lieutenant nodded. "Good plan, sir. Will you direct Dawson to do the same?"

"No. Taking out this troop already suggests a larger footprint than is comfortable for a successful mission without unintended consequences to the timeline. Some of these military personnel may be your ancestors." *Or mine.* "Many of the Traditionalists originated from military families and ICE agents. Dawson's men can handle the physical exertion required to traverse the terrain."

The Lieutenant laughed. "Glad Dawson didn't pick me to be on his team."

"Dawson," O'Rourke barked into his communication device.

"Sir?"

"New plan."

†

The control room was already overcrowded when Mavis strolled in, bringing her larger-than-life energy, along with her beloved Buttercup, who clung to her side. She set Buttercup's mat next to the array of Dynamic Surface Displays.

Saron and Gloria had moved to a corner of the room to work on adapting the cache of automatic weapons. The process was easy enough. Saron worried more about how long it would take to install them on the perimeter. The less exposure to the outside, the better.

"You two look cozy over there." Mavis narrowed her eyes. "Gloria, I don't think you're Saron's type. Now, Avery…" Mavis cackled.

"Oh, for fuck's sake, Mavis. You have got to stop imagining crazy shit. And did you honestly think it was a good idea to bring Buttercup to this crowded room?"

"She was getting antsy," Mavis defended. "Buttercup isn't used to not being able to roam about freely in the sunshine."

"So take her to the garden," Gloria answered.

"I think it's time for me to leave now," Rachel remarked before making a quick exit.

"For the record, a blind person can see the sparks between Avery and Saron," Gloria continued, ignoring Rachel's hasty departure. "You know you're the only woman for me."

Saron's head popped up, and she was sure her eyes grew wide as the women casually discussed their growing affection for one another.

Gloria chuckled. "You know it's not a secret, Saron."

"There is nothing happening between Avery and me. She is my responsibility, as you all are."

"Mmhmm," Gloria answered. "Whatever you say, boss."

"I am not your boss, either," Saron protested.

"Did you need something, Mavis?" Gloria redirected her attention to Mavis, smiling broadly at her fusion partner.

"I'm scheduled to take over for Rachel," Mavis answered as she slid into the seat Rachel had recently departed. Buttercup promptly flopped on the lambskin mat next to her with an exaggerated huff, as if to say, "I'm so over this adventure."

"Good, I'll be able to keep my eye on you. Make sure you aren't causing trouble." Gloria winked.

"Trouble? You know I only ever cause good trouble," Mavis teased. "You weren't complaining last night."

"I never complain," Gloria answered.

"Can we please return to adapting these weapons? Then we need to discuss how you plan to install them on the perimeter. Perhaps you can walk me through your thoughts on that. I would prefer to be the one to deploy the system."

"Fuck that. My system, my install. It'll be much quicker if I do it myself than if I try to explain it to you. Besides, you let me attach the mini panels to the roof by myself."

"That was before we learned of the destruction to those solar fields. I cannot allow you to place yourself at risk. For reasons I cannot divulge," Saron added.

Gloria squinted at Saron. "We're connected in some way," she guessed. "Oh, my Goddess, I'm like your great, great, great, great, grandmother or something—not sure how many greats to add to get us to the right century. Right?"

"I cannot answer your question."

"What the hell?" Mavis exclaimed. "You fuck a man, Gloria? I thought I only had to worry about your dalliances with other women."

"I have never once 'dallied' with another woman. You broke up with me. I was free to see other people," Gloria defended. "None of them meant anything. It was more like a *friends-with-benefits* situation. I have needs, and you weren't meeting them after we split."

Saron sighed. "Gloria does not have relations with a man. Of that, I am sure."

Saron remembered how she had tried to avoid staring at Mavis's cool gray eyes, so similar to her own, but without the pale violet tint. Obviously, Gloria and Mavis remained together long enough to have a child, and now Saron was convinced that Mavis was most assuredly her other direct familial ancestor, not just Gloria's fusion partner who helped raise her daughter. Turning her gaze to Mavis, she once again landed on those compelling eyes. Yes, that confirmed her sudden epiphany. Saron had Mavis's eyes.

"What are you staring at? Oh…" Mavis said with a sudden flash of clarity. Her expression softened.

Frak! Nothing about this mission was going the way Saron had anticipated. The complications kept adding up to one big shit show. That was 21st-century slang, which Saron immensely appreciated.

"Do not make assumptions you cannot confirm," Saron weakly argued.

Gloria looked from Mavis to Saron. "Oh, oh…Holy shit! We're going to be parents, Mavis. Avery does it! She really does it! Is that why you volunteered for this mission? Do we have a boy or a girl? Holy fucking shit. Do we have more than one child? Do our children conceive naturally or through the Avery method? Should we name it that, the Avery method? No, that's probably stupid, because aren't major breakthroughs in science given the scientist's last name, or do the stupid men appropriate her breakthrough research?" Gloria's rapid-fire questions took Saron off guard.

The only response that came to mind was "frak," which she inadvertently expressed without censorship.

Mavis grinned. "Aw, come on, my brave, multiple greats, granddaughter, which, from this point forward, I will shorten to great-granddaughter. Give us the deets. The cat is already out of the bag."

"Don't you mean the horse has left the barn?" Saron attempted to distract.

"I like cat out of the bag better. So spill," Mavis ordered.

"I honestly don't possess all the details. I was only aware of my connection to the Sapphites. It wasn't until I met Gloria that I pieced together the bond. And then we visited your junkyard…"

Mavis smiled. "You have my eyes. Well, almost. Did they do a little genetic modification to get that exact color?"

Saron shook her head. "I believe it's a side effect of Simpson Ova. In the initial stages of Simpson Ova, many heterosexual couples chose this breakthrough method of conception, rather than conceive naturally. The unusual eye colors were considered captivating at the time. My eyes are no longer considered remarkable."

"One thing I don't understand is how Mavis and I have a child together. Avery is working on self-fertilization of eggs, not splicing the DNA of two eggs."

"Simpson Ova is the name attached to both processes. According to history, she wanted to give women a choice. For those who wished to have a baby with their fusion partner, she did not want to force the couple to decide which ova to use. Sometimes, that choice left one person feeling disconnected or less intimately bonded to their child. Whether this is true or not, it is what is taught. The first successful birth is a self-fertilized egg. They taught us in school that this weighed heavily on Avery when she eventually made a commitment to her lifetime fusion partner."

Having explained this to Gloria and Mavis, Saron was reminded of the fact that Avery would eventually marry. This thought created a kind of pit in her stomach. She did not belong in this time, nor was she destined to become Avery's fusion partner.

Gloria placed her hand on Saron's arm. "Cheer up, Saron, perhaps you are her lifetime fusion partner. Stranger things have happened. Would it be so bad to remain with us? If that convoluted storyline works for *The Terminator*, minus the dude's death at the end, why can't it happen here?"

Now Saron had a queasy feeling for an entirely different reason. Saron could not be responsible for raising a child who would eventually, over many generations, result in the birth of her beloved Jasmine. That was too much. Wasn't it? Hundreds of years separated this child from Jasmine. Perhaps getting to know and raise the child would be a balm for her still-gaping wound. Saron had a lot of thinking to do, as her fondness for Avery grew exponentially with each passing moment in her presence.

CHAPTER NINETEEN

Partially disintegrated bodies of soldiers littered the already devastated field of solar panels. Along with that horror, lay five naked men, their necks all arranged at an unnatural angle. Anyone chancing to come upon the gruesome scene wouldn't be able to synthesize what lay before their eyes.

Dressed in military fatigues, O'Rourke's men climbed into the sturdy vehicle and headed in the direction of their next target. The radio hissed, then crackled to life as a commander from Old America queried on the status of the solar field.

Taking a chance that he could respond appropriately, O'Rourke answered with vague information, indicating their inability to comprehend the scene before them. Before he'd killed one of the soldiers, he'd heard him describe what he saw and repeated his words. The Army would send more men, but at least he'd given his troop more time to reach their next target. The vehicle was primitive, but O'Rourke got the hang of it soon enough as he traveled the highway. It was actually fun to operate. He might have to locate an antique when he returned if they were still available. The toy would have been beyond his means as a commander, but with his promotion to general and new appointment, everything became possible.

†

Their new target was vast, at least ten times the number of panels of the previous solar field. While it was unlikely that the women had tapped into this particular source of energy, O'Rourke had to cover all their bases. Unfortunately, cutting the energy source to something this massive would undoubtedly increase the heat to their operation. It was unavoidable. As soon as the surrounding residents lost power, the authorities would come running.

O'Rourke wanted to evaluate the technology before attempting to disrupt the power source, even if they accomplished disruption in a less dramatic fashion this time. Perhaps he might be able to decipher the work of Time Agents and only disrupt the Sapphites' power source. *Frak.* He should have exercised the same caution with the two previous fields. Impulsivity was both a blessing and a curse. Often, that instinctive need to act had served him well. However, on occasion, it had caused issues. That might have been the reason he remained a commander rather than rising to the rank of general. He shrugged off any acknowledgement of that perceived weakness.

"Stay close to the vehicle while I check things out. If anything moves, phaser it," O'Rourke ordered.

Scanning the area, he walked through the field and bent low to the ground when he came across an uneven surface. Then, he saw it—a slight discoloration, as if someone had disturbed this particular patch in the last several months.

O'Rourke called out to his lieutenant. "Lieutenant, come take a look at this."

"Sir?" The lieutenant hurried to where O'Rourke was inspecting the ground.

Pointing at the area slightly different from the rest of the field, O'Rourke continued, "I want you to take a good look at this slight discoloration, uneven surface, and tension cracks. If you find this anywhere else in this vast field, use your phaser to penetrate the ground and uncover the cable below. As a comparison, use your phaser to dig multiple areas that don't look like this, but don't destroy the cable yet."

Pointing his phaser at the ground and starting on the lightest setting, O'Rourke began to disturb the ground, sending dirt, grass, and weeds flying until he'd uncovered the thick cable below, enough for him to conduct an in-depth inspection. The cable looked to be in pristine condition. Shifting to another area, he repeated the process and found the cable was severely discolored, brittle, cracked, and corroded compared to the newer appearing cable.

"Not so smart now, are you!" Accessing his communication device, he barked, "Dawson. We found them. Instead of the previous rendezvous point, I need you and your men to make your way to our location. I'll send an echo ping to your map. Take one of the military transport devices and clothe yourselves in their uniforms. Use your wide beam to eliminate the rest. We won't be creating a stir in this location, so we should have ample time to smoke out the Sapphites."

O'Rourke walked over to his lieutenant, who continued to search the ground.

"I'm sorry, sir, I haven't found any similar discoloration," the lieutenant answered apologetically.

O'Rourke grinned. "That's okay, Lieutenant. Get the rest of the men. We're going to follow this cable to those fraking bitches." Scanning the area, he saw the line, clear as day. It seemed to extend for miles. *They thought they were so smart.*

†

Saron had finally agreed to work alongside Gloria to install the automatic security system. She had once again used 26th-century tech to quickly create the hidden ascending and descending platforms. The sooner the system was up and running, the better. Saron hoped they wouldn't need it, but she wasn't that naïve. When Mavis's voice crackled in her ear, she knew their luck had probably run out.

"Uh, Saron, that monitor, sorry, Dynamic Surface Display, that you connected to the solar field, is showing a single military vehicle. These guys look off to me. I've been around Army guys before, and they don't act like this. Whoa, nope, they aren't the Army. Pretty sure they're those Traditionalists. What they just did to the ground with some fancy weapon is a major clue. You'd better get back to the control room and see for yourself."

"Frak," Saron muttered. "Gloria, time to go inside."

"Just a few more minutes to install this last one."

"We might not have a few more minutes," Saron barked. "I need to see what's happening inside the control room, and I can't have you unattended out here. You'll be a sitting duck."

"Screw that. I have my own specially engineered weapon if I run into trouble." She pointed to the automatic weapon strapped to her body. "Mavis can let me know if anyone approaches. I promise, I only need five more minutes, and then we're set."

Saron reluctantly agreed, mainly because she suspected they would require every advantage, and Gloria's automatic weapons system was nothing short of brilliant. "All right. But if you're not inside within the next five minutes, I will personally drag your ass down into the Safe Haven. I don't care if you're my direct familial ancestor and my elder by hundreds of years."

"I look pretty good for my age," Gloria preened.

"The clock's ticking," Saron yelled over her shoulder as she made her way into the dilapidated cabin.

†

Moving quickly through all of Gloria's newly established security checkpoints, Saron entered the control room and focused on the Dynamic Surface Display she'd connected to her surveillance equipment at the solar field.

The men were moving methodically along the line of cable leading directly to the cabin. It would take them at least thirty minutes to arrive. Saron quickly calculated the time it would take for her to prepare an assault. There were five men. That would be easy enough to handle. Especially with Gloria's automatic weapons system, now refitted to deliver a phaser burst intended to stun versus kill. She'd needed to attach one of the precious power cells to the system, putting a strain on the entire system with one less power cell connected to the mini panels. Still, that decision was necessary for their ultimate safety. After stunning the men and returning them to the 26th century, she could disconnect the automatic weapons system and reconnect the power cell to the mini panels, so Saron wasn't too concerned.

†

Five minutes had come and gone. Just as Saron was about to make good on her promise to drag Gloria back inside, the woman stood and quickly made her way to the cabin. Saron breathed a sigh of relief when she heard the click of the door to the control room, and Gloria sauntered inside.

"Easy peasy." Gloria grinned.

"You're a stubborn ass, love," Mavis barked over her shoulder, not taking her eyes from the Dynamic Surface Displays.

Gloria leaned over Mavis. "So, those are the assholes causing all the commotion, eh? They don't look that tough to me."

"Remind me why we're only going to stun them?" Mavis asked. "I hope you aren't going to make me turn my trusty shotgun into some pussy ass stun gun."

"Avery," both Saron and Gloria answered.

"Oh, right, the pacifist."

"That's Ms. Pacifist to you," Avery quipped as all eyes pivoted to the woman who had just entered the control room. "What's going on?"

"We will have unwelcome visitors in approximately thirty minutes," Saron answered. "Nothing we can't handle. Gloria's automatic weapons system is up and running. We didn't have the opportunity to test it out, but I'm confident it will work."

A second vehicle roared into focus just as the five men moved outside the view of the Dynamic Surface Display Saron had installed at the solar field.

"Frak," Saron exclaimed. "Ten men," she muttered. "That's still manageable."

Saron followed their progress as they climbed from their vehicle and followed the upturned dirt path created by the phasers.

"What do they say about a watched pot?" Gloria joked. "Let me know when they show up on the other displays. I'll just grab a snack and be back in time for the fireworks."

"Don't you dare treat this like it's some everyday normal occurrence," Mavis barked. "And don't go leaving this room. Aren't you the only one who knows how to operate your fancy defense system?"

"We have time, don't we?" Gloria directed her question to Saron.

"Fifteen minutes," Saron instructed.

"I thought you said they won't be here for thirty?" Gloria asked.

"Let's exercise some caution and give ourselves plenty of time to act. I need you at one station, while I woman the other one."

"Huh? I never thought that saying would catch on. I've used it," Gloria noted. "Saron, when did 'woman the station' become a commonplace saying?"

Saron crinkled her nose. "It hasn't. I thought I was using a term understood in the 21st century. We generally say, 'crew the station.'"

"That works for me," Gloria noted. "All right, I'll be back with snacks in fifteen minutes." Gloria danced out of the control room, grinning.

Saron turned her attention to Avery. "Avery, is there a reason for your visit to the control room? I thought you'd be working in your lab all day."

"We've done it. The egg is dividing," Avery announced.

Even surly Mavis whooped in delight. Saron could not think of a time when she'd been prouder of someone's accomplishments. She would have a front-row seat to this historic moment. Her feeling of indescribable joy at sharing this monumental breakthrough with Avery was almost too much for Saron to handle. She felt the tears of joy slip from her eyes. Running to the woman she could no longer deny her feelings for, she scooped her into her arms and held on like her life depended on it. Which in reality, it did.

"Congratulations, Avery," Saron whispered into her ear, taking a few moments to breathe in her scent. "I wish we had more time to celebrate your success, but I have a more pressing issue to attend to." Saron reluctantly let go and took a step back.

"Can I help?" Avery asked.

"Not unless you are willing to do whatever is necessary to stop these assholes, Ms. Pacifist," Mavis quipped. "Personally, I'm happy to bring out my trusty shotgun if Gloria's fancy defense system fails."

"I think your time and attention are best suited in the lab," Saron gently suggested.

"All right. I guess I'll shuffle my pacifist ass to the lab and allow the big, bad butches handle everything. Let me just don a pair of these, and you can call me when everything is all taken care of." Avery grabbed a pair of earbuds, then leaned in and placed a gentle kiss on Saron's lips. "Please be careful."

Mavis relaxed in her chair and crossed her arms. "Mmhm. Nothing happening between you and Avery, huh? If it makes a difference, you have my approval. Gloria's, too, I suspect. And you should always respect the opinions of your elders."

"It's not that simple," Saron mumbled.

Mavis chuckled. "Every complicated problem has a simple solution. You listen to your great-grandmother. The same logic applies to referring to you as my great-granddaughter—I'm not adding the appropriate number of greats, because that would be ridiculous for a title," she added with a smirk. "I may not act like I know what I'm talking about because I don't always take my own advice, but I am wise about these things."

Avery's face turned into a mask of confusion. "Great-grandmother?"

"Long story that I don't have time to share at the moment," Saron answered. "Please, Avery, return to your lab. I can't have the distraction."

Avery nodded and turned to leave, sharing one last look at Saron, filled with an emotion Saron wasn't quite ready to deal with yet.

"Yup, the lovely Avery has it bad. And from the look on your face, you do, too." Mavis chuckled.

Chapter Twenty

The rest of O'Rourke's men had joined them twenty minutes ago, catching up quickly by following the unearthed cable. It had taken them longer than he expected because the cable weaved along a heavily forested area leading to a small wooden structure, cleverly hidden in the copse of trees.

They were still several hundred feet from the rickety old cabin as O'Rourke squinted at the dilapidated home. Inching closer, he was about to warn his men about a possible ambush when ancient automatic weapons rose, sitting solidly on multiple platforms that seemed to emerge from the ground. His familiarity with the destruction of those ancient weapons caused him to yell to his men.

"Take cover," he barked.

As his head swiveled to take in the scene, he noticed an unusual light blast out of the weapons, almost like a phaser. Eight men crumpled to the ground before he was able to fall back into the dense cover of the forest. Only Dawson remained by his side.

A quick scan of the area revealed that his men's bodies remained intact, but none of them were moving. He couldn't believe his luck. The stupid bitches had only stunned his men. Depending on the setting of the stun, they'd be functional within the hour.

He needed to travel closer to their modified weapons to render them inoperable. His phaser set to maximum should do the trick, but for that to work, he'd need to advance within one hundred yards of the platforms and set his phaser to wide beam, capturing them all at once. Hopefully, the phaser had enough energy to perform the task.

†

O'Rourke watched in horror as each automatic weapon descended one by one into the ground as if by magic. *Not so stupid after all,* he thought. Still, Saron would need to emerge from whatever hole she had temporarily hidden in before sending his men forward in time directly to the Ministry. When she surfaced, he'd attack.

Dawson slowly progressed along the forest floor until he was close to O'Rourke. "Your orders, sir?"

"It won't take long for Saron to make her move. We'll wait."

Before O'Rourke's words had barely left his mouth, each of the eight men lying on the ground dissipated, as if a time-travel device had activated remotely.

"How in the frak did she manage that?" O'Rourke exclaimed. "Oh, clever, clever girl."

"I believe we're in a digital deadlock, sir," Dawson remarked.

"Let's see who is the more patient warrior," O'Rourke noted.

Dawson frowned. O'Rourke supposed that reaction was fair; he wasn't exactly known for his patience.

"Do you think their compound is hidden underground?" Dawson asked.

"Most definitely."

"Is it possible to use our phasers to penetrate all the way to where we can get to them?"

"Interesting idea. We'll need to recharge our phasers. It's taken nearly all of our phaser energy to follow the cable and eliminate the military personnel who posed a threat to the mission. How many power cells do you have left?"

"All three, sir."

"I have three as well." O'Rourke removed his ModuPak and rummaged inside, laying each power cell on the forest floor. Dawson followed suit, setting his ModuPak on the ground before retrieving his supply of power cells.

"Sergeant Collier. I assume you've been monitoring everything," O'Rourke barked into his communication device.

"Yes, sir." Collier's voice crackled in his ear.

"I'll send our position. There's no need to monitor the other solar fields. All the action is here now. We may need your stash of power cells. Find the closest vehicle and make your way to this location."

"On my way, sir."

"I still like our odds. Three elite warriors against a band of clearly pacifist women. They didn't even use the power of those ancient automatic weapons," O'Rourke spat out in disgust.

"I wouldn't underestimate them, sir. They did manage to take out eight of our men and send them back to the Ministry. We'll need to assume that any intelligence our warriors possess about our capabilities will find its way to Saron Bahl, who has proven a formidable opponent."

"She has," O'Rourke agreed.

A blast of light burst inside the shadowed forest. Dawson slumped, forming a crumpled mass mere feet away. And then there was one.

†

O'Rourke panicked as he looked around for the source of this latest attack. Moving quickly away from Dawson's prone body, he narrowly avoided the next phaser blast. However, this time, he clocked the direction of the flash. It was coming from above. Movement in the trees caught his attention. And there she was, gracefully traveling along the sturdy branches. Yes, Saron Bahl was a formidable opponent. He raised his phaser and aimed, narrowly missing the woman, but catching the branch she precariously stood on.

Saron tumbled from the tree, landing right in front of O'Rourke. She'd obviously hurt her ankle, but quickly recovered, ready to do battle. Whatever it took. This would be fun. He tossed his phaser aside and relished the chance at hand-to-hand combat with his enemy. O'Rourke wanted desperately to end Saron Bahl with his bare hands. The pleasure of seeing the light leave her eyes, up close and personal, would exceed his wildest dreams.

†

Saron grabbed her phaser and headed for the door. While she trusted Gloria's automatic weapons system, she was also a firm believer in backup plans that would inevitably be needed when things went terribly wrong. The chance of stunning ten men before they recognized what was happening and retreated to safe territory was much higher than she'd revealed to Gloria and Mavis.

"What the hell are you doing?" Gloria asked.

"I trust you and Mavis to operate your weapons system. Take out as many as you can, as quickly as possible. I recommend waiting for all ten of them to come into focus before blasting. I'm going to hide in the forest and take care of the stragglers."

"I don't believe Avery is going to like that—you going all GI Jane," Mavis interjected.

"What is the saying, 'what she doesn't know, won't hurt her?'"

"Keep in contact, okay?" Gloria requested.

Saron offered a quick nod, and she was off.

†

Moving briskly to the heavily forested section of the property, which was just outside the perimeter where Gloria's automatic weapons reached, Saron scanned the dense foliage, looking for an advantage. She assessed her ability to dig a hole and pop up ready for battle, but without an exact location where the men would retreat to, she quickly discarded that option. Then she looked up and smiled. People rarely scanned the sky when searching for their enemies. An aerial view would provide the strategic advantage she needed if several men survived the first wave of attack.

Saron scrambled up one of the larger trees and waited. If needed, she could move along the treetops until securing a strategic vantage point to carry out a targeted attack.

Saron heard the men before they entered her visual frame. They weren't even attempting to be stealthy in their approach. Big mistake. Tracking their progress once they came into view, Saron plotted the best place to settle should Gloria and Mavis fail to take out all ten men.

†

Eight men, not bad. Saron was proud of Gloria and Mavis. She grinned as the leader cursed when the transporters activated, and the men disappeared. She honestly hadn't expected it to work, but Gloria had given her the idea when she'd joked about her dream of developing heat-seeking bullets that would be far more efficient, and did the 26th century have anything like that? Adapting the tiny transporters to eject in the stream of phaser particles had been far easier than anticipated. She'd had to use a precious power cell to replicate a large enough number of transporters to achieve success, and then she'd sent prayers to the universe for the idea to work.

Saron waited patiently as the second man moved into range along with the leader. She was almost happy that there were two men left. She needed their power cells.

Patience had served her well in the past as she waited for the right moment to attack. As it turned out, that was a smart move indeed, uncovering critical intel. The leader had ordered a third man to remain behind as a central monitor, acting as a one-man field control room unit. Interesting. So they knew who she was. She'd heard enough. If there was additional intelligence, the Neuro Analysis Unit would do their job and relay that information to Saron. She would require an update regarding their progress of disbanding the Traditionalists' stronghold, anyway.

A wave of sadness overwhelmed her. If the Ministry was successful in relocating the Traditionalists and this was the last of their rebel time travelers, she would have no reason to remain in the 21st century. She shook her head and returned her focus to the men below.

Moving quietly, she grabbed her phaser and pointed at the man closest to her. In a matter of seconds, he was down, and she trained her fire on the leader. Her second shot barely missed, and when his head turned in her direction, and he fired, she got a good look at his face before the thick branch she was perched on vaporized and sent her tumbling to the ground below, minus her weapon.

Landing awkwardly on her ankle, she was sure it was broken, but she couldn't worry about that now. Shaking off the pain, she confronted her attacker, who had opted to discard his phaser and face her without weapons. *Good.* She was about to wipe that smarmy look off the man she hated with a passion. Donovan O'Rourke was the mercenary who was responsible for the death of the love of Saron's life.

Sorry, Avery, I cannot let this man live.

†

The feral expression on Saron's face undoubtedly gave the man pause before he adopted a fighting stance. While

O'Rourke had the advantage of size and brute strength, Saron was quicker and more agile, even with a broken ankle. She used his bulk against him, narrowly avoiding a blow to her head as she spun around and assisted his forward momentum, sending him to the ground and landing an elbow to the back of his neck. A grunt of dissatisfaction was her reward. But he was quicker than she anticipated, instantly rolling over to sweep her legs and slam a booted foot on her broken ankle.

Saron cried out in agony before setting her pain aside and grabbing his leg, and with a quick twist, she dislocated his knee joint. Her adrenaline was in high gear now. Fury overtook all sense of restraint. She didn't wait long to grab the nearest rock and smash it against his face, hearing the crunch of his nose. *Ooh, that's got to hurt*, she thought with renewed relish.

O'Rourke flailed, grabbing her hand and twisting with a fury of his own. The snap was loud enough to hear over her roar of pain. He now had the advantage with two of her limbs essentially out of commission.

She sent a prayer to the deity she no longer believed in to give strength to the Sapphites. She had to trust that Mavis and Gloria would defend the Sapphites with their last breath. Maybe all was not lost.

As Saron resigned herself to her fate, she heard a most glorious sound, followed by an unnaturally loud blast.

†

"Hasta la vista, fucker," Mavis yelled. "I don't need to stay on Avery's good side, and I didn't make any asinine promises, either. You okay, Saron?"

Saron shook her head as she pushed O'Rourke's literally dead weight off of her. "I thought I told you to stay back."

"Yeah, well, I'm not too good at taking orders," she answered unrepentantly.

Saron chuckled. "No, I suppose you're not. Help me up. I must send the other guy back. But before I do that, I'll need to remove the evidence of your…" Saron let the words trail off as she reached for her discarded phaser, lying only a few feet away. Mavis gently lifted Saron to a standing position, and Saron pointed her phaser at the body, promptly turning O'Rourke into a pile of ash. She wanted to kick at the ashes to spread them over the forest floor, making it difficult for anyone to find, but with only one good leg, this was impossible.

Mavis saw her staring at the pile of ash and asked, "What do you need, Saron?"

"Can you spread the ash, while I hobble over to the other guy?"

"Just hang on, and I'll help you after I've hidden the evidence. That's what you need, right?"

Saron nodded and tried to ignore the throbbing in her ankle and arm. It was going to be a miserable trek to their Safe Haven. She wasn't sure how she would manage the steep descent into the tunnel.

After Mavis kicked around the ashes until they thoroughly blended into the dense foliage, she murmured into her communicator. "Saron's hurt. We need an assist."

Saron shook her head. "No more people need to be out in the open. One more man is coming. In fact, I need you to head back. Now!"

"Fuck that. Let's go." Mavis moved to wrap an arm around Saron's good side. "Lean on me. Can you put any weight on your foot?"

Saron shook her head. "I'll crawl on my own to the cabin if I have to. Just help me to the other guy."

"No, you most certainly will not. I guess you got that stubborn streak from me." Mavis shrugged. "Or maybe Gloria. She gives me a run for my money, too."

"Mavis, please," Saron pleaded. "The third man will be here soon." They moved slowly to where the other warrior lay in a heap, and Mavis helped Saron to the ground. Attaching the device to the man, she hit the button, and a flash of light preceded his disappearance.

"Neat trick, now none of that bluster, you need our assistance," Mavis practically growled. "So shut the fuck up and let us help you."

†

Gloria and Avery charged into the forest, and Saron sighed. She was completely ineffective in getting these women to listen to her.

"Right ankle's broken, and you can see her left arm is useless as well. I'll grab under her armpits. You two each carefully find a spot on one of her legs, and we'll carry her," Mavis directed.

"Wait. Someone needs to gather their ModuPaks and power cells. We need those power cells and any other tech that cannot land in the hands of anyone else of this time."

"I'll take one if you can get the other, Avery," Gloria directed.

Avery nodded and reached for the ModuPak closest to her position. She gathered the power cells and shoved them inside before putting the ModuPak on her back while Gloria secured the other one. "Ready?" Receiving nonverbal acknowledgement, she announced, "I'll take her right side."

Saron winced when the women each took a position on her body and lifted. "Oh, Saron," Avery declared, a pool of unshed tears welling in her eyes. "I'm so sorry. I'm trying to be gentle. I know it hurts."

"I'm fine. Can we please hurry?"

Every step caused a new wave of misery. The adrenaline had worn off, and Saron was feeling the full effect of her broken bones. She'd never wished for 26th-century technology more than she did now. Perhaps with all the extra power cells, she could replicate a bone mender to hasten her recovery.

The last man standing might not be as challenging to overtake as the others, but Saron was never one to underestimate her foes. She was glad O'Rourke was dead and would have made the decision to end his life regardless of the consequences. Ten years was a long time to hold a grudge and remain unfulfilled. Would Avery understand her need for revenge?

†

Sergeant Collier scanned the forest. He could almost feel the line of worry form in the middle of his forehead. He'd attempted to contact his commander for the last twenty minutes to no avail.

Scrutinizing his FlexiPad, he noted that he was standing on the exact spot indicated by the red dot. Crouching, he explored the foliage, looking for any clue that would enlighten him to what had occurred. He found a spray of fresh blood on a fern and pulled out his lab analyzer, confirming Commander O'Rourke's blood.

Looking closely, he could see evidence of a struggle, but no bodies, not even ash residue. Did that mean his entire troop was sent back to the 26th century, undergoing the sickening, invasive neuro-analysis? Perhaps he needed to track the unique energy signature left over from phaser fire. Pointing his detection device in various directions, it lit up like the massive Christmas tree the Traditionalists still put up every year to celebrate the birth of their Lord and Savior. He looked beyond the dense forest to a more sparsely populated area, where an old cabin, barely visible, still stood amongst the trees.

Before venturing from the coverage the forest provided, he needed to submit an emergency transmission to obtain further instructions. Why hadn't they made contact with him already? Retrieving the transmission device from his ModuPak, he made several attempts to contact Central Command.

Finally, a harried voice on the other end answered, "This channel isn't safe. Stop calling."

"Wait. This is Sergeant Collier. I appear to be the only surviving Apex Warrior."

"Then finish the fraking mission. It's our only hope. The Traditionalists are no more. The Ministry of Time Politics cleared out our compound. Only a handful of men and women remain. We're all in hiding. Sorry, I have to end the transmission. You're our only hope to set things right. Frak—"

The transmission ended abruptly, and Collier stared at his device. He'd get no assistance from the Supreme Exarch, nor any of the other blowhards in leadership. Peering at the edge of the forest where he'd first noted the dilapidated cabin, something in his gut told him that making a dash for the protection of the cabin would result in inevitable failure. Based on the residual energy signature, that area was a risky venture. He'd bide his time in the forest and camp out like old school survival training had adequately prepared him for. This is why he had trained. He could do this. He'd be the hero.

No sense in making this mission unnecessarily uncomfortable. That's what his power cells could do—replicate whatever he needed to wait the Sapphites out. Then he'd strike like a deadly cobra. That was his nickname, and he'd make sure he earned the moniker given to him in his youth.

CHAPTER TWENTY-ONE

Avery was a researcher, not an orthopedist. Sure, she'd gone to medical school, but only to achieve her ultimate goal of researching different means of reproduction. When Saron passed out, Avery nearly went apoplectic. It didn't take medical training to understand that was Saron's body's reaction to the intense pain. The Safe Haven had medical supplies, but they weren't equipped for surgery, and Avery suspected that was what Saron needed. Both breaks were bad. She didn't even want to imagine how Saron had managed to break her ankle on one side and her arm on the other.

When they reached the tight space allowing them to descend to the tunnels below, Mavis, who'd taken control of the situation, quipped, "I don't suppose y'all have an engineer hiding within your ranks, do you?"

"Why?" Gloria asked.

"Because I suspect we're going to need one to figure out how to get Saron down those stairs without messing her up more than she already is."

"Could one of us carry her on our back?" Gloria asked.

"I'm not sure any of us are strong enough to carry her all the way down, plus Saron will have to be awake and hold on with her good arm. I don't believe she can handle that right now."

Saron stirred and mumbled something unintelligible.

†

Avery peered at the cement staircase as if that would provide inspiration to her. She met Rachel's eyes when the young woman looked up at her and began to climb, carrying a pack on her back and two long poles.

Rachel smiled. "I saw everything happening on the monitor and got someone to watch while I pulled together a few things that might help us move Saron into the complex."

Avery felt a rush of relief. She'd forgotten how talented Rachel was with building things and her past experience with backcountry rescues.

When Rachel made it to the top, she set the poles on the ground and slipped the backpack from her body. "It won't be elegant or anything, but I'll fashion a field gurney to carry her down as gently as possible." She assessed the three women. "Gloria, it looks like you and I will each take an end. Mavis and Avery can provide support in case we falter on the steps. It'll be like carrying a mattress down a flight of stairs, but we'll need to do it more carefully."

Mavis raised her hand. “I’m a lot stronger than I look. We don’t want to be responsible for causing Saron any more pain than is absolutely necessary. I’ll take Gloria’s place.”

Rachel nodded and took quiet control of the situation. She pulled a blanket and a roll of duct tape from her backpack. “We need to fold this blanket around those poles, then use the duct tape to secure the blanket. Gloria, can you grab those poles for me and set them just far enough apart to hold Saron’s body?”

“Got it,” Gloria answered.

“Avery, can you help me secure the blanket?” Rachel asked.

Avery jumped at the chance to be useful; it was a rare circumstance when she didn’t feel in complete control of a situation. She was entirely out of her element. She watched the pain so clearly etched across Saron’s face. Her complexion remained a ghostly white, and beads of sweat glistened across her forehead.

It didn’t take Rachel and Avery long to fold the blanket over the poles and secure the makeshift stretcher with duct tape. Mavis, Avery, and Rachel gently carried Saron’s battered body to the field gurney.

“Replicate a bone mender,” Saron mumbled, as she stirred on top of the blanket.

Her eyes blinked open, and Avery tenderly brushed a lock of hair aside. “Shhh, it’s all going to be okay. We’ve got you.”

“I’m ready to lend my muscle to this operation,” Mavis announced.

“All right, let’s do this,” Rachel directed. “Avery and Gloria, you go on ahead. I’ll be walking backward, so any verbal commands will help as we traverse the steps. Slow and easy wins the race."

Avery moved into position and perched on the second step. "I'm ready."

Gloria slipped past Avery and took a position on the third step.

As they slowly carried Saron down the cement staircase, Avery made sure to direct Rachel's movements, allowing Mavis and Rachel to descend one step at a time. When Avery reached the bottom step, she clambered to the side where Gloria waited. Then they both helped guide the stretcher down the tunnel that was barely wide enough for Gloria and Avery to take positions on both sides. It took a few minutes for everyone to get in position, and Avery felt a flood of relief that they were almost to the Y in the tunnel. From there, she wasn't sure how to proceed, but they would figure that out once she had Saron laid out on the bed.

"Take me to the control room," Saron announced a little more clearly than her previous fevered ramblings.

"Honey," Avery brushed her hand along Saron's forehead, "we need to get you to a bed, and then we can evaluate your injuries."

With Herculean precision, Saron articulated, "The replicator is in the control room. A bone mender will speed up the healing process."

"Oh, thank the Goddess for that," Avery said in relief.

†

Damn her fraking reaction to pain. Once the adrenaline subsided, this always happened to Saron. Intense pain caused Saron's body to essentially shut down. It was irritating. At least it had never occurred during battle. It was as if her brain had communicated to the rest of her body that she could relax now and take a short nap. Unfortunately, it took her a little while to recover enough from the temporary rest to have coherent thoughts. She'd tried to communicate her need before, but they'd misinterpreted her words as incomprehensible ramblings of a seriously injured team member.

Finally, Saron was able to make them understand. She'd still be out of commission for a while, but the bone mender would do an adequate job of setting her bones without the need for their antiquated 21st-century answer to complicated breaks. She shuddered at the thought that they might attempt surgery. With the acquisition of additional power cells, she could afford to replicate a bone mender.

Saron was still in considerable pain, but the women were gentle enough not to cause further damage as they carried her to the control room. Using every ounce of energy she had, she focused on the task at hand.

A small smile reached her lips when Buttercup cautiously approached and offered a gentle lick to her cheek.

"Buttercup, mat," Mavis commanded.

"It's fine. That was sweet," Saron whispered as her good arm reached to stroke Buttercup's massive head. "Good girl."

After receiving affirmation of her good deed, Buttercup moved to her mat and settled with a satisfied grin.

Avery must have sensed Saron's need to keep the group of women exposed to advanced technology small, because she glanced at the woman sitting in front of the monitors and quietly directed, "Thanks for filling in, Katy, we can take it from here. I'm sure you have tons of work to set up your space. Don't let Nora sweet talk you into giving up more of the garden," she teased.

Saron saw Katy look at the group of women who had obviously been through an ordeal as she paused, before asking, "Are you sure you don't need my help?"

"No, we've got this," Avery answered.

Katy's brow furrowed as she looked over her shoulder, seemingly reluctant to leave, but taking the subtle cue from Avery.

†

After Katy left the control room, Saron pointed to the ModuPak she'd shoved into the corner and croaked, "Can you hand me that ModuPak?"

Gloria retrieved the ModuPak for Saron and handed it to her. She was supporting her body with her one good arm. "Can I help you?"

"Maybe prop me against a wall or something while I retrieve the confiscated replicator. Then I'll need one of those power cells from the ModuPaks you picked up in the forest."

Gloria nodded. "I know what the power cells look like."

"Good."

After the women had repositioned Saron against one of the walls, she rummaged in her ModuPak and pulled out the replicator. Connecting it quickly to the power cell Gloria had handed her, Saron didn't even try to hide what she was doing as the blue light glowed brightly in the room. A newly replicated bone mender appeared, and Saron shakily held it in her hand. Passing the device over her arm, a green light pulsed until Saron felt a modicum of relief. She'd still need to be careful, but she'd be good as new in another week or so.

"Do you need help with your ankle?" Avery asked.

Having completely given up on keeping this future tech out of the hands of the Sapphites, Saron nodded. "Press this button and pass the bone mender over the area of my ankle that's swelling to the size of a watermelon."

"Okay, I think I can handle that," Avery answered. "Will you be able to walk after this thing fixes your ankle?"

Saron shook her head. "Not without some discomfort, but with assistance, I may be able to put a small amount of weight on it. Enough to move around. If you have a crutch I can use for the next week or so, that would be good. If not, I'll replicate one. I won't spend the energy to replicate a hover assist."

"Hover assist?" Gloria asked.

"Never mind. It's something normally used for recovery of major or multiple injuries."

"I don't suppose you want to explain that technology to us?" Gloria teased.

"No, you already possess too much knowledge of the 26th century."

†

Saron hadn't even seen Rachel leave, and her return to the control room was just as quiet. She held out a pair of crutches and a large plastic boot. "I kept these from an old basketball injury. I thought they might help. The boot should provide a modicum of support." She set the crutches next to Saron, along with the boot.

"Thank you, Rachel, that was very kind of you. Do you have mind-reading skills? That's quite a rarity," Saron said seriously.

"Uh, no, not mind-reading, just old-fashioned common sense. Do people in your time mind-read?" Rachel stuttered, then blushed, appearing uncomfortable with Saron's focus on her.

"Yes, it is a specialty that was used extensively in the Neuro Analysis Unit until a neuro engineer refined the technology that is used today. Often, mind-reading is an imprecise science. Before you came to the rescue, I was talking about how one of your ancient crutches might help me move around more easily. Until my arm heals in about a week, two wooden sticks would be uncomfortable. The boot will help."

"I hope the boot fits. Perhaps you should ice your ankle first." Glancing at Saron's ankle, then shifting her gaze to Saron's injured arm, her brows furrowed in confusion.

"Yes, I suppose replicating a cold compression unit would constitute wasted energy consumption when frozen water is an adequate cooling agent. At least the bone mender sped up the healing process. I will only need these ancient assistive devices for perhaps a week," Saron responded to Rachel's look of confusion. She began to push her body to a semi-standing position. Avery was right beside her, helping her to stand, as she tentatively put a small amount of weight on her ankle. "Still a little tender," she noted.

"Bone menders, neuro-analysis, and cold compression units, I don't really know what you're talking about, but—"

Breathing heavily, Nora barreled into the control room and almost comically skidded to a stop when she saw Saron.

"Whoa, what happened to you?" She looked around the room. "What did I miss? I didn't hear any alarms."

"Nora," Avery patiently drew her focus, "is there a reason you came into the control room like we're on the Titanic and about to hit an iceberg?"

"No. At least I don't think so, but the news is reporting that nearly an entire troop, actually two, are destroyed," Nora relayed. "Really gruesome scene. They found the partially disintegrated bodies of both troops and ten naked men with broken necks at two different former solar farms. The military is in a tizzy right now, and they're tracking two missing vehicles. I think they're desperate for information because the military I know, never provides this level of detail when things go wrong."

Saron began laughing, and the looks she received from Rachel, Gloria, Mavis, Nora, and Avery, suggested they thought she'd finally lost it.

"That's what they get for not thoroughly researching this time," Saron remarked through her laughter.

"Hon, you aren't making sense," Avery said.

"I'll admit, I've gotten a few things wrong, too, but forgetting that the vehicles of this time have a primitive, but effective GPS tracking system is a major frak-up. I suspect I won't need to deal with the remaining Traditionalist. He might have superior weapons, but one man against the entire pissed-off military is not something I would depend on. I wish we had surveillance covering that forested area, so I could know for sure."

"Um, Saron, I hate to burst your happy bubble, but aren't you concerned about the military discovering 26th-century technology?" Gloria swiveled away from the Dynamic Surface Displays to address Saron.

"Frak! I can't let them find our tech. I'm going to have to deal with this before they arrive."

Leaving the boot behind, Saron grabbed one of the crutches and began hobbling to the door.

"Saron," Gloria's voice wobbled. "I think the military is already here. I see flashes of light in the forest."

Mavis grabbed her shotgun. "I'm coming with. I don't even know how you can drive right now."

Rachel and Avery chimed in with, "Me too."

Saron sighed. She was in a no-win situation. She didn't like putting any of the Sapphites in danger, especially these three, but she wasn't sure she could do this all by herself. Unfortunately, Rachel was now added to their inner circle. Saron supposed that was okay since Rachel had been the one to engineer that clever makeshift gurney.

Glancing at her Universal Temporal Watch, she noted the cracked screen. The damage must have happened in her fight with the leader. *Double Frak*. If the Ministry had tried to send an event horizon transmission on the Safety Broadcast Network, she'd probably missed it. She'd have to worry about that later, because right now, her priority was gathering the lone Traditionalist's ModuPak.

"All right, come on. Let's go."

CHAPTER TWENTY-TWO

Collier heard the convoy before he saw them, even with his optic scanner, because he'd been too focused on the cabin. How had the military tracked him?

The soldiers were like a swarm of bees, combing the forest. It was only a matter of time before they found him. Grabbing his phaser, he verified that it was set to a wide beam. He'd only get one more blast before needing to recharge it. Three power cells, which had seemed more than sufficient for the mission, now appeared woefully inadequate if they expected him to go to war with the entire United States military of the 21st century. They had ample firepower to take on one man.

After he'd blasted the first wave, he reconsidered his options. He couldn't win this battle. Either he could hide and hope they didn't discover him, or he could return to his time. But what would he go back to? The Ministry had scattered the Traditionalists, leaving them unorganized and in crisis mode. His homecoming would be far from glorious. Shuffling his options like a deck of cards, he landed on hiding as the best plan. Let them discover the stolen vehicles. Moving quickly through the forest, he looked for somewhere to hole up until this all blew over.

A quick blast disintegrated the camping gear he'd replicated to make his wait in the forest more comfortable. No sense in leaving a trace behind. Perhaps they'd give up in a day or two when they didn't find anything besides the stolen transportation. Of course, the vast destruction of the first troop was more than enough evidence of his existence, but he hoped that, when that was all they discovered, they would move on. It was wishful thinking; he knew that. Suddenly, he felt like one of the lab rats the Traditionalists still used for their experiments. He was in a cage of his own making.

†

Attempting to catch his breath, Collier crouched behind a large tree and noticed a new vehicle coming from the opposite direction from where the military was swarming. Maybe his luck was turning around. If he could just get a good shot at the tire to stop the vehicle's movement, that would be his way out. He knew he wasn't a good enough shot to hit the driver. That would require an expert marksman rating, which he did not possess. Would the stun setting work for his purpose? He wasn't sure how the technology functioned. Flesh and blood were different from inanimate objects. But he'd rather repair the tire instead of replicating a new one. Stopping the transportation was his first priority. He could deal with the occupants after that.

Changing his phaser setting, he took aim, narrowly missing the tire on his first try. Taking aim again, he celebrated with a fist in the air after realizing he must have clipped one of the tires. The vehicle fishtailed down the gravel road, coming to an abrupt halt in the middle of the road.

Expending the rest of his energy as his adrenaline kicked into high gear, he ran at full speed toward his transportation and salvation, only to be met with a shotgun blast that narrowly missed. The occupants of the vehicle had teeth.

He narrowed his focus, clocking four women inside. The Sapphites. He didn't have time to change the setting on his phaser as he took aim, but before he fired, he registered the tell-tale light from a phaser and rolled just in time to avoid a direct hit. Unfortunately, in the process of evading the phaser fire, he lost his own weapon.

†

Three women scrambled from the vehicle, as a fourth struggled to emerge, holding a phaser unsteadily in one hand while propping her body against a wooden stick. *That must be the famous Saron Bahl,* he thought. One of the scowling women pulled hard on the top of the shotgun, and a spent shell ejected as she pointed the weapon at Collier.

"Mavis, stop. Don't kill him?"

He squinted at the attractive woman, and recognition came quickly. Why would his Lord play this cruel joke on him? Avery Simpson stood before him. Arguing to save his life. She was right there. So close. The target—the woman who would have brought him glory had he managed to send her to Hell. He closed his eyes, accepting his fate. The crazed look in the other woman's eyes told him all he needed to know.

"Why the hell not? He wouldn't think twice about turning us into dust."

With one last act of defiance, Collier opened his eyes and spat on the ground. "Frak you. Glory to our Creator who will welcome me into Heaven. Go ahead and do it already."

"Don't, Mavis. We've already attracted too much attention with the first shot. Let me handle this," Saron ordered. The next thing Collier knew, the phaser landed a direct hit, and his body went rigid. He tried to get his brain to send a signal to his limbs, any signal. Nothing moved but his eyes. Saron hobbled over and attached a transporter to his wrist.

"Grab his ModuPak," Saron directed.

The quiet one, who seemed to observe without comment, cautiously approached.

"Don't worry, I've stunned him. He can't harm you."

The woman nodded and struggled to remove the ModuPak from his stiff body, but finally managed to confiscate his belongings. She took several steps back, holding his overstuffed ModuPak in her hands.

Saron nodded to the woman and turned her attention to Collier. "Hope you have a nice trip home. Say hello to the Information Retrieval Agent for me." She pressed the button on the transporter, and Collier felt the familiar queasy feeling associated with time travel.

†

"Wh..what…happened to him?" Rachel stared wide-eyed at the spot the Traditionalist occupied before Saron sent him to the 26th century.

"He's back where he belongs. Come on, we don't have much time unless you want to explain what we're doing in this forest to a bunch of hyped-up soldiers, who won't take too kindly to a shotgun-toting woman as they search for terrorists."

Mavis grinned. "This shotgun-toting woman saved your ass earlier."

Saron hobbled to Rachel and asked her to open the ModuPak. "If we're lucky, we'll find a universal repair kit. It works on various 21st-century materials—rubber, steel, aluminum, fiberglass…" Saron shrugged. "You get the picture."

Pulling the small black device from the confiscated ModuPak, Saron quickly moved in the direction of the Land Cruiser. Aiming the device at the back tire, she used a sweeping motion that sent the green light moving eerily over the damaged tire until it was operable.

"Let's go. Try to avoid coming in contact with any military patrols. Just in case, is there somewhere to hide that shotgun?" Saron asked.

"Why don't you disintegrate it or whatever you do with your phaser?" Avery suggested.

Mavis held the shotgun close, practically hugging it to her chest. "No way, you aren't touching Gloria."

Avery laughed. "You named your shotgun? Gloria, huh?"

"It was as close to Glory Be as I could come up with. Because my shotgun is the only deity that I'll pay homage to. Glory Be to Gloria has a nice ring to it, doesn't it?"

"Mmhm, and you didn't name it for the other love of your life? I can't wait to tell Gloria you named your beloved shotgun after her," Avery teased.

"Please don't. Gloria will be absolutely insufferable if she hears that."

Saron didn't have time for this. "Can we tease one another later, please?"

†

The women hurried to the Land Cruiser, and Mavis tucked her shotgun in the back under a blanket. They traveled down the road with Mavis driving and Saron in the passenger seat, until they came upon the roadblock. Saron nearly instructed Mavis to turn the car around, but one of the soldiers waved them forward and held his hand out, motioning for them to roll down their window. Another man approached with his gun in the nearly ready position.

"Saron, let Mavis do the talking," Avery suggested.

"I'm sorry, ma'am, I can't let you pass. This area is restricted." He narrowed his eyes. "What are you doing on this forest road?" He peered into the car.

"We live around here," Mavis answered amiably.

"Haven't you heard about the terrorist attack? You shouldn't be out and about. It isn't safe. Especially for a group of women."

"We're kind of isolated from the city because we prefer our privacy." Mavis smiled at the young man, and Saron hoped it would disarm what appeared to be growing skepticism. "We haven't been following the news. Gosh, we'll just turn around and head home. We don't need to be involved in anything dangerous."

"I recommend evacuation until we sort out the situation. Have you seen or heard anything unusual? The only thing we're asking from the public is to report events that are out of the ordinary."

"We saw a flash of light in the forest about ten minutes ago. Thought that odd, but we were too far away to see what it was all about."

The man frowned. "That's it?"

"Yes, sir. Sorry, we were curious, so we thought we'd check it out. I know it isn't like the Northern Lights, but we hoped to encounter a similar phenomenon, you know. Maybe even an alien spaceship. It's stupid, we know, but things get kind of boring out here. It's the most excitement we've had in years. We'll take your advice and leave our cabin. We just need to collect a few things before we go. It isn't much to look at, but it's been home for us. Thanks for the warning and for your dedicated service." Mavis closed the window before the young man could protest and turned the vehicle around, waving at him with deference.

As soon as they turned around, Saron directed, "Let's see about a route through the forest that will take us to the back of the cabin as quickly as possible. I'm glad this Land Cruiser can function off-road. If the military gets curious, we'll need to make the cabin look lived in but temporarily abandoned while we wait for the military to leave the area." Saron removed a small device from one of the pockets in her cargo shorts and stared at the topographical map of the forest, looking for a route Mavis could take through the dense copse of trees. "Veer to the left, and I'll direct you."

"You got it, Saron."

"By the way, good job, Mavis," Saron noted.

Mavis grinned. "You didn't think I had it in me to be polite and demure."

"I think it's best if I didn't weigh in on that," Saron quipped. Now that they were out of immediate danger, she relaxed into the fake leather seat.

†

Avery, Gloria, Rachel, and Mavis organized a small group of women who made quick work of turning the cabin into something a little less frightening. Some women gave up their own Afghan blankets and comforters, along with bedding, to outfit the two rustic bedrooms. A little dusting and surface cleaning, along with scattered pictures and other personal belongings, gave the cabin an almost homey feel.

Katy grumbled about the need to fill the pantry with canned vegetables and other staples. She also transferred a small amount of her store of several meats and various refrigerated items to the old refrigerator. Saron prayed it would work once they plugged it in and connected it to their solar panels. They were careful to stock the freezer and leave the fridge sparser, so it appeared as though someone had emptied it of the more perishable items, as if the occupants would be absent for an extended period.

Gloria volunteered to move the Land Cruiser far enough away from the cabin so that Mavis's cover story would ring true. Retreating quickly to the underground complex, Saron marveled at the resilience of these women. They seemed to take everything in stride, not questioning the need to relocate or create a false home above the Safe Haven.

†

When the small group returned to the control room, Rachel took her leave, and Saron watched as a military vehicle approached. Four men surrounded the cabin, guns lifted in the ready position as they failed to knock, kicking down the door and sweeping the place, before yelling, "Clear."

"Rude," Mavis noted.

"The military is not known for subtlety," Avery answered ruefully. "At least they didn't try to drag us out of our vehicle and shoot us like ICE used to do. I still remember that awful time when the ICE Gestapo indiscriminately killed people, starting with Renee Good. Although I was a child at the time, even I understood the significance of what was happening in our country."

"Yeah, that was dark days, indeed. It hasn't really improved much today," Mavis added with a hint of sadness in her voice.

"This must be the cabin those strange women mentioned," stated the young man who had halted them. "I guess they're legit. What a shithole. Why would they live out in the boonies like this? Crazy dykes." He shook his head.

"I don't think they were all queer. Maybe just the driver and the other one in the passenger seat. The other two were hotties."

The young man scowled. "That's what those dykes do. They recruit attractive women. It's that fem/masc thing. Instead of going after their own, they steal our women. A buddy of mine had that happen to him. His wife left him for a woman who looked so much like a man, she had to prove she was a woman every time she went into the women's restroom."

"Damn. Maybe they're part of that cult I heard about. Didn't they settle in this part of the country?"

"Nah, I don't think so. This place isn't big enough for an entire cult or weird commune, whatever they are," another man with owlish eyes said.

"Why does everyone think we're a cult?" Gloria snorted.

"Come on, nothing here to see. Sarge said to check it out. We've done that. The action was in the forest," the young man announced.

"I'd rather not be a part of what happened to the Recon Platoon. Fucking scary." He shuddered. "The bodies looked like someone poured acid all over them. My dad said China has a new weapon, and that's what they used. That's three platoons, just gone in the blink of an eye."

"China doesn't usually send terrorists. I'll bet it was the Iranians. Although I didn't think they were that sophisticated."

Mavis rolled her eyes as they continued to chatter inside the cabin before they marched outside and headed toward the forest. "Please tell me a more intelligent military survived in your time."

"We have no use for military forces," Saron answered as she turned her attention to repairing her Universal Temporal Watch now that they'd narrowly escaped further scrutiny. After fixing the critical device, the auto-looping beep blared inside the control room.

†

Since Saron had already revealed a great deal, she was no longer concerned with particular members of the Sapphites learning too much about the future. She touched the dial and answered, "Officer Saron Bahl, authorization 6257634, ready to receive the transmission."

"Saron, thank the Goddess you're still alive," Captain Grimes exclaimed.

"Sorry, Captain, my Universal Temporal Watch took a beating in a small skirmish with one of the Traditionalists."

Saron could almost see the captain nodding on the other end of the transmission. "I thought that might be what occurred after we received your gifts. I did anticipate hearing from you much sooner, though. We've been sending transmissions for hours now."

"I'm afraid the Traditionalists have made a mess of everything. I've needed to prioritize to remain on top of the mission."

"That is why we attempted to reach you. The time map showed a large irregularity, but we assumed it was part of protecting Avery, rather than a warning of additional potential changes to the timeline. The Traditionalists are in panic mode. Whatever occurred in the 21st century has caused nearly half of the Traditionalists' colonies to simply disappear. There wasn't much left to disband and relocate. Unfortunately, because of the disarray, a few stragglers took flight. We're attempting to track them down, but we can't be sure they haven't taken time-travel technology with them. I'm afraid we'll still need you to remain in the 21st century until we sort out this mess. There are opposing views on how to handle the obvious impact on the original timeline. Some are arguing to let it stand, good riddance and all that to the Traditionalists, while others, who retain a purist view of protecting the timeline, believe it would set a dangerous precedent to allow changes of this magnitude, yet vigorously preserve the original timeline in a similar situation. The enormity of change is causing quite a stir."

"We've never had a similar occurrence, but I think I can guess what happened, Captain. The Apex Warriors practically declared war on the military when the government sent their forces to investigate the destruction of multiple solar fields, devastation that left millions of people without power. This government assumed it was a terrorist attack. Since many of the ancestors of the Traditionalists were members of the military, eliminating the military troops resulted in their own self-destruction. I'm on the side of those who wish to let the timeline stand. Karmic justice."

"Hmm, that's helpful information. Rumors of a wide-beam phaser appear to be true. We'll need to look into that as well. There's one more thing, Saron. The leader of their team, Commander Donovan O'Rourke, the man responsible for Jasmine's death, did not return to the Ministry with his men. Sergeant Collier believes something happened to him, and he's dead, but we're unable to confirm that."

"He's dead," Saron verified. "I didn't kill him, but I would have. If you need to put an official corrective chronobrief in my file, I understand."

"No, Saron. I can't say I would have reacted differently. Both of you were like daughters to me. Despite how far we've come as a society, we're still only human. Jasmine's bright light deserved to shine much longer than it did. We'll let you know when we have a definitive answer on whether there are a handful of Traditionalists still at large who possess illegal time-travel technology. Stay safe, Saron. End transmission."

"Sorry, I didn't mean to eavesdrop, but does this mean you're staying with us?" Avery asked.

"Yes, at least for now," Saron answered. "I don't believe we're in any immediate danger, but we'll still need to lay low until the attention from the military dissipates."

"Good. You deserve a well-earned rest. Can I take you to our pod and pamper you? You never iced your ankle or arm like Rachel suggested. I don't suppose you'll accept any pain medication, either."

"No, dulls the senses. But I will consent to a bag of frozen water."

"You know, the 21st century has cold compresses designed specifically for your type of injury. We won't have to use ice."

"Good to know." Saron stood and gestured with her head for Avery to lead the way.

CHAPTER TWENTY-THREE

Avery didn't know how to broach the topic of Jasmine. It was the huge elephant in the middle of their pod. Saron, of course, pretended that Avery hadn't overheard every word of Saron's conversation with the captain.

"You don't need to babysit me." Saron limped to the bed, laying the single crutch to the side as she flopped on top, not bothering to pull back the covers. "I'll probably crash for a few hours while there is a lull. I intend to take full advantage of this quiet interlude. You need to get back to your lab and finish your research."

"Who's Jasmine?" Avery decided to rip the band-aid off. She had an insane desire to understand what the captain was talking about and why she called out this man, O'Rourke, by name, in connection to someone clearly important to Saron.

"I had hoped to avoid this chat. I suppose a holograph is worth a thousand words." Pointing to the corner where she'd stowed her ModuPak, Saron asked, "Can you please hand me my ModuPak?"

Avery picked up the large backpack from the floor and set it next to Saron, then joined her on the bed.

†

Saron pushed herself up against the headboard before digging inside the bag and retrieving the FlexiPad. She'd loaded the holographic images into the confiscated FlexiPad from her Universal Temporal Watch, wanting the crystal clarity the FlexiPad offered over the tiny screen on her watch. Accessing the screen, she scrolled to the control button that opened her personal holographic images. A shimmering holograph appeared of Jasmine and Saron wrapped in one another's arms, smiling brightly as they posed for the invisible display recorder. The image turned in the center of the room, and Avery gasped.

"Your fusion partner who died? We're related, aren't we?"

"I am intimately connected to the Sapphites in so many ways. Gloria and Mavis are already aware of my familial ties to them. I recognized the physical attributes attached to my ancestral line, distinctive bits from both of them. Initially, I only knew of my connection to two founding members of the Sapphites. My captain also knew this detail. The digital photographs of you displayed in the Enforcement Strategy Nexus at our daily infosync had an eerie similarity to Jasmine. I suspect Captain Grimes did not miss that detail, either."

†

"Similarity is an understatement," Avery deadpanned. "Is that why you volunteered for this mission? Were you looking for a replacement for Jasmine?" Avery's tone came out harsher than she intended.

"Yes and no. Of course, it was self-serving to protect Gloria and Mavis, and I suppose also you, because what little time I had with Jasmine, I didn't want erased from history. But I swear, I was not looking for a replacement. That would have been impossible, anyway. I can't remain in your time, and you can't travel to mine."

"Why not?"

"It's against the rules," Saron answered, as if that were obvious.

"And you've never broken a time-travel rule before?" Avery challenged.

"Only the minor ones. The type that I categorize as guidelines."

"You mean like the ones likely to cause an 'official corrective chronobrief?'"

Saron winced. "I'm no angel."

"Well, that's a bit debatable. You're as close to a guardian angel as I'll ever come into contact with. I suppose getting involved with your deceased lover's, what…direct familial ancestor, is out of the question?"

"It's unconventional at the very least. Probably unethical, and definitely, a horrible idea."

"Just answer this next question honestly, please. Do you want to become involved, despite all the reasons you believe we shouldn't?"

"Goddess help me, I do," Saron whispered, barely loud enough for Avery to hear, then moved her ModuPak to the floor.

"That's good enough for me. Can you please turn off that holograph? It's creeping me out," Avery said as she repositioned her body.

After turning off the holographic images and setting the FlexiPad onto the nightstand, Saron slowly turned to face Avery and pushed a lock of hair aside as she let the tips of her fingers brush along Avery's jaw. "You are so beautiful. It's taken every ounce of willpower not to let my feelings run wild."

"I wish you weren't so good at that. Go ahead, succumb to the temptation. I don't mind."

Saron began to close the distance when Avery placed her hand on Saron's chest. "Wait, are you up for…whatever is about to transpire? Your injuries."

"As long as you don't try to position my limbs into a pretzel, I'll survive. Even if I reinjure myself, it will be worth it," Saron added before capturing Avery's lips in a searing kiss that sent tingling up and down Avery's body.

"Holy shit, you aren't augmented with some 26th-century tech, are you?"

Saron chuckled. "No, just good old-fashioned foreplay."

"Foreplay? Is that what you call toe-curling kisses? You can lose the 26th-century vernacular for making love, but I won't be opposed to you replicating 26th-century sex toys."

"I do not need sex toys to elicit an Elysium surge," Saron declared with mock indignancy.

"A what surge?"

"Elysium is a term in Greek mythology for a paradise-like state. Thus, the term Elysium surge is used to describe a particularly powerful orgasm. It caught on in the 25th century and kind of stuck."

"But the sex toys are fun in the future, right?" Avery asked.

"They do allow for different sensations. I used to have a cache in my youth."

"Can we try them?" Avery pleaded. "I'm always up for new experiences."

"It would be a wasteful use of the replicator," Saron argued.

"Oh, come on. We absconded with several of those precious power cells and another replicator. Surely this is one of those guidelines you like to sidestep."

"You are very difficult to resist. Perhaps, after I heal completely…"

"Deal, now where were we?" Avery pushed Saron on her back and climbed on top. "I believe I need to demonstrate my skills in helping you achieve an Elysium surge." Avery pushed on Saron's shirt, indicating her desire for Saron to undress. "Let me help you rid yourself of this constrictive clothing. I imagine, in the future, clothing is easier to remove?"

"Not really, but it is more comfortable," Saron noted as she pulled off her shirt, revealing perfectly rounded breasts, not too large, but not too small. Avery wondered how she hadn't recognized that Saron wasn't wearing a bra, even if her breasts were on the smaller side and unprotected, thus not likely to bounce. She should have guessed after that first night together when Saron had stripped to her tight black tank top and form-fitting briefs.

†

Avery's hand traveled reverently down Saron's body as the tips of her fingers mapped every ripple in Saron's abdomen. Saron's muscles were on full display. Her body was a glorious representation of a woman in top athletic form. Avery wondered what kind of exercise would be needed in the future to achieve these stunning results. Her own body lacked the same definition, and she hoped she wouldn't be a disappointment to Saron.

Shaking those thoughts from her mind, Avery refocused on giving Saron pleasure. Her index finger traveled slowly to the top of Saron's cargo shorts, deftly undoing the top button as she slowly pulled on the zipper, revealing the soft black curls beneath.

"No bra, no sexy black briefs? How lucky am I?"

Saron reached for Avery, but she pinned Saron's arms to the sides, careful not to reinjure her broken arm. "Can you relax and enjoy this. I promise to let you touch me, but I'm in control for now."

Saron chuckled. "Yes, ma'am. I do have one request. I've been dreaming of seeing you naked for some time. Will you bring that dream to life?"

"Only if you remove this final barrier. There is nothing quite like skin-to-skin contact."

"No, there isn't in the 26th century, and apparently that holds true for the 21st century as well."

"Some things never change," Avery quipped as she rolled to the side to let Saron undress herself, while she removed considerably more clothing than Saron's functional attire.

†

Saron had already broken so many rules. Succumbing to her overwhelming feelings for Avery, which had only grown exponentially in the last two days, paled in comparison to the physical sensations now practically overwhelming her nerve endings.

She'd revealed future technology, killed a Traditionalist in self-defense, admitted to her relationship to Gloria and Mavis, and now, she was about to have a divine connection with her primary mission's vulnerable entity. Correction, she was about to allow Avery unfettered access to her body and heart. Because Saron knew, without a doubt, she'd not only unravel under Avery's touch, but she was well on the way to losing her heart.

Nothing would prevent the inevitable. If she were honest with herself, she recognized this was fated to happen. Did Captain Grimes realize this as well? That wily older woman had to know. Maybe she approved.

†

Avery took her time as she explored every inch of Saron's body. Just as Saron thought she couldn't take another touch before exploding, Avery would back off, slowly building her arousal to an even higher pitch until Saron believed she wasn't capable of more.

"Avery, please," she begged.

Avery had been using her tongue in combination with her curled fingers, causing Saron to lift her hips to meet every stroke inside.

Finally, the rhythm was too great, and Avery commanded, "Come for me, Saron."

Saron exploded in a veritable symphony of sensation as her release pulsed vigorously against Avery's still embedded fingers. Eventually, the spasms slowed, and Saron's breathing returned to almost normal.

Avery crawled up Saron's body without removing her fingers and brought their lips together, molding them into a sensual link, before slowly pulling her fingers from inside Saron. Still on top, Avery moved to allow full access to her fingers, which she took her time to lick clean.

"Better than a gourmet meal at a Michelin-star restaurant."

"Will you allow me the honor of the first step in a fusion partnership?"

"Is that 26th-century code for making love to me?" Avery asked.

Saron smiled. "Yes. Not all divine connections lead to fusion partnerships, but one cannot exist without satisfying Elysium surges. Compatibility with physical pleasures is a critical component. No one enters into a fusion partnership without divine connection."

Avery smiled. "Good to know. You keep referring to sex as divine connection. It's such an interesting way to describe such a broad array of pleasurable activities, putting all forms into one category. Is there a reason there's only one name for physical intimacy?"

"What else do you call it?"

"I suppose it depends. Fucking, making love, banging, muff diving, sex of course, plus a whole lot of other less appealing descriptors."

"Why is a swear word attached to such a beautiful experience?" Saron asked.

"Good question. I'm sure if we searched the origin of the word, we'd find out. I think it's Germanic. I never really thought about it."

"I will stick with 'making love' or 'divine connection.' May I touch you now?"

"Yes, please."

Saron found every one of Avery's erogenous zones and was pleased by her enthusiastic vocal response. That was something new to Saron. Fusion partners didn't often express their pleasure so ardently. She kind of liked it. The sounds of pleasure did something to her own arousal.

†

Saron hadn't meant to fall asleep, but their divine connection had taken everything out of what little reserve Saron retained. A quiet knock on the door caused Saron to bolt upright in bed.

Avery slowly opened her eyes and groggily announced, "I'll get it. Relax. They aren't pounding, so I suspect it isn't urgent." Avery strolled into the bathroom and returned, tying her robe. She walked to the entrance of the pod and pressed the button. The doors slid open to reveal Gloria smiling broadly.

"Nora and Katy have prepared a feast. The only place large enough to accommodate everyone is the garden. They've temporarily set aside their differences and sent me to fetch you. I wouldn't normally disturb you, but you'll hurt their feelings if you don't come. Saron, too. It's their way of thanking her."

"Give us ten minutes, okay?"

"You got it," Gloria answered. "You look truly well fucked. Well done, Avery."

Avery chuckled. "Don't say that in front of Saron. She prefers divine connection."

"Okay, you look completely divinely connected," Gloria quipped. "It'll be kind of odd to welcome you to the family as my great-granddaughter's lover."

"Right, I almost forgot you said that before. I never followed up on the whole story. Saron and I have only just scratched the surface of these familial relations."

"Cool, huh?"

"Oh, you have no idea how interesting the connections can get," Avery answered.

Saron took that as her cue to hobble to the door with the bedcover wrapped around her body, noting how the bone mender had done a remarkable job, allowing her to put more weight on her ankle than she thought possible. Everything about the Sapphites and her connection to this amazing group of women was astounding, but in an admittedly good way.

"Looking good, Saron. Um, I'll just leave you two to dress," Gloria choked out, waving to a naked Saron wrapped in the blanket.

†

Avery looked at the spread Nora and Katy had prepared for the Sapphites. They'd even collected decorative flowers and laid them on the table surrounding the food. She knew this was their language of love. Something to show appreciation for all Saron had done to protect them.

The atmosphere was festive as women milled about, drinking homemade wine and beer. Wine was Nora's specialty, and beer was Katy's. The two good-naturedly argued about which was better.

Gloria approached and slipped her arms around both Avery and Saron, leading them to the long table. "Sorry, we didn't wait. Dig in before this crowd of locusts gobbles up all the good stuff. I know you'll want a glass of wine, Avery, but I don't know Saron's preferences. Do they have wine and beer in the 26th century, or are y'all too health-conscious?"

"Mostly, we have replicated beverages called synthahol that are similar to the old ales and wines. I prefer ales."

"Perfect," Gloria exclaimed. "Katy is quite pleased with her latest batch of nut-brown ale with a hint of blueberry flavoring."

Saron crinkled her nose. "That sounds like an interesting combination."

"It's good, trust me. Mavis and I both had one, and the challenge will be to stop at two. They're big bottles." She giggled.

Mavis strolled up to Avery and Saron, a mischievous look on her face. Buttercup walked by her side and nosed Saron's hand, initiating a quick pat. "So, the lovebirds finally came up for air. Is my great-granddaughter good in bed? If she is, she got it from me. If she isn't, she got it from Gloria."

"She must be a chip off your old block, Mavis," Avery teased back. She refused to feel embarrassed about enjoying her time with Saron.

"Hey," Gloria playfully smacked Mavis, "I don't hear you complaining. In fact, your moans are loud enough to wake the dead."

"It's good to know that people of the 21st century can speak so freely of physical pleasure. I've read about the times in history when it was a cultural null to discuss intimacy."

"I'm going to have to get used to 26th-century lingo. I assume cultural null means taboo," Avery said.

Saron smiled. "Yes, sorry. Remember, although I've had instruction in 21st-century slang, there was so much to memorize."

"So, people fuck like bunnies in the 26th century and like to talk about it?" Mavis asked.

Saron shrugged. "Divine connections are celebrated."

Avery cupped her hands and whispered, "Sex, she means having sex."

"Yeah, I remember. That's a hard one to forget. Divine connection. I love it," Gloria announced. "Tonight, you and I are going to have a marathon divine connection if you behave."

"Where's the fun in that? I thought you liked it when I misbehaved," Mavis retorted.

Gloria winked. "Depends on where you do the misbehaving and with whom."

Avery was going to have to get used to thinking of Gloria and Mavis as Saron's great-grandmothers—the shortened title thanks to Mavis. With them all around the same age, it was a little disconcerting, especially with those two, who tended toward the outrageous.

"I assume you are talking about misbehaving during divine connection," Saron interjected. "Can you explain what exactly that entails. It sounds like Gloria enjoys it."

"Aren't you just a little tweaked out about discussing divine connections with your technical elders?" Avery asked.

Saron furrowed her brow. "Why? Divine connections are often discussed in detail with family members who have greater knowledge, especially when we're younger. Granted, I've had numerous conversations with my sisters, mothers, and grandmothers, but one can never have too much information. This would be a fascinating class to offer: *Historical Techniques and Origins for Divine Connections*. Perhaps each century would have something to add. I think I'll suggest that."

Mavis slung her arm over Saron's shoulder. "Let's go have a beer, and I'll tell you all about it."

Buttercup dutifully followed her mama and new best friend, as Saron limped along while appearing to focus intently on what Mavis was whispering in her ear.

Avery smiled as she watched Mavis interact with Saron. It was as if she had become a whole new person. None of the drama remained between Gloria and Mavis. Perhaps knowing a smidgeon of their future, and the fact that they would have a baby together, solidified her belief that they would make it for the long haul. Avery wondered what the future would bring for her. Besides knowing she was destined to make a baby with one of her eggs, Saron had left the rest purposely fuzzy.

CHAPTER TWENTY-FOUR

Saron was becoming increasingly worried as the days flew by, and she still hadn't received the final word from the Ministry of Time Politics. Fortunately, they had kept her up to date, revealing that whatever had occurred to alter the timeline had affected far more people than the Traditionalists. They'd even lost a few good Time Enforcers. Reports of disappearing loved ones were popping up all over the world. The Ministry was getting a lot of pressure to do something about it, but time was a fickle mistress.

Saron could understand why they hadn't come to a collaborative understanding of how to approach the situation. This was the first time in the Ministry's history that they weren't able to prevent a disaster from unfolding. It was highly likely that sending someone back in time to capture and imprison Commander Donovan O'Rourke wouldn't necessarily accomplish their goal of readjusting time. If it were as simple as that, Saron would volunteer for the mission and request that the Ministry send her back in time to just before Jasmine went on her first mission. But how would that change her current mission? It was all so confusing. All this ruminating over the different possible scenarios didn't matter because the Ministry would never authorize that.

Small changes in history were often overlooked, lest the Ministry's authorized interference result in a less favorable outcome. There was always a risk of that occurring when messing with the normal course of history, which is why the Ministry generally took a more conservative, proactive approach by stopping a major breach before it unfolded. Critics might complain when they were personally affected by minor blips, but the needs of many outweighed those of the few. If only Saron had stopped the commander before his wave of destruction.

The military wasn't giving up. The Traditionalists had wreaked havoc on the neighboring communities, and Old America's government was out for blood. Whose blood the intelligence community could never agree on, since the government was left with mass destruction but no way to tie it to the usual suspects.

†

In the meantime, the area was flooded with emergency management personnel, caring for the elderly, the sick, and the poor, who were unable to leave the area. Returning power to so many homes was a monumental task, especially since a vast number of solar panels had been obliterated by O'Rourke's indiscriminate use of phaser fire. Saron seethed at his completely ignorant and callous disregard for human suffering. She was glad Mavis had killed him. Fortunately, most of the activity surrounded the devastated solar fields, and Saron was able to retrieve her 26th-century surveillance tech.

Saron was nearly ninety-nine percent recovered from her injuries and paced the floor of their bedroom. She was itching to go topside and see for herself the level of anguish the absence of power caused those who depended on it. No one had expected a large-scale power outage connected to the solar grid; backup generators were a rarity.

"Hon, you'll wear a groove in the floor," Avery noted with a hint of mirth.

"I feel useless. And responsible."

"Responsible? How are you remotely responsible for what is happening in the neighboring communities? We all want to help, but with the military still hanging around, I don't see how it's feasible."

"I should have known the Traditionalists would send warriors who have no regard for human life. I could have stopped O'Rourke before he started his path of annihilation. They've always been a selfish society, prone to ensuring their own prosperity and power, without consideration for anyone else. In their communities, wealth is still hoarded by the few, while the many merely scrape by."

"You're basically describing the world I live in now. The gap between rich and poor is wider than it's ever been in the United States. It began during the MAGA era and never improved. You'd think we would have learned our lesson after that president nearly destroyed our country. I'm just happy to hear that it eventually gets better."

Saron stopped pacing and smiled. "You're not making it sound very appealing for me to remain in this time."

"Didn't know that was a viable option." Avery offered Saron a smoldering look. "Weren't you the one who said the turning point in history starts with my research? Don't you want to have a front row seat to this amazing time?"

"I do, and I probably will. The Ministry doesn't seem too keen to pull me anytime soon. Initially, I thought it might be best to leave well enough alone, but others were affected by O'Rourke's actions. It wasn't just the Traditionalists."

"That isn't all you've been obsessing over, is it?" Avery guessed. "You can tell me anything. You know that, right? Have you been thinking about the possibility of changing Jasmine's fate? O'Rourke is the linchpin in this mess, isn't he? Remove him from the equation, and the timeline might return to its original state."

"That isn't my call to make. Besides, the Ministry would never authorize that."

"But if they did? What would that mean for us?"

"I don't know, it's like thinking about which came first—the chicken or the egg. It's an impossible brain twister. One that not even the most brilliant mind has ever provided an adequate answer to."

"Actually, as a scientist who specializes in ova, the paradox is not difficult to solve at all," Avery stated matter-of-factly. "The egg came first, of course. Zoologists all agree on this. From an evolutionary perspective, chickens are relatively young, like maybe 10,000 years old, give or take. Since they evolved from birds, which are millions of years old, it's pretty logical to state with confidence that the egg came first. Only hard-core bible thumpers say the chicken."

Saron began laughing, then joined Avery, who was lounging on their small love seat. "It's a causality example that goes back to Aristotle. A philosophical dilemma arises because our human brains struggle to sequence events where one thing depends on another. Time travel and the effects on the timeline create a brain twister on steroids. But your explanation is priceless. It's why I love you so mu—"

Saron stopped herself mid-sentence, realizing what she'd just admitted, as Avery blinked rapidly in response to her confession.

"I…uh…it's a common turn of phrase…" Saron began.

"Don't you dare take that back or make light of it because I am one hundred percent certain that I love you, too. And it's going to hurt like hell when you leave us."

Saron captured Avery's hands in hers. "Judging by how the Ministry doesn't seem in any big hurry to find the rogue Traditionalists, it could be years before they call me back."

"I'll take whatever time I can get."

†

The steady beep on her Universal Temporal Watch alerted Saron to an emergency transmission.

"Officer Saron Bahl, authorization 6257634, ready to receive the transmission."

"This is Captain Grimes, Saron. The Ministry has made a decision. There were profound, far-reaching changes, affecting too many people, including some families with considerable influence. With your familiarity of the time period and Commander O'Rourke, they've requested your assistance with a new mission."

"What about the Sapphites? Have you rounded up the rogue Traditionalists?" Saron asked.

"They are in such disarray right now, it's not an immediate concern. If you're successful with the new mission, we should know right away. Then we will return to our original plan of relocating the entire Traditionalist colonies to inside the walls of a new Restorative Justice Facility we're in the process of building."

Saron noticed the frown on Avery's face at the mention of relocating the entire Traditionalist colonies.

"Captain, is it fair to the women and children who were not at all a part of any violation of the Accordium to place them in the Restorative Justice Facility?" Saron asked.

"Mmm, yes, you've landed on one of the livelier discussions. A process for evaluating the appropriate placement of the women and children, and even some of the men, particularly the younger men, will take place under the direction of Dr. Wise at the Information Retrieval Center. I suspect many will be integrated into our communities."

"I worry about their integration, especially the innocent children. There are still many affected by the raids, and the anger runs deep. We should take great care not to ostracize those who had nothing to do with the violence."

"That's a very mature and sensitive observation, Saron. However, our focus at the moment is on restoring the timeline."

"I'll be going after O'Rourke, I presume," Saron stated.

"Yes, it's the least disruptive action."

"How far back in time?"

"One year. That should provide adequate distance from the current timeline without creating a broader impact."

"So, going back ten years is out of the question?" Saron asked.

"I think you know the answer to that already, Saron." Captain Grime's tone softened.

"What authority do I have with O'Rourke?"

"I think you know the answer to that as well. Capture is preferable, but do what is necessary to achieve a successful mission. Hundreds of thousands are counting on you to make this right."

"And if I reject the mission? What are the consequences?"

The captain sounded genuinely confused. "Saron, what's going on?"

"Has anyone ever stayed, you know, after a completed mission?" Saron asked.

"You want to remain in the 21st century?"

"I have nothing waiting for me in the 26th century," Saron stated. "My life is all work. At some point, I'll be forced to retire because I can't physically handle the more challenging missions. I'm simply asking to push up my retirement date."

The captain chuckled. "No, you're not. You're making an unprecedented request, and you know it."

"How about if I offer an enhanced proposition? I'll go on this one final mission, but then the Ministry must agree to send me back to the 21st century as a permanent designation. You know that protecting these women is the most important assignment in the history of the Ministry. Call it insurance to safeguard the Age of Enlightenment. When I restore the timeline, it may take a much larger effort to round up all the individuals in the Traditionalists' colonies. You've already admitted to the challenge of tracking down rogue players."

"Interesting proposition. I'll confer with the council and let you know the Ministry's answer. I hope she's worth it, Saron."

"She is. You know she is," Saron declared.

"I'll get back to you. End transmission."

†

"You want to stay in this time, with me?" Avery asked, the delight clearly bubbling to the surface.

Saron nodded. "I do."

"But you'll be giving up so much. The utopia you describe in the 26th century…" Avery's words trailed off.

"I meant what I said. Sure, it's a comfortable life. No one wants for the basics. My physiological and safety needs on Maslow's hierarchy are well met. To some degree, I also have love and belonging, at least with my family. I *will* miss my sisters, mothers, grandmothers, and nieces, but perhaps I can send and receive family transmissions. I thought I had achieved esteem and was well on my way to self-actualization, skipping over a major part of love and belonging, but now I am convinced that I haven't fulfilled my potential. I'm finally on my journey to self-discovery, and I believe with all my heart, my destiny lies with you. I was meant to protect the Sapphites."

"When will you have to leave?"

"It hasn't been approved yet, so I'm not sure."

"It will be. I feel it in my gut," Avery declared. "You're meant to remain in this time. I just need your assurance that you will return to me after dealing with O'Rourke."

Saron stroked Avery's cheek. "Scientists don't go by their gut," she teased. "They use empirical evidence. I can't make any promises, but the empirical evidence suggests I will complete a successful mission. I've not failed one yet."

†

Two days later, Avery recognized the particular tone of the sustained beeping on Saron's watch. Avery had almost memorized Saron's security code. While Saron was ready to receive the transmission, Avery wasn't too sure she was. Her heart beat so rapidly in her chest that she thought it might burst from overexertion.

"Officer Saron Bahl, authorization 6257634, ready to receive the transmission."

"Saron, Captain Grimes here."

Saron chuckled. "I know, Captain, I recognize your voice. It's rather distinctive. Although I've always wondered why the Ministry doesn't have authorization codes for those sending transmissions. Anyone could replicate a voice synthesizer that makes it virtually impossible to tell the real person from the synthesized voice."

"Hmm, good point, Saron, I'll run that up the hierarchy stream. I blame artificial intelligence for the technology that ironically took hold in the 21st century. Perhaps you can influence that after you return from this mission," Captain Grimes joked.

"Are you communicating to me that the Ministry accepted my ultimatum?"

Captain Grimes chuckled. "I'm glad you recognized your idea as an ultimatum. Fortunately, I have enough strategic wherewithal to have presented it with a touch more tact. It took a bit of convincing on my part, but eventually they saw the wisdom of this combined solution designed to meet both the spirit and the written text regarding the Ministry's vision and purpose. No one wanted to see your current mission ultimately fail because we can't secure all known and unknown threats still remaining with those stragglers."

"Thank you, Captain. When am I expected to return to obtain the mission infosync?"

"Will twenty-four hours be enough time?"

"Yes, Captain. See you soon."

"Saron, I know I don't need to tell you how dangerous O'Rourke can be. He's unpredictable and arrogant, which can end up being a blessing or a curse. Make sure you give yourself time to say goodbye to Avery..."

"Twenty-four hours is ample time, Captain."

"I hoped you would say that. End transmission."

†

Avery's joy was quickly extinguished as she listened to the captain's warning and encouragement to say goodbye, suggesting something might go awry with Saron's new mission.

"Just how dangerous is this new mission?"

Saron shrugged. "I've defeated O'Rourke before; I can do it again."

"Mavis is the one who ultimately defeated him," Avery countered.

"Ouch." Saron grinned. "Have a little faith."

"I'm a scientist. Faith never enters the equation."

"All right. Let me provide you with the data necessary to soothe your jitters. Jitters is a word you still use, right?"

"No," Avery answered. "Forget 21st-century slang. Give me the goods. Data, please."

"I've gone on four hundred and seventy-two missions, seventy-three if you count this one that isn't finished. All have resulted in a positive outcome. Mission accomplished. The average duration of each mission is forty-eight hours, with a range of as little as two hours to my longest assignment, which lasted one month. Collateral damage, as in human casualties, prior to this mission, was zero, unless you count a few of my opponents."

Avery whistled. "Impressive. You must be considered the best of the best."

"I am the officer selected for the more intricate and dangerous missions," Saron responded, as if reciting a fact rather than bragging. It was one of the things Avery loved about Saron. She took her job seriously without boasting.

"Is that why they chose you to protect us?" Avery asked.

"No, I volunteered before Captain Grimes could ask."

"So, do they select you for the more intricate and dangerous missions, or do you volunteer?" Avery teased.

"A little of both, I suppose," Avery answered with a shrug.

"Is it selfish of me to keep you mainly to myself over the next twenty-four hours?"

Saron shook her head. "No, but I would like thirty minutes to say goodbye to Mavis, Gloria, and Rachel."

Avery arched her eyebrow. "Rachel, huh? Should I be worried you want a divine connection with Rachel?"

"No, of course not," Saron sputtered. "Rachel reminds me of my youngest sister. The 26th century may have enlightened views surrounding divine connection, but incest is still considered unacceptable."

Avery held out her hand. "We really shouldn't waste a minute of our time together. The clock started ticking the minute Captain Grimes ended her transmission. I say we give that cyberstrap of yours a spin. Ooh, or maybe the synthstimupulse. That was a lot of fun."

"I could replicate a holotouch divinator?"

"How does something with holo in the name even work? I'm picturing futuristic porn displayed in glorious 3-D detail."

Saron wrinkled her nose. "Not exactly, but it does combine three senses, sight, touch, and sound, and can be programmed in thousands of different play scenarios."

"Yes, please, replicate a holotouch divinator."

"I really shouldn't have replicated any of those items. If Captain Grimes knew how many rules I've broken, I doubt she would have advocated for me."

"Hmm, we have an old saying, 'what they don't know, won't hurt them.'"

"Yes, I am familiar with that phrase, but prefer to use it sparingly. Lies of omission are still lies," Saron noted.

"Oh, don't be such a Girl Scout. I promise I won't ever keep the big things from you."

"Girl Scout? What does an organization known for baking cookies have to do with wanting to be honest?"

Avery laughed. "The scouts don't actually bake the cookies; they sell them. Honestly, whatever classes you took on the 21st century clearly got a lot wrong. The very first Girl Scout law was, 'I will do my best to be honest and fair.'"

"So, the Girl Scouts were a society with laws?"

"Not exactly, but close enough. The scouts were a bunch of goody-two-shoes, but at least they didn't turn away lesbians."

"I'm not going to even ask what goody-two-shoes means. I can take an educated guess."

CHAPTER TWENTY-FIVE

Saron and Avery had taken advantage of every possible minute together, talking, laughing, and engaging in both gentle and enthusiastic divine connections. It was almost time to leave, and true to her promise, Avery gathered Mavis, Gloria, and Rachel for Saron to offer a proper goodbye.

Rachel looked confused about why Avery wanted her to come to their pod, but as if they truly did have mind-reading skills, Mavis and Gloria knew what was coming.

"It was good getting to know you, kid." Mavis turned her head and pretended she wasn't wiping away a tear.

"Wait, what? You're leaving?" Rachel looked between Avery and Saron. "What if the military finds us and starts asking questions?" she asked with a touch of panic in her voice. "They're assholes."

Saron laughed. "Some of them, probably, but not all. I'm going to do everything in my power to return and make this my home. Now give me a hug." Saron opened her arms and folded Rachel inside. “Thank you for everything, all of you were literal life savers.” She released Rachel and looked each woman in the eye.

“You can’t guarantee you’ll return to us, can you?” Gloria noted.

“There are no guarantees in life. Any of us could choke on a chicken bone or get in a transport crash…. If possible, could you hold off venturing topside until the military personnel have cleared out? I know that will put a strain on your resources, but Nora and Katy are nothing if not creative. A little less meat is probably good for everyone, anyway.”

“Hippy dippy vegans, ick. I knew this was like a cult. It’s like a vegetarian cult or something,” Mavis grumbled. “You sucked me in with Katy’s meat stores, and now you’re going to take it all away.”

Gloria bumped her shoulder playfully with Mavis. “You’re just grumpy because you don’t know how to tell Saron you’re going to miss her, and that you love her. How many times do I have to tell you we aren’t a cult?”

“Gloria, I’m going to leave the power cells here with you. If I don’t come back, I need you to rewire your mini panels and reconnect the Safe Haven to the solar field two miles away. You have to promise me that you’ll destroy every power cell after you’ve reconnected the system. I’m already bending the rules by leaving them in place. Like the prime directive in that old show *Star Trek*, leaving future tech behind violates the Ministry’s prime directive.”

“What if I promise not to take them topside? We can keep them down here where no one will ever find them. They’re just so efficient,” Gloria argued.

“No, I’m sorry, I cannot allow that.”

"All right, Saron," Gloria agreed. "I promise. I don't suppose you'll leave one of your phasers and a replicator behind?"

Saron chuckled. "No, I'll be transporting all the tech we commandeered from the Traditionalists back to the 26th century. I've already gathered it." She pointed to the pile of ModuPaks. "I'll take hugs from the rest of you now. You included, Mavis."

As each woman took turns hugging Saron goodbye, Avery waited until Mavis stepped aside. She held on tight for at least a minute, then cupped Saron's face and brought their lips together. "I love you. I'm going to send my request out to the universe for your safe return, but I want you to know I don't regret a single moment of the time we spent together."

"Nor do I. I love you, too."

"Any chance you can leave behind the 26th-century sex toys? What's the harm in that?" Avery teased. "Because I know you won't bring them when you come back to us."

Saron smiled and shook her head. "Maybe I'll smuggle a few of my favorites upon my return."

"I'll hold you to that," Avery answered.

Before Saron completely lost it, she turned the dial on her Universal Temporal Watch and activated the daisy-chained transport setting that included the ModuPaks. She'd be home in a matter of seconds, but home didn't feel like home anymore.

†

Saron sat and waited patiently in the Collaboration Nexus. She wasn't sure she trusted this space anymore after the breach they'd only discovered when it was a little too late to do anything but react.

Captain Grimes strolled confidently into the room. "Saron. It's good to see you looking well. It's quite remarkable that after battling the Apex Warriors, you don't appear to have sustained a single injury."

Saron wouldn't look the captain in the eye, but could she really keep that detail to herself? "Actually, Captain, I made an executive decision to replicate a bone mender after falling from a tree and breaking my ankle, then breaking an arm in hand-to-hand combat with O'Rourke."

"I see. And where is the replicator and bone mender? I assume you took the replicator from one of the Traditionalists."

"Yes, Captain. I brought both back with me, along with other tech confiscated from the Traditionalists. I didn't want to waste good tech." Would failing to share that she'd left the power cells with Gloria be such a sin? Saron didn't think so. She decided to shift the conversation in another direction. "Captain, I'm not sure I feel comfortable conducting the infosync in this room. There *was* a breach."

"I'm aware of that, Officer Bahl," Captain Grimes snapped. "We've taken precautionary measures after the breach, and this room is scanned regularly."

"I didn't mean to overstep…"

Captain Grimes sighed. "No, no, you're absolutely right, we should be reminded not to loosen any security protocols, and to periodically evaluate whether we need to add to those practices."

"If you're satisfied that the room is secure, then so am I," Saron declared.

The captain pulled out a FlexiPad and brought up the schematics for the Traditionalist colony that they suspected O'Rourke had chosen to settle in. "This was difficult to obtain, but we have a defector with us who was very helpful in filling in the gaps. O'Rourke uses the ExoGym almost religiously every day at the same time. And because he's an entitled prick, he insists on reserving that time without any disruption from others, including his fellow warriors. That will be your best opportunity to catch him."

"Perimeter security at the colony?"

Captain Grimes nodded. "Heavily guarded. However, you'll be able to carry the latest tech in your ModuPak since you're only traveling back one year. A cloaking prototype is currently undergoing final testing. I hate to provide you with tech that is still being tested, but it should give you cover to bypass the guards. We'll also alter your appearance to look like the Supreme Exarch's daughter. Once inside the colony, this should give you easy access. The only downside is that women are not allowed in the ExoGym. That is restricted to men only. They believe athletic women, or those obsessed with their bodies, are distasteful, promiscuous, and unattractive. You'll need to sneak in well ahead of O'Rourke's ExoGym time and wait for him."

"Understood."

"Saron, get in, send him directly to the Ministry, and get out. Don't get caught. Even though the Traditionalists have completely violated the Accordium, thus far, we have not. Sending you in to remove O'Rourke is a clear violation."

"Do I have authorization to extinguish his life?" Saron asked.

"Your orders are to send him to the Ministry, but I would not be unhappy if you think you have no other choice. I argued in favor of extinguishing his life, believing it would be a better option. The council did not agree, likening it to stooping to their level of savagery. Keeping him alive creates additional diplomatic problems because it violates the Accordium. My official directive is capture. Unofficially, take the bastard out."

Saron grinned. "Understood."

"Follow me, and I'll take you to where you can be outfitted for the mission." Placing her hand on Saron's shoulder, she asked, "You'll be happy in the 21st century? With Avery?"

"I will. I love her," Saron stated with more emotion than she believed she was capable of.

"I'm glad to hear that. You've got some of that spark back. I thought we'd lost you to grief. You've been an empty shell for the past ten years. It's pained me to see you like that. Have a good and full life. Perhaps the history books will include your contributions. That is a possible change to the timeline that was acceptable to the Ministry."

CHAPTER TWENTY-SIX

With her ModuPak stuffed to include everything she would need for her mission, Saron rotated the dial on her Universal Temporal Watch and prepared for the relatively comfortable trip back in time. Traveling one year was nothing like returning hundreds or even thousands of years into the past. It was incredibly rare to venture that far back because not many individuals sought to change the timeline prior to the industrial age, and they were more cautious about altering the past, when there were fewer humans on Earth.

Not even a flutter occurred in her stomach when Saron found herself approximately one mile from the Traditionalists' border. She wanted to be more precise with her location before moving closer to her target, and Saron had plenty of time before dark to make her approach. She dug into her ModuPak and retrieved the latest version of the popular FlexiPad. Captain Grimes was right; she'd never been so prepared with tech before. Saron had the latest and greatest toys to aid her in this mission.

The Ministry must have received an overwhelming number of complaints about the changes to the timeline. It probably only took one important delegate to raise a ruckus about a missing loved one for the pressure to become too overwhelming. Frankly, she was amazed it had taken them this long to make the decision to remove O'Rourke. Perhaps they were a bit queasy about using Saron for this mission. They knew full well her connection to him and the likelihood she would extinguish his life, versus sending him to the Ministry for the Information Retrieval Agents to dig inside his brain.

†

Saron settled on the ground and waited. Soon, it was dark enough for her to begin her trek to the border. Far enough away from the perimeter where she could barely see the posted guards with her high-powered optic scanner, Saron initiated the cloaking device.

When she approached the invisible fencing, she was just about to disrupt the barrier when lights and bells sent several guards running.

"Breach on the south border."

"I don't see anything."

"Energy signatures don't lie. I heard they're testing cloaking devices at the Ministry for Time Politics."

"Why would the Ministry be interested in cloaking? Aren't they a bunch of peace-loving degenerates?"

"Don't know and don't care. Just lay some phaser fire over there." The massive guard pointed to the exact spot where Saron stood.

Frak.

Saron had to act fast, or she'd be literal dust. Tucking and rolling, she flung her body to the ground and belly crawled to a safe location. The phaser fire lit up the evening sky but remained several inches above her head. As she moved farther into enemy territory, inch by excruciating inch, continuing to crawl on the ground, it seemed to take forever before she reached a main road. She still couldn't chance uncloaking, but at least her initial approach had redirected the guard's focus. Pulling herself to a crouching position, Saron exploded into a dead run, traveling quickly along the main road until reaching a thoroughfare leading into the center of town. A quick glance at her map showed the location of the ExoGym.

Knowing that the energy on the cloaking device was getting dangerously low, Saron had to chance decloaking as she slowed to a leisurely stroll along the surprisingly old-fashioned storefronts. She had heard that the Traditionalists enjoyed the times of old, but this was like traveling back to the 21st century.

Before decloaking, Saron swiveled her head, ensuring her sudden appearance on the street would not attract attention. Glancing at her clothing, not the most practical for a mission, she looked for a place to send her ModuPak back to the ministry, minus the smaller flexipouch preferred by debutantes in the Traditionalists' colonies. *Frak.* She looked a mess after her time on the ground. She'd need to fix that. The long dress with the high collar itched, but she was supposed to be Zyria Ritter, the Supreme Exarch's daughter.

Saron hadn't planned on uncloaking this early, but she remained flexible and adjusted to meet the mission demands, something she excelled at. A large waste receptacle caught her eye. It would have to do. Crouching behind the receptacle, she hoped the large container would conceal the short burst of light. She'd really rather not destroy her ModuPak because it contained cutting-edge tech that was probably worth quite a bit to the Ministry. Now, to repair the tears and stains on her dress.

†

Turning the corner after getting rid of her ModuPak and fixing her dress, Saron came face-to-face with an amiable-looking young man, who appeared surprised to see her.

"Zyria? What are you doing walking about unaccompanied? And at this hour?"

Sizing up the young man, Saron guessed he might be a possible suitor. That was the ancient term the Traditionalists preferred. He was well-dressed, which meant he was a member of the upper class.

She'd heard rumors that some of the younger Traditionalists were making waves, especially those from the most prestigious families. They wanted more freedom to move about and form relationships without the overbearing interference from their fathers. Saron took a chance.

"I had a fight with Father and just needed a bit of air," she answered. "I'm on my way back home."

He nodded sympathetically. "I understand. Shall I walk you back?"

"That's kind of you to offer, but I would really like a little time alone before I face Father again."

"If you're sure…"

"I am. It might be hard to explain why you are accompanying me home without permission. My father doesn't even know I've left the house. It might make him come to the wrong conclusion. I wouldn't want him thinking ill of you. That would result in an end to your visits."

"Perhaps your father will allow another visit soon," he asked hopefully.

Saron offered a demure chuckle. "I'll need to make nice with him before I ask. He is not too happy with me right now. But you'd better move along quickly. My father has eyes everywhere. If someone reports seeing us together, my father might come to the wrong conclusion and refuse to consider you as a legitimate suitor."

The young man's eyes darted around, tracking the guards and the distant commotion still occurring close to the border. "I was on my way to see if my assistance was required, anyway. I thought I saw a light in the alley and was going to investigate it. Something is happening at the border." His eyes scanned the perimeter.

"Go, go, that most certainly takes precedence." Saron waved her hand in the air. "You are so brave to run into the middle of danger."

The man beamed with pleasure at the compliment, and before hurrying to where Saron could still see flashes of light from phaser fire, he called over his shoulder, "Hurry home, Zyria, it's not safe out here."

Saron nodded and quickened her pace, hoping not to run into anyone else before she made it to the ExoGym. She supposed the commotion she had caused was a good thing, redirecting attention to the border versus the center of town.

Slinking around another corner, she found what she was looking for and pulled the small replicator from the flexipouch. Replicating a lock disengagement tool, she made quick work of the back door and slipped inside.

Stripping off her clothing, Saron replicated more appropriate attire for battle. Gathering the bundle of clothing and the small flexipouch, she moved in the cover of darkness until finding the perfect place to hide out and wait.

Not wanting to spend another minute disguised as Zyria Ritter, she retrieved the surgical change unit and waved it over her face. She felt like herself again, moving around her mouth and flexing her face, finally able to relax.

Where she'd chosen to hide wasn't the most comfortable location, but she would endure the long wait until O'Rourke arrived. Setting the haptic notification for thirty minutes before O'Rourke's reserved time at the ExoGym, Saron closed her eyes as she relaxed inside the maintenance tunnel directly above the rack of weights and fell into a light sleep.

†

Saron's eyes blinked open, and she was now wide awake after the haptic notification vibrated against her wrist. Had she misjudged the time? Someone was stirring below. Saron carefully aimed her phaser at the floor and adjusted the setting, creating a small peephole for her to look through.

A servmaid methodically walked around the exercise equipment, sterilizing every piece. At this rate, she would still be attending to the room when O'Rourke arrived.

Frak. Frak. Frak.

The servmaid did not deserve to be collateral damage in her mission. She'd never harm the woman, but she couldn't be sure that O'Rourke would care enough to avoid hitting her in the crossfire, should it come to that. The paranoid bastard always had a phaser with him, even during his daily exercise routine. It was like a second penis.

There was nothing she could do but watch and see how the events unfolded. If she was lucky, O'Rourke would bark at the servmaid to leave the room. Saron could only imagine what demented routine he engaged in during his daily exercise. It must be something he didn't want anyone to view. She wouldn't wait long enough to find out, though.

†

Right on time, O'Rourke crashed into the room, his eyes landing on the servmaid. "What the frak are you doing in here right now, you little domestic whore?" He sneered. "No one is supposed to be in this room."

"Sorry, sir. I'm assigned to clean the ExoGym."

"You must be new. Get the frak out before I phaser your tits off and make you eat them," he growled.

Reduced to tears, the young servmaid scurried from the room, and O'Rourke grinned in satisfaction.

Prick.

The sooner Saron crashed through the ceiling and took care of him, the better. With his back turned, he admired himself in the floor-to-ceiling mirror, preening as he flexed his muscles. Saron used her phaser to cut a hole large enough to fit through. He stroked one of the largest cylinders on the rack and slotted it into one end of the bar. Selecting several more, he continued to prepare the free weights on the rudimentary bench press. After carefully moving the circular piece to the side and changing the setting to kill on her phaser, she silently jumped from the hole to the spot behind the bench where he sat, preparing to lie down and begin his first set.

His reflexes were faster than she remembered as he scrambled from the bench, pivoted, and took aim. But Saron wasn't injured this time. Performing an acrobatic move, which made her so lethal, and one which none of her colleagues had a good defense for, she managed to avoid the phaser beam and sweep his legs. Her senses were on full alert now, and she was tired of messing with this piece of shit.

"I'd hoped we would meet someday, Saron Bahl," he jeered as he jumped to his feet, phaser in hand.

"We've met," she deadpanned, anticipating his next move with a phaser blast expertly aimed at the hand holding his phaser. The dust had settled on the floor before O'Rourke could even react. A quick death was too good for him. She probably should have just ended it with a well-placed shot to his chest, but she couldn't resist taunting him. "I know you don't like your women trained to fight, but I'll match my athleticism with yours any day of the week."

An evil grin appeared on his face. "Excellent. Old school."

Saron tossed her phaser aside. "I wouldn't want to claim an unfair advantage. Best to give you a sporting chance."

Saron and O'Rourke traded blows, with Saron connecting more solidly than O'Rourke as she moved out of range, increasingly frustrating him. Of course, he wouldn't play fair, growling as he removed the backup phaser from his high-top kinetickicks. But Saron had anticipated this move and rolled to where her phaser lay on the ground, aiming at the large mass in front of her and sending O'Rourke directly to hell with a direct hit to his chest.

Spitting on the pile of ash, Saron snarled, "That's for Jasmine."

The new phasers were remarkably efficient as his massive body had turned to ash almost instantly. His phaser beam, barely missing her, had scorched her favorite outerwear. She still believed he got off too easily, wanting him to suffer just a little longer, but she thought better about tempting fate.

"Fraking asshole. I paid good money for this outfit," she announced to the empty room. "Oh well. Easy come, easy go. I'd love to stick around, and I hate leaving a mess for the servmaid to deal with, but…" Saron shrugged before turning the dial on her Universal Temporal Watch, sending herself back to the 26th century.

She breathed a sigh of relief that it was all over. Now, the real test: did her mission yield the results the Ministry was hoping for? She'd know soon enough.

CHAPTER TWENTY-SEVEN

Saron transported directly into her eco-dwelling sphere. She needed a moment. A shrine to Jasmine still occupied a prominent space in her domicile. Holo images floated and danced in the air, rotating like an old-fashioned slide show. That was all she had left now to gaze upon. She almost felt guilty leaving it all behind, but hadn't she mourned long enough? Jasmine would want this for her. She was sure of that. How would she honor Jasmine's memory, yet still move on?

Her front door buzzer chimed, alerting her to her duty. *That didn't take long.*

"Come." The doors swished open, and Captain Grimes stood politely outside waiting for the invitation to enter.

"Did you bring the good stuff?" Saron asked.

"Yes, but you can't open the bottle until after the situation recap. I've been sent to gather you." She held up her hand. “Don’t worry, you’re not in trouble. I figured you would come here first.”

“How much time do I have?” Saron asked.

“As much as you need. Everyone at the Ministry is considerably less disquieted because of the success of the mission. The restoration of the timeline was better than they’d hoped. I think they worried that removing O’Rourke would not yield the desired outcome. They were wrong.”

“Yeah, he was a bastard of epic proportions. Stupid and arrogant. I suspect whoever was sent in his place was more judicious in their approach. I wonder how I defeated the new leader?”

“I have something to show you when you arrive at the Ministry. The minute I realized you had succeeded, I went to the historical archives.”

Saron arched an eyebrow. “And…” she prompted.

“I think I’ll wait to share it with you. Seeing it in black and white is a near-religious experience. I want you to feel the full effect of what you’ve accomplished and your decision to return to the 21st century. Let me know when you’re on your way, and I’ll try to make the situation recap as quick as possible.”

“Who else will be there?”

“Just Minister Barnes and I.”

“Thank you, I know that was your doing. I respect Minister Barnes as much as my mother. I appreciate only having to report to the two of you. The whole council would have been overwhelming, even with my mother there to keep them from bloviating.”

“You’re welcome, Saron.” Captain Grimes offered a quick squeeze to her shoulder before saying, “I’ll leave you to it.”

†

After Captain Grimes departed, Saron looked around her cozy eco-dwelling sphere and wondered if Galena, her traveling younger sister, was finally ready to settle in one place. She would love to gift the eco-dwelling sphere to Galena. After completing her medical training, Galena traveled the globe from one natural disaster to another. Earth still had a lot of healing to do after centuries of abuse to the planet.

Saron supposed there would always be natural disasters; they had occurred well before the industrial age and the heavy use of fossil fuels, but she suspected they would eventually slow down. The scientists had made tremendous progress over the last century, reducing the need for the Healthsphere Alliance.

Saron didn't know exactly how to say goodbye to her life. Should she pack up all the memories and take her belongings? Or perhaps give it all to the Matter Regenesis Center? Maybe she could seek the wisdom of her mothers.

†

After they finished the situation recap, Captain Grimes led Saron through the Ministry's massive complex to the archives. "Time is still a bit of a mystery. I believe you will find this interesting." She pulled a hardback from the shelf and handed it to Saron. "Page 263 is particularly fascinating."

Saron glanced at the title, *The Life and Times of Avery Simpson*, and opened the ancient book to the page the captain suggested she read.

Scholars debated for years whether Avery Simpson received outside assistance on her breakthrough research, making sperm obsolete for procreation. Some attributed her success to advanced technology provided by aliens.

With the discovery of her journals, a new theory emerged. Saron Bahl, her longtime companion, suddenly appears in her journal entries. There is no mention of her as an original Sapphite nor any record of a Saron Bahl of that approximate age living anywhere in the United States prior to 2045. It's as if she appeared out of nowhere.

In an early entry about Saron, Avery describes her joy at learning that she will remain with the Sapphites. The conspiracy theorists began weaving the tale of Saron as a time traveler who provided Avery with advanced technology from the future.

While most scholars discarded this notion, as well as the theories of alien influence, the theory took root with a handful of scholars disgruntled by the notion that a woman would even dare to cut men completely out of the reproductive process. The answer remains a mystery to this day.

Most scholars simply accept the most likely answer—Avery Simpson was a brilliant scientist, far ahead of her time in so many ways. Her contributions will live on as one of the most consequential events in human history. No doubt Saron Bahl was a tremendous support to Avery, and clearly the love of her life, but a time traveler seems unlikely.

"Can I keep this for a little while?" Saron requested. "I'd like to read the whole book while I still have time. I won't leave for another six or seven days while I attend to my affairs. I'll need that much time to say goodbye and wrap things up in my eco-dwelling sphere."

"Just let me know if you need any assistance."

"No, I need to do this on my own," Saron answered.

"The menders of the historical archives are already working on a holotext to correct the record. I thought you might find it interesting that your decision to return to the 21st century is already reflected in the historical archives. When I read the book *The Life and Times of Avery Simpson* prior to your mission, there was no mention of you."

"I joked with Avery about time being a head scratcher for me and brought up the paradox of which comes first, the chicken or the egg. She, of course, schooled me on the science, stating that irrevocably, the egg came first. I wonder what she'll say about this. Did time actually change the minute I accepted this mission?"

"Perhaps. I admit, I didn't check the archives until after it was clear that your second mission to take O'Rourke off the board was obviously successful. On a lark, I pulled out the book and scanned the text, finding your name. I'd prefer to provide you with the electronic version. Taking hardbacks from the archives is not permitted."

"Of course, that makes sense," Saron answered. "I almost forgot that in the mid to late 21st century, electronic books were even more popular than hardbacks."

"I confess, it's a guilty pleasure of mine to read from a hardback. It's why I love visiting the archives."

"Is there anything else you need from me? I'd like to visit my mothers now and begin the long goodbye process. I know they'll understand, but I worry a little about Mama Astraia's reaction. She's certainly more emotional than Mama Emily."

Captain Grimes chuckled and nodded. “On the outside, maybe, but Emily is so proud of you and loves you like crazy. She just has a different way of showing her love. They’ve both been so worried about you since...”

“I know.” Saron offered a sad smile, then shifted the conversation. “I’ll bet Mama Emily was a right pain in the ass with the council.”

“Well, if rumors are to be believed…”

†

“Daughter,” her mother opened her arms wide, “I had expected the mission to protect the Sapphites would profoundly change you, but I never expected…” Mama Astraia’s words were lost in a desperate attempt to control her emotions.

Saron fell into her mother’s embrace. “Does Mama Emily know why I wish to return to the 21st century?”

Mother Emily, as a council member at the Ministry of Time Politics, had been the primary influencer in her decision to become a Time Enforcer. Saron had always looked up to her formidable, accomplished mother.

“What do you think, my daughter? You know the gossip at the Ministry leaks more than a failed power cell. Obviously, as a part of the council, she was involved in the discussions on this new mission. Of course, she knows. I believe she was afraid to tell me, knowing I’m far more emotional about these things than she is. Can you imagine your Mama Emily being afraid of anything? She’s expected home any minute.”

Saron took a step back and smiled, assessing her Mama Astraia. “You look well, Mama A.”

Her mother patted her stomach. “I’m getting fat with the food your grandmothers insist I eat rather than a replicated meal. Speaking of your grandmothers, they’ve requested we host a feast before you leave, with, of course, meals lovingly prepared by their hands. How much time will we have with you?”

“I’ll take six or seven days to put all my affairs in order,” Saron answered. “Perhaps they will leave some meal preparations for when they arrive. I’ve missed working side by side with them on organic meals,” she added wistfully.

“I’m sure they would enjoy that as well. Goodness knows I never took to learning organic meal preparations. Oh, Daughter, when you speak of putting your affairs in order, great Goddess, it sounds as though you are choosing conscious departure. There hasn’t been a single instance of that in over one hundred years. None of us knows how to handle your decision. Of course, we will respect it. Your mother used her influence to approve this most unprecedented request from you. She worked hard to remind me that you are a grown woman. Will she make you happy?”

Saron smiled brightly, thinking of Avery. “Very happy, Mama. I only wish you and Mama Emily could meet her.”

Astraia nodded. “Emily is working on authorization for you to take limited technology with you on your journey of no return. Mainly, communication devices that will allow us to remain connected. I wanted her to push for in-person visits, but she said that would be a harder sell. This is territory none of us are prepared for. Not even your stoic Mama Emily. It’s like the Ministry has to evaluate new laws and guidelines.”

Saron grinned. "Good, it's about time they flexed a little bit. I've occasionally found their rules a bit restrictive. While I understand the need, especially after the recent chaos…"

"Which you brilliantly fixed. Captain Grimes has insisted on an honor ceremony. They wish to present you with the Nova Star Medal of Valor. You are the toast of the planet, you know."

Saron groaned. "Oh, fraking hell, do I have to attend?" Saron whined.

Astraia chuckled. "I may need to rethink your mother's insistence that you are a grown woman when you act like a child."

†

The doors to their modern dwelling sphere swished open, and her Mama Emily strode inside. "Daughter."

"Mother. You are looking well."

"You have made me very proud, Saron."

"Thank you for being my advocate. Mama Astraia spilled the beans."

Emily waved her hand in the air. "The council members are a bunch of stodgy old men and women, minus me, of course. They're nearly as bad as the Traditionalists."

Saron fake gasped. "Blasphemy, I say, blasphemy. Trust me, Mother, they are nothing like the Traditionalists."

"Perhaps." Emily grinned and opened her arms. "I will collect my annual hug now."

Emily held on for much longer than usual, and Saron suspected she also wondered if this would be the last time they would hug.

"Will you stay with us until you leave?" Astraia asked. "Your sisters have made it a point to travel home and remain until you depart."

"There won't be enough room for the entire Bahl brood," Saron answered.

"We'll replicate restpods and set them up in the main living space. The kids will love it. It'll be like urban nature syncing," Astraia explained.

"Before they descend on the relative peace and quiet we're enjoying right now, I wanted to seek your counsel on something," Saron requested.

"We are always here to provide counsel," Astraia answered. "Too bad we didn't have the opportunity to provide counsel on your decision to return to the 21st century," she teased. "I assume that is not what you seek counsel on."

Saron smiled. "No, but it's a related topic. I'm struggling with what to do with my belongings and all the memories attached to them."

"Why are you not taking your belongings to the Matter Regenesis Center?" Emily inquired.

Astraia shook her head at her legal fusion partner. "My love, you know I adore and respect you, but they are not simply belongings to discard; they hold memories of Jasmine."

"Oh, I see." Emily had her contemplative face on. "We are still debating what you will be allowed to take with you. Do you believe your new fusion partner will object to holo images of you and Jasmine?"

"I don't know. I showed Avery a hologram that I had loaded onto a confiscated FlexiPad. I believe it startled her. The resemblance was quite unsettling at first."

Emily nodded. "Yes, I've viewed the archival pictures myself."

"Those pictures do not do justice to her beauty or to the almost unnatural likeness. But Avery is not Jasmine. I need you both to know that I haven't fallen in love with her simply because she looks like Jasmine. She's a remarkable woman in her own right."

"Of that, we have no doubt, Daughter," Astraia assured.

"I recommend making sure Avery understands your feelings. Tread lightly, my daughter. No one wants to have to compete with a dead fusion partner," Emily advised.

Astraia offered Saron a sad smile. "As an individual prone to elevated emotion, I can assure you that while it might be difficult for Avery, if she loves you, she will understand and accept that you had a life before her, including a great love. She cannot expect you to erase Jasmine's memory."

"I will advocate for the allowance of your holograms," Emily stated in her practical, no-nonsense manner. "The rest of Jasmine's belongings should probably have been taken to the Matter Regenesis Center long before now," she gently chastised.

"I wasn't ready before, Mother. I am now."

"We all grieve in our own time and in our own ways. Emily, dear, you cannot force your way upon others," Astraia cautioned.

Emily sighed. "I suppose not. Perhaps I should keep from running my mouth. In matters of the heart, you are much better counsel, Astraia."

"Not true, Mother. I needed the combined counsel. Thank you both." Saron lifted her head to the commotion outside her childhood home. "Looks like the brood has arrived."

"Ah, yes, that's Lyra. Her hovercraft needs a maintenance check. It's terribly loud, much like her brood," Emily stated.

"Emily, that was rude," Astraia chastised. "You love seeing the girls."

†

Saron's two sisters, her nieces, and her oldest sister's fusion partner rushed inside.

"Aunt Saron," her nieces exclaimed in unison as they ran to Saron, each taking a side to hug her.

"Is it true you're going to live with the dinosaurs?" Keziah, the youngest, asked.

"Not exactly, Keziah. But I will be living in the 21st century."

Keziah's eyes began to water. "That means we won't ever see you again, doesn't it?"

Astraia approached Keziah and stroked her fine blonde hair. "Your g-ma Emily is working on that."

"Will we be able to visit you in old-timey 21st century?" Dulce, the oldest, asked. "I've always wanted to time travel. I'm going to be the best Time Enforcer once I graduate," she declared.

Saron chuckled. "Well, you still have many years of study before you can join the academy. If you think your studies are rigorous now, wait until you have to study and memorize thousands of slang phrases and learn about machinery from an earlier time."

Dulce crinkled her nose. "I won't mind the slang. I like researching old sayings. I'm not as good with technology."

“I have faith in you,” Saron responded before turning her attention to her sisters, who waited patiently for their turn. “Do I not deserve hugs from you two?”

“No, I’m angry at you for keeping such a big secret from us,” Galena grumbled.

Saron laughed. “When do you suppose I had time to track you down and update you on my love life? Get over here and give your big sister a hug.”

Galena folded her body into Saron and squeezed. After she let go, Lyra approached, pulling Saron into an equally fervent hug, whispering, “Welcome home, Saron.”

“Good to see you again, Saron,” Melina, Lyra’s fusion partner, said. “We are all so grateful for your service. You brought back my favorite aunt. She went missing in the timeline chaos.”

“Come, let’s all settle in the other room. I’ve prepared a few treats to nibble on. However, the real delicacies will come when the grandmothers arrive,” Astraia directed.

CHAPTER TWENTY-EIGHT

Avery was losing her mind. It had been eight days now, and nothing. It didn't make any sense to her. Nora kept everyone informed, and they'd all whooped with joy when she reported on how the news seemed to abruptly switch to another story about President Whitmer's dramatic new budget proposal that would cut medical research, humanitarian aid, and most of the social safety nets, while adding to military spending and tax breaks for large corporations. Not a single word remained about the terrorist attacks.

Gloria had ventured topside to confirm the absence of a military presence in the woods adjacent to their Safe Haven. It was as if they'd never been there at all. By all indications, Saron's mission was a success, but something was clearly wrong because she hadn't returned. Maybe Saron had changed her mind? Now she was pissed, along with her profound distress over the possibility that Saron had died while completing her mission.

Gloria didn't even wait for Avery to invite her in as she barged inside with Mavis in tow. "Enough wallowing. You've locked yourself away for the past four days. This pity party you're throwing yourself is not going to result in that breakthrough research that Saron risked her life for. Mavis and I want our baby."

"What?"

"You're going to find the key to splicing the DNA of two eggs together, or whatever technical term is used that allows Gloria and me to make a baby," Mavis stated. "Do not forget that Gloria and I are both Saron's biological great-grandmothers."

"Dispermic chimerism," Avery answered absently. "I knew your connection to Saron but didn't exactly consider my role in this since my focus has been on single egg fertilization."

"Well, now you know the whole scoop, so chop chop, let's go," Mavis ordered. "Time to get back to your lab and make this possible for us."

"I don't think I'm in the right headspace for that."

"Now, you listen to me." Gloria gently grabbed Avery's chin, forcing her to meet Gloria's eyes. "You cannot let Saron's sacrifice be for naught. Fulfill your destiny. Do it in memory of our beloved Saron." Unshed tears glistened in Gloria's eyes. "We'll have a service for Saron if that's what you need to move on."

Avery's head dropped into her hands as she quietly sobbed. Gloria had just laid out a truth she hadn't wanted to acknowledge.

†

The door to the pod whooshed open again, announcing another's presence in what had become her sanctuary.

"A service? I think I've had enough of those to last a lifetime," Saron quipped.

Avery's head popped up, and she launched into Saron's waiting arms.

"Saron," she breathed out. "You're back. What kind of twisted society has a service for someone before they're certain you're dead?"

Saron arched an eyebrow. "You were about to do just that," she quipped. "But, no, not that kind of service. They did this whole pomp and circumstance thing and presented me with the Nova Star Medal of Valor. Actually, we call it an honor ceremony, but I suspect you would consider it a service ceremony."

"Kid, you gave us all a scare," Mavis noted as she appeared to scrutinize Saron. "You're looking a little pale."

Saron smiled. "Time travel is hard on the body. It will pass. I know I'm your direct familial ancestor, but referring to me as 'kid' seems a strange choice, considering I'm probably older than you are, or at least the same age."

"Good point, but a lady never reveals her true age, so you aren't wheedling that out of me," Mavis teased.

"She's thirty-four," Gloria interrupted with a grin. "But more importantly, where's my hug?"

Avery watched the women embrace and sent a silent mantra to the universe for answering her pseudo-prayers. As a scientist, she couldn't legitimately call them prayers because she didn't believe in a deity. But certainly, there was a higher power at work. Someone had sent Saron back to them, and she appeared relatively healthy and completely uninjured.

When Gloria and Saron separated, Avery asked with a smidgeon of irritation, "Where the hell have you been for the past eight days?"

"I'm sorry, I didn't consider that my absence would concern you so greatly. I had many loose ends to tie up and some tough goodbyes."

"Shit," Avery exclaimed. "I'm being a selfish bitch. You've a whole other life that I've forced you to leave. With family and friends. Can I claim emotional distress as an excuse, thinking something may have happened to you?"

"I understand," Saron stated as she brushed her fingertips over Avery's cheek. "The extra time with my family and the Ministry helped to make the case for limited time travel. I'll be able to see my family once a year. We're still in discussions over special exemptions for individuals not directly involved in time enforcement to engage in minimal and specific time travel. I am the first to request a permanent assignment in an alternate time. My family is eager to meet you, especially my niece, Dulce, who is many years away from entering the Time Enforcement Academy. I have so much to share with you."

Mavis cleared her throat. "I think it would be best to leave these two alone while they reconnect. We have plenty of time with Saron now."

"Oh, right, yes, good plan," Gloria added. "I'm so glad you made it back to us."

†

After Gloria and Mavis left, Avery pulled Saron to her and practically devoured her lips in a searing welcome-home kiss. When they finally broke apart for air, Saron grinned and said, “I have gifts from the 26th century. The council saw no harm in holographs and other treats I knew you would appreciate.”

“You brought me sex toys?”

“Oh, yes. A wide variety,” Saron confirmed.

“What else did they allow?”

“Not much. However, I was granted authorization to continue using the power cells. The Ministry has a vested interest in keeping the Safe Haven operating with full efficiency until your research has been completed. There’s a revised edition of a book about your life in the historical archives, and I’m in it.”

“Really?”

“Yes, apparently, someone in the future finds your journals, and the conspiracy theorists went wild.” Saron winked.

“I’ve tried to be prudent with what I share. Perhaps I should scale back my exuberance for you.”

“Don’t worry, the Ministry is correcting history. It does bring about some existential questions about time, and specifically when and how it changes based on interference from the Time Enforcers.”

Avery sighed. “The chicken and egg paradox again?”

“I have an electronic copy of the book for you to peruse.”

“You mean an ebook?”

“Isn’t that what I said?” Saron countered.

“Not exactly, but close enough. It’s so good to have you back. Any chance we can break out those 26th-century sex toys?”

"I'm going to have to get used to your name for my cyberstrap and the other items I've brought for you to try."

"What do you call them other than sex toys?"

"Divine connection assistive devices."

"Sounds way too clinical and frankly not something as fun as I know them to be."

Saron wrinkled her nose. "Perhaps you're right. Sex toys, it is?"

"Oh, we are going to have so many glorious years together. Now that I know someone is going to read my journals, I plan on being a little more judicious about what I choose to share."

"I'd appreciate that. I suspect my mothers will read those journals. And while we take a more relaxed view of divine connection, I don't relish the teasing I will get from my sisters. I hope you don't mind that I've brought with me a few cherished holograms of my time with Jasmine. I couldn't completely wipe her from my memory. It doesn't mean I love you any less."

"Of course it doesn't. I don't want you to forget Jasmine. Memories of her are important in every timeline."

"Thank you. In the book, I'm referred to as your longtime companion. I'm honored to embrace that old moniker as long as I get to spend the rest of my days on the planet with you. I never thought I'd find love again."

"I'm eternally grateful the Ministry sent you. I will love you until my last dying breath."

"As will I," Saron promised. "I'm going to make damn sure nothing changes this moment in time or the many precious future moments we shall have together."

GLOSSARY OF TERMS

***Author's Note*:** While most, if not all, of these terms are easily understood or explained in the book, they are here as a reference just in case!

Accordium: A treaty or agreement between parties with differing views.

Adaptive Mobility Unit: Futuristic version of a motorized wheelchair generally used by senior adults who need assistance because they are unable to walk.

Apex Warrior: Specialized military personnel for the Traditionalists.

Automated Luxury Restorative Justice Unit: Prison of the future.

Biofluxscent: Adolescent.

Bond Initiators: Prospective suitors.

Bone Mender: A medical device to repair broken bones.

Cipher Directive: Secure electronic briefing with details on a mission.

Classified Operations Chamber: The most secure room in the Neuro Analysis Unit.

Cloak Agent: A spy or undercover agent.

Collaboration Nexus: A secure conference room for private discussions.

Conscious Departure: Suicide in lieu of providing the enemy with intelligence.

Culinary Hub: Kitchen.

Divine Connection Assistive Devices (Cyberstrap, Synthstimupulse, Holotouch Divinator, Vibesync): A general term for various sex toys.

Divine Connection: Sex or intimate relations.

Dwelling Sphere: A general term for a 26th-century home.

Dynamic Surface Display: A computer monitor or television display.

Eco-Dwelling Sphere: A general term for a 26th-century more compact home, probably similar to a condo.

Elysium Surge: An orgasm or release after sex.

Enforcement Strategy Nexus: A central room for Time Enforcers to meet and receive regular briefings.

Event Horizon Transmission: Confidential transmission intended for Time Enforcers on a mission in a different time.

ExoGym: A workout facility used by the Traditionalists.

Frak: The replacement swear word for fuck.

Fusion Partners: A committed couple.

Heritage Warrior: Military-type personnel for the Traditionalists, similar to the personnel in the Army.

Holo-novel: An enhanced version of an ebook or audiobook providing the option to have a visual representation of the words spoken or in electronic form.

Information Retrieval Agents: Specially trained individuals who work in the Neuro Analysis Unit, who are responsible for obtaining intelligence through a process called neuro analysis. A replacement for interrogation or torture.

Infosync: Confidential in-person briefing.

Justice Participant: A prisoner residing in the Automated Luxury Restorative Justice Unit.

Kinetickicks: A form of athletic shoe.

Knowledge Synthesis Report: Top secret briefing on missions.

Matter Regenesis Center: Recycling center.

Ministry of Time Politics: Ministry for short. A department within the leadership structure of the World Council that establishes all the rules and laws related to time travel and the maintenance of the timeline.

ModuPak: Backpack for carrying gear used by both Time Enforcers and Traditionalists.

Nature syncing: Camping in the woods or anywhere outside.

Neuro analysis: A safe process to elicit critical information through technology. It is a highly effective method with no chance of hiding information from the Information Retrieval Agent who asks the questions. A replacement for mind readers.

Neuro Analysis Unit: Another department under the Ministry of Time Politics used for the interrogation of spies or individuals who may possess critical information.

Official Corrective Chronobrief: Formal disciplinary action.

Omni-tolerance: A philosophy adopted by the World Council to accept differences in cultural norms.

Optic Scanner: A powerful form of binoculars.

Phaser: The primary weapon of the 26th century.

Power Cell: The primary energy source in the 26th century. It is used for everything from recharging phasers and replicators to supplying energy for anything that requires energy to run.

Replicator: Tool to replicate both organic (food) and inorganic materials (tools and tech).

Safe Haven: Like a safe house, usually established by Time Agents.

Safeguard Broadcast Network: System for sending Event Horizon Transmissions.

Sapphites: An Influential group of queer women in history that formed their own society and were responsible for the breakthrough scientific discovery of egg fertilization without sperm.

Spector Corp: A unit similar to the Navy Seals or Army Rangers that exists within the Traditionalists' military structure.

Supreme Exarch: The recognized leader of all the Traditionalist colonies.

Sustenance Packs: Food that is similar to Meals Ready to Eat.

Time Agent: Personnel who work for the Ministry of Time as support staff for the Time Enforcers. The Ministry deploys these agents to prepare moments in time for future missions that Time Enforcers may need to go on. This is a less dangerous role.

Time Enforcer: An officer who works for the Ministry of Time to ensure there aren't changes to the original timeline. They are very similar to elite units in law enforcement.

Time Travel Enforcement Unit: A unit under the direction of the Ministry of Time Politics designed to enforce the laws related to time travel and breaches in time that could affect the original timeline.

Traditionalists: Rogue colonies with their own governing structure, separate from the World Council. A patriarchal society with severe conservative values, laws, and societal norms. The men are the head of the household and hold all the power. Strict religious teachings play a large role in their beliefs.

Transporters: Small devices that Time Enforcers use to attach to individuals to send them back to their original time.

Ultimate Expedient: Disbanding and resettlement of separatist colonies that fail to adhere to the World Council's laws.

Universal Temporal Watch: A universal tool used for many purposes, including time travel, communication over timelines, tracking, and other basic tools. This is a staple for Time Enforcers in a watch format that is adapted to whatever time period the Time Enforcer travels to.

Vibesync: Vibrator that adapts to personal preferences.

Vibradate: A date with a person someone has a romantic interest in.

World Council: The overall governing body for planet Earth. Borders and the separation of countries are no longer present in the 26th century.

ABOUT THE AUTHOR

Annette is an award-winning author, published by Affinity Rainbow Publications, who lives in the beautiful Pacific Northwest with her wife and their four furry kids. With over thirty published novels, six Lesfic Bard Awards, and one Goldie Award for her fourth novel, *Locked Inside*, she finally feels like a real author. Annette is as much a reader as a writer and is always looking for the next sapphic novel to queue up. She came up with the *One Fan at a Time* tagline, because it rolled off the tongue much better than *One Reader at a Time.* After pondering who she was at her core, she feels it was all about connecting to each reader on a personal level. Annette would be the first to admit she doesn't do well with the masses. If someone picks up her book and it touches them, she believes she has achieved what she wants with her writing by reaching each reader. It is who she is at her core. Drop her a line. She loves to hear from readers.

Email: annettemori0859@gmail.com.Sign up for her Substack: https://annettemoriauthor.substack.com/

Check out her blog: Everyday Occurrences: https://annettemori0859.wordpress.com/

Visit the Affinity Rainbow Publications website for her books and many other outstanding authors: www.affinityebooks.com

Other Affinity Books

Noble Intentions by LJ Reynolds

Agent Charlie Matthews returns to her hometown to piece together the remnants of her once-perfect life, only to hit the ground running on what may be the most significant case of her career.

Detective Noble Gentry's sole focus is ending the hunt for the killer before additional lives are lost.

Two strong women, both dedicated to their jobs. Thrown together, they unite on a mission to stop a killer with nothing to lose.

Will they catch the killer?

Will their growing attraction get in the way? Sometimes love is closest when it seems gone forever.

The Princess Needs a Wife by JM Dragon

Since birth, Princess Sophia Osric has led a charmed life. When a family tragedy forces her to shift from casual obligations to specific royal duties, it results in a decree from her father to find a wife or risk losing her special privileges. But there's always a catch—it must be a commoner. How on earth can she do that? Where will she find a commoner other than someone to wave or smile at?

Perhaps fairytale romances happen for princesses, too.

Without Borders by Stacy Reynolds

When the opportunity to become a war correspondent opens at her news agency, journalist Nicole Sheppard jumps at the chance to go to Ukraine. Her lifelong goal to gather news firsthand in the heat of battle and to test her mettle against the turbulence of war will finally be realized.

What she doesn't anticipate is having her heart and emotions tested as well when she meets the beautiful French doctor, Marie Dubois. As Nicole dodges bullets and Marie extracts them from the wounded, the two women struggle against a growing attraction to one another.

But when Nicole and Marie are kidnapped by a ruthless Russian mercenary, they must work together to find a way to escape.

The only thing they can't escape is falling in love.

The Invisible Woman by Annette Mori

In a world where logic meets the extraordinary, Tamara, a brilliant forensic scientist, discovers a mysterious purple plant that blesses her with superhuman abilities, including invisibility. Teaming up with her best friend, Annalise, a passionate FBI agent haunted by scars from her past, the two friends embark on a quest to bring down a brutal serial killer known only as The Hunter. As the danger intensifies, their bond deepens, and secrets are revealed. Will Tamara and Annalise finally admit to their feelings despite being polar opposites? Join these extraordinary women in this gripping tale of love, friendship, and the fight for justice, where heroes are born from pain.

Never Too Late by Glenda Poulter

After the death of her long-time partner, and a scandal at the school where she taught music and art, Janice Halston emerged as a shadow of herself. Feeling shaken, cautious and artistically blocked.

Tam Murphy lost her wife and son within a short time of each other. She tries to fill her emptiness with her daughter Mae, and granddaughter, Ocee.

Janice and Tam are brought together by the precocious Ocee. As their friendship deepens, so do their feelings for each other. Their deepening feelings send both women spiraling…in different directions. One toward what could be, the other away from fear of another loss. Will their spirals lead them back to each other, or further apart?

Nothing But Net by Ali Spooner

Hunter James, a rising star in college basketball, has her career and life sidelined after experiencing a family tragedy.

An opportunity for a fresh start opens the door to return to what she loves most: playing basketball. Hunter rushes through that door to make the most of her second chance.

Back in the basketball arena, doing what she loves, will she open herself and her heart to another chance to forgive herself and fall in love?

The Kitten Trap by Annette Mori

Inspired by the classic movie, *The Parent Trap*, two adorable black kittens, Midnight and Onyx, play matchmakers for their human mothers, Mac and Carmen. Struggling with the complexities of farm life, Mac can barely believe her beautiful girlfriend, Carmen, has agreed to move to the drafty old farmhouse to live with her and her beloved

Pops. When Carmen is forced to leave the farm to care for her ailing mother, Midnight and Onyx as well as Mac and Carmen must struggle with the difficult separation. Just when it appears Carmen and Onyx may come back home to the farm, cruel fate raises a further challenge, one that will need the help of two mischievous kittens to overcome.

To Autumn by Katie M Hall

Sixteen-year-old Robyn Gale, along with her younger sister Anne, is sent away for the summer holidays of 1997 to stay with her grandmother at a caravan park in Devon. Robyn's had a tough few months: trying to cope with the fallout of their mother's attempted suicide, messing up her GCSEs, and finding herself attracted to girls. Perhaps getting away from her real life is just what she needs…she can focus on finding a boyfriend, watching *Neighbours,* and swimming. A solid plan, until she meets charismatic Australian lifeguard, Autumn, and her life is turned even more down under.

Fairytail Farm by Ali Spooner

Dr. Hill McCall and her wife Alice dreamed of developing a sanctuary for unwanted cats and dogs to live out their lives as a retirement project. Hill has secretly worked on the project for months when a wealthy benefactor surprises her with a large donation, allowing Hill to be more aggressive with the project's opening. A group home operator approaches Hill about summer volunteer positions for four girls as Fairytail Farm becomes more than just a sanctuary for the animals. It creates an environment of love and kindness for the animals and all that support the project. Several love stories develop from first love to mature couples who have found their forever person. Fairytail Farm is more than a dream come true. It is a home for happily ever afters.

The Love Demand by Annette Mori

In the dazzling realm of reality television, where love and drama entwine in a complicated dance as old as time, a groundbreaking series emerges that transcends the ordinary. *The Love Demand* is not your typical reality show. Lacey Fellows isn't sure she wants to subject herself to further humiliation, however, on the off chance her girlfriend may agree to accept a second marriage proposal, Lacey reluctantly consents to participating in the new reality show. What she doesn't count on is meeting a kindred spirit—one she can't seem to shake from her thoughts. Jaimie would do almost anything for her girlfriend, including following her to the ends of the earth and participating in a conniving television show that puts her in front of a camera, which happens to be her least favorite place. Her girlfriend, Sabina, hasn't met a camera she doesn't like. They couldn't be more opposite, but Jaimie still hopes Sabina will want marriage, kids, and the whole shebang. The last thing she expects is to fall in love with someone else. Let the games begin.

Sullivan's Trace by Ali Spooner

Micah "Sully" Sullivan has settled into a solitary life at the family horse ranch after her father's death. When her long-term vet, Doc Barton, plans to retire, his granddaughter, Bryn, arrives to take over his practice. An attack on one of Sully's prized horses throws Sully and Bryn into a whirlwind as they fight to save the young animal. Just as Sully is becoming comfortable with her growing attraction to Bryn, tragedy occurs, and her brother and his wife are killed in an accident. Sully's solitary life drastically changes when a family of three is born.

Love Sins by Annette Mori

Jessica Green's life is predictable and boring. As the chief engineer for Solar Flair, her career is right on track. Her love life, not so much. The last thing she expects is a call from her estranged father's attorney. Too curious to ignore the message, she can't resist meeting with him and discovering more about specific instructions related to his estate, as well as the letter her father left for her. Rattled by what she finds at her father's home, she promptly dials 911.

Special Agent Amanda Forrester is perplexed by a call to join a homicide investigation until she arrives at the scene and learns the victim is not only a serial killer but an elite assassin the authorities have been after for years. To Amanda's increasing irritation, the daughter recognizes a picture of the last target and insinuates herself into the investigation. As the case takes a surprising turn, Amanda finds she has landed smack dab in the middle of a complicated and dangerous situation. The facts lead her to a puzzle weaving together the recent suicide of a wealthy businessman with the activities of several prominent politicians. Amanda must join forces with a mysterious organization and the persistent woman she finds increasingly hard to resist. Her instinct to protect the alluring and vulnerable Jessica Green kicks into high gear, taking the reader on a roller-coaster journey for the last book in *The Next Generation* series.

Affinity
Rainbow Publications

eBooks, Print, Free eBooks

Visit our website for more publications available online.

https://affinityebooks.com/

Published by Affinity Rainbow Publications
A Division of Affinity eBook Press NZ LTD
Canterbury, New Zealand

Registered Company 2517228

www.ingramcontent.com/pod-product-compliance
Lightning Source LLC
LaVergne TN
LVHW020702110826
845149LV00012B/2072

* 9 7 8 1 9 9 1 3 5 7 3 6 6 *